HARRY KERN

EDWIN RITTS

Produced by Publish Pros
www.publishpros.com

DEDICATION

I wish to thank my dear wife Susan for granting me the time to spend at my writing table, following the lives of my characters and writing down their thoughts and deeds. Also, I thank my colleagues at Publish Pros, Rich Carnahan and Mary Hall, who guide my writing efforts at every phase. Finally, I want to thank my sister Cathy for her editing talents and tenacity.

CHAPTER ONE

1910

The boys awoke to a dark, mid-winter morning on the farm. Twelve-year-old Harry Kern and his six brothers shared the attic of the ramshackle wooden house their father had purchased after the first two boys were born. The space had a window at each end for light and, when opened, a breeze in summer. But now bits of snow blew in through the layers of wooden boards serving as both interior and exterior walls, and there was no heat. In winter it was not uncommon for the boys to awaken to beds laced in snow. The cold was combatted by heavy woolen quilts and blankets their mother would create when all her other chores were complete. She worked fast as she sat near the first-floor fireplace, seemingly always heavy with another child on the way. The boys slept in their daytime clothing—even their shoes and woolen hats. They knew no different and were content, even healthy, as they adjusted their coverings from fall to winter. Eventually three additional brothers would inhabit the attic space before a sister would end the line of siblings and have a small room of her own on the first floor.

The rooster was reluctant to crow in winter, so the boys took their cue from the dimly rising sun coming to bear in the east. Winter chores were not as extensive as in the rest of the year, but there were some to be done, and the brothers drew straws daily to determine who would be up just after dawn. This particular morning Harry and his brother Graham drew the short ones and groaned loudly as they pushed free from their bedding. There were probably a few eggs to gather, and the cow would need milking. One of the two would start a fire in the kitchen stove for Mam and fill the coffee pot with water and grounds.

The family gathered at six fifteen for breakfast and discussion, led by Pap, about the day's activities. Winter days, aside from the few farm chores, amounted largely to book learning for a few hours at the elbow of their father. None of the children attended a formal school. Pap, whose given name was Thomas, was once a rural schoolmaster, but he now considered himself a gentleman farmer, having purchased ten acres of land fifteen miles east of Ashtabula, Ohio. He was something of a Utopian and perhaps a bit of an anarchist, with a fondness for afternoons spent reading and re-reading the works of Emerson, Charles Dana, George Ripley, and William B. Greene. He often spoke of wishing he'd been born earlier so he could have lived and farmed at the utopian Brook Farm Ripley had created. Tom decided to look for personal fulfillment by working his land and enjoying "what could be brought about from my own energy." His own energy, as well as the considerable energy of his dear wife, was most notably manifest in the bringing about of ten healthy children in their first twelve years of marriage.

The Kern family originated in Germany, with the first immigrants arriving in Buffalo, New York in the late 1860s. These were three teen-aged brothers, of whom only one stayed in Buffalo. The other two moved west by boat along Lake Erie to the town of the same name, where the brother who would become Tom's father settled. The second, based on his occasional letters, wandered west to Chicago. They never saw one another again. Tom's parents and their family prospered in Erie, where his father worked on the lake's cargo docks. After graduating high school, the first Kern to do so as far as anyone knew, Tom and his young wife Mary moved west toward Ashtabula, her hometown. It was there Tom taught school, though after several years he tired of the structure of teaching and his students.

The farm provided food for the table and included a cow, some chickens, a horse, and an acre pond for fishing. When surplus crops were harvested, they were sold in town on Saturday mornings, summer and fall. Several of the boys would hitch the horse and wagon and before dawn travel the fifteen miles to market. At day's end, proceeds would be turned over to Mam, official family treasurer, and in turn she dispensed a cent or two to each son who had made the trip. Harry made the trip most often, enjoying the freedom the ride allowed, the energy of being among non-family members, and talking with customers and exchanging ideas. He would be the first of the Kern boys to leave the farm, having no interest in working the soil, preferring mechanical pursuits, particularly the workings of gasoline engines and the kinds of vehicles they could propel. He was a tinkerer, very good at fixing things.

At sixteen, he constructed an open wheeled racer made from automotive and other machine parts he begged for or salvaged around Ashtabula. When running, his contraption made an awful noise, and the faster it ran the louder it was. The noise frightened the cow when pasturing and kept her off the farm's dirt roads; it didn't do much for her milk either! His goal, in the spring of 1914, was to enter a much-discussed road race for amateur drivers, from Ashtabula to the metropolis of Cleveland on Route 20. A trip of eighty-three miles running through Geneva, Painesville, Mentor, and East Cleveland before finishing in Public Square on Superior Avenue. If he completed the course, the finish line would represent the farthest distance Harry had ever been from the farm. He knew it was questionable—his machine could blow a tire, or any of its myriad mechanical parts could malfunction. Cash prizes would be awarded to drivers with the best overall times and least fuel consumed. Third prize was enough to keep him in spending money for a year. The Akron-based General Tire Company was sponsoring the race to highlight its factory and newest line of automobile tires. The fact the race was to end in Cleveland and not Akron did not seem to matter to anyone, even the sponsor.

Harry's machine was of his own design. Built on a Ford Model A chassis, it was a single seat affair. Its Hart Parr Model 3 two-cylinder tractor engine was mounted perpendicular to the chassis in the front of the vehicle. The drive shaft was a short steel pipe that held a forged metal wheel out the engine's end. A leather belt ran to its rear axle. It exhausted vertically and could reach eighteen horsepower when the belted drive was fully engaged. It was a rough affair, with no unifying paint color to disguise its homemade look. For Harry though, it was a work of art. He raised the five dollar entrance fee by working additional chores at neighboring farms, and his brothers made financial contributions to the adventure. Mam was against the entire idea but made him an overcoat "duster" from canvas material left over from porch awnings, despite her feelings. Pap worried Harry would be so very far from the farm if he made it to the finish line. He knew his number-three son was not cut out for the life he had chosen for himself. But Cleveland? The city was filled with sin and temptation.

CHAPTER TWO

Mam rose from a nap on a kitchen bench, stretching to her full four-foot, eight-inch height. She had been up this day since the rooster's crow and now finished preparing the noonday meal for her nine sons. She walked onto the kitchen porch and looked over the crops coming up from the rich earth. She told Mary to yank the braided rope of the cast iron dinner bell. With just a few pulls, both women knew the boys would be at table in less than ten minutes. From a farm family herself, Mam made up for a lack of formal education with common sense and organizational ability. She ruled all in her domain.

The boys arrived for dinner from their labors, assembling around the long table and its steaming plates of fried chicken, corn, green beans, onions, tomatoes, and melon.

"Worked off breakfast by ten, Mam! Thought dinnertime would never come," said Ben, her oldest.

"Comes the same time every day," she said with a smile. "Don't none of you eat too fast, the fields will be there when you get back, and your Pap won't want you complaining cause your bellies ache."

"Rhubarbs comin' right along," second son Dick said through a mouthful of corn bread. "We'll have some ready for market by Friday."

"I'll want some of that for pie, Richard," she responded. "Remember to bring a half bushel tonight when you come in. And if some of you boys want to take some cats from the lake this afternoon, I'll fix 'em for supper."

With full mouths her sons nodded in anticipation. *It's good to have them together. Won't always be this way,* she thought as she looked over at Harry seated among his brothers.

As progenitor of the family, Pap felt he should be permitted to bestow given names on the children. Mam agreed so long as she could bestow the name "Cabot" as a middle name to each of them for a presumed esteemed ancestor, John Cabot. She maintained that Cabot, the first European to reach the mainland of North America at the end of the sixteenth century, was a relative.

That she had had ten children seemed perfectly normal as her mother had bore an even dozen. Secretly, Mam felt she had outdone her mother even with fewer children, as hers were all male, except for the last. It had been after Mam delivered Lester that Pap decided it was time to buy a farm. If they were lucky, he thought, summers would be warm for growing and winters cold for reading and reproducing. They had met when she was in her early teens and Pap was in his early twenties. The couple married after a brief courtship. Her mother's people were of English lineage, while Mam's father was German and Dutch. He was pleased with the match and saw no reason why an able-bodied female should not be breeding and be some other man's responsibility. A few years later, the young couple, with baby Richard on the way, headed west for North Kingsville, between Erie and Ashtabula, where Tom's position as schoolmaster awaited. A small cottage was provided, along with an annual salary. He would teach all grades to the fourth; younger students in the morning, older ones after dinner, and none at all during harvest and planting seasons.

CHAPTER THREE

As the day of the race approached, Harry planned practice runs around the farm, each of two-mile lengths. He thought the number three would be a good omen for the racer as it was his family position and painted it in barn-red paint on the seat's base, the machine's only flat horizontal surface. Ben and Lester said they would help with these practices, and Harry marked a course mirroring the race's first miles on the dirt road through family land. He wanted to make good runs in terms of minutes, watching his speed and fuel intake and making adjustments to the leather drivetrain to avoid its slipping to one side or the other and causing unwanted delays.

The first trial occurred on an early spring afternoon, the leaves budding out light green against blue sky. With Harry behind the wheel, Ben gave one crank to the motor, then another, and the engine came to life. It was so loud the three boys stuffed rag pieces into their ears and communicated with hand gestures, pointing at what had caught their interest or concern. Harry dropped the clutch, the leather belt tightened, and he and the racer were off. Lester was posted at the first half-mile mark, and as the racer lurched forward, he began counting, "1001, 1002, 1003," until Harry passed his vantage point—one-and-a-half minutes total time by his reckoning. Harry charged ahead toward a white rag tied to an ash tree, marking the third mile. Looking quickly at the leather belt as he passed Lester, he noted it was slipping to the left but was not off the steel cylinder welded to the rear axle. Still, there would need to be an adjustment. As he pushed the accelerator harder, he saw the rag ahead, as well as the cow running opposite his mark, ahead of the noise. *Milk will be soured a little tonight.* He laughed and pulled the gear to disengage and slow his approach. The racer came to a stop just past the rag, missing the cow that had made an abrupt turn to enter the creek. He checked his gas tank's level before re-engaging the drive belt to move the racer onto the path for a second run. There was no reverse!

✿✿✿

Race day broke overcast on the farm. As always, there were eggs to collect and udders to squeeze. Harry felt different. The farm looked so beautiful to him, as if he were looking at everything for the first and perhaps last time. As he walked from the barn, milk sloshing in the metal pail he carried, he felt his stomach turn. Sweat broke out on his forehead, though the morning was still cool. He sat in a chair on the kitchen porch, the milk and four cats beside him, and thought about giving up on the race.

"You feeling sick, Harry?" Mam asked, looking at her nearly grown third son through the open door.

"Not really Mam, and yet my belly ain't right and I got this race comin'."

She dried her hands on the rag near the washbasin and walked out to the porch. She ran her short fingers through his light brown hair. "You'll be fine son, it's just that this is a new beginnin'. You're just a bit jittery 'cause of the race and how it's going to change everything you've known before. I remember feeling the same way before marryin' Pap. You'll be fine just as soon as you crank that machine of yours and head out. You'll see. Go in the kitchen and eat a little somethin', then go get yourself ready."

Harry did as his mother said. He felt terribly alone as he scrubbed his face and combed his hair back from his forehead. He dressed in overalls and his work boots and five minutes later walked to the far end of the barn where his racer sat, covered by a large tarpaulin. As he pulled the stiff, oily covering off, Pap came around the corner.

"Here's a day that will probably change your life, son. Sure is going to change mine. You're a man today, the third of my boys to reach that state of being. I know you will always make Mam and me proud." Pap reached in his overall pocket and produced five dollars. "Here, you take this for your trip and what you may need. Mam and I been puttin' back a bit."

A tear welled in Harry's eye as he took the money. "Won't let you down, you or Mam," was all he was able to get out. "I'll be back, just you wait."

As Pap helped his son fold the tarp, Mam appeared with a paper bag of food. Harry climbed aboard his machine while Pap gave the engine a crank. It roared to life. Harry wedged a small cardboard suitcase between his right leg and his seat. It contained a fresh shirt, the canvas duster his mother had made, a comb, and a hat. Harry smiled at his parents.

"You'll see, I'll be back—if I make it to Cleveland at all!" He pushed the accelerator, engaged the belt drive, and the racer moved forward. "I'm off!" he shouted over the noise.

CHAPTER FOUR

The sun was now up and warming as Harry drove into town. The starting flag would wave down on the racers at one o'clock and he needed to stop at 5 Star Hardware for an oil can and a pint of oil to keep the leather drive belt and metal gears cool as his speeds increased. It was eleven as he neared where the race would begin. An air of excitement greeted him, with people waving at each of the racers in turn. Flags flew, and red, white, and blue banners decorated porches of homes and buildings leading in and out of town. At the hardware store, he waved to Mr. Rainey, its proprietor, with a grin.

"Top of the day Harry! What may I do for a local boy lookin' to make good?"

"Just a few last-minute things, Mr. Rainey. Need a good oil can and some number thirty weight."

Harry inspected the three different oil cans being offered and decided on the one with the easiest trigger to operate. Mr. Rainey filled it near to the top of its neck then wiped the excess away.

"Won't do to have it slip from your hands, my boy," Rainey quipped. "This one is nice and light with a good handle."

Harry squirted a bit out and agreed.

"Let's see," said Rainey. "Comes to about thirty cents with the oil."

Harry dug deep into his overall pocket and came up with the funds. Above the cash register he saw several pairs of goggles Rainey had gotten in for the race. They had chrome eyepieces and thick leather straps.

"How much would a pair of those set me back, Mr. Rainey?"

"They'd be..." He looked at them and considered. "'Bout another thirty cents I guess."

Harry considered his funds, the fact that he would need to purchase gas at least twice more, stay two nights at boarding houses should he actually make it to Cleveland, and eat what he could.

"They're awfully nice but not in my budget this time, Mr. Rainey."

Rainey reached up and pulled a pair off its hook. "Here ya' go Harry, a gift. Do your best and we'll consider it fully paid."

Harry thanked Rainey profusely and adjusted the goggles right then and there, picked up his oil can, and left wearing a smile and the new goggles.

✵✵✵

At 12:45, the racers approached the starting line. Each was given a stop-watch to keep his time and report it to officials at the end of each of the three sections of the course. The first run would be from Ashtabula to North Perry, a distance of about twenty-three miles; the second, from North Perry to Mentor, was a distance of about fifteen miles; the finish to Cleveland's Public Square made up the final forty-five miles. Every racer's gas tank would be filled with exactly five gallons of the same grade gasoline at the beginning of each day's run. Harry knew his racer used more fuel than most, so he had practiced going out of gear down hills to minimize fuel consumption. Twenty drivers began the race at one o'clock sharp. The sun continued to shine, making the day increasingly humid. Harry found himself in the second row of vehicles. He knew a couple of the other racers from summer vegetable forays into town, but none with whom he was terribly friendly. His was certainly the most homemade-looking vehicle in the mix, and he felt anxious as motors raced, awaiting the starter's flag. Wearing his duster buttoned up the middle, he pulled his cap tightly to his head and adjusted the new goggles.

The mayor himself shouted out from the small grandstand, "Gentlemen, on your marks...get set...go!"

A red flag waved, and the drivers were off to North Perry in a thunderous roar of engines. Within the first half mile, Harry wedged into an opening between two racers who had lined up in the first row and he managed to stay pretty much in that position for the first day's run. North Perry would be a good test of his race strategy, constantly hovering near the leader and keeping a steady speed, watching the leather belting as it ran between motor and axle pulleys.

The first day's run was a thrilling blur. He finished ahead of the middle of the pack, making about ten to fifteen miles per hour and using just two of the five gallons of gasoline he carried. He heard reports of some breakdowns that had occurred and was pleased his automobile had performed well. Those drivers were out of the race now, and with fewer entrants, Harry felt his chances improving. Day two's run was a short jump to Mentor—about an hour's distance at the speed he had maintained that day. Day three would be the test for all concerned: forty-five miles in four to five hours without a stop. Harry spread a blanket on the ground beneath his racer and settled in, deciding to save the cost of a night's boarding. He opened the paper bag Mam had packed him that morning, pulling out one of the onion and ham sandwiches it contained. A tear again came to his eye thinking of her, so small and humble, and of Pap, who had somehow looked frailer than he had the day before.

✯✯✯

The second day began very much like the first—a starting time of noon, bunting festooning a grandstand assembled a day or so before. Harry's first day's statistics had moved him into an early lead, so his racer was now in the first line of vehicles. He wished he could somehow let his family know.

They were off again with a roar. He saw a horse buck as he passed a turn in the road. The first day's run had not worn on the leather belt, but he worried about tomorrow's long day and how all the mechanical parts he had scraped together would hold out. *Just get us to Cleveland, old girl*, he found himself thinking. The second day's course contained a series of curves in which he planned to use his coasting technique to save on gas. As he approached the first of these, he noted the road not only curved, it dropped down a considerable hill. He thought he would break only if his machine's belt seemed to want to slide to the left and then re-engage the belt and power through the curve.

The second day was over before Harry knew it, but it had at least given him some good experience with coasting and coming out of turns. Again, his gasoline usage was less than the other drivers, which put him ahead statistically, if not physically. This fact would again put him near the very front of the pack for the forty-five-mile charge into Cleveland. A news reporter for the *Mentor News-Herald* wanted a few moments as Harry's score was announced that afternoon. He found it extraordinary that "...a farm boy driving a...well, what would you call it?...a machine, could capture the lead two days in a row."

Harry was news.

CHAPTER FIVE

"Oooo!" Kathleen James whispered within earshot of her sister as she devoured Harry's photo in the morning's *The Plain Dealer*. "I'm sure he's even better looking in person." She scanned the article again to find his name. "Harry Kern is definitely someone I'd like to get to know!"

Her sister rolled her eyes. Sixteen that year, Kathleen was decidedly self-assured and ready to begin her adult life.

"It says this Mr. Kern is just off the farm! Says he is the leading driver in the race that ends here today, downtown." Kathleen handed the paper to her sister to show her the article and Harry's picture. "He looks so dashing in his duster and goggles," she carried on. "Perhaps we should greet the racers this afternoon."

Like a majority of young Clevelanders, Kathleen James knew of the automotive extravaganza concluding at Public Square that day. Her interest had not really been piqued until she saw Harry's picture.

"He's good-looking Mary, don't you think?"

Mary James looked at the photograph, scanned the article, then returned the newspaper to her sister. "Broad shoulders do it for you every time Kate," she said. "I expect this Mr. Kern spends a lot of time baling hay and tending to livestock. I think you should be more interested in boys whose houses have indoor plumbing."

"I think I can have diverse interests in men at this stage of my life," Kathleen responded. "He's good looking and obviously has a good sense of what he's doing in this racing endeavor, and I think that should be appreciated. Come on now." She smiled at her sister. "What can our going to watch the end of this race hurt? I'm sure Father will be down there."

The girls' father was a patrolman with the Cleveland Police Department. He had reached a sergeant's rank, which paid for a large three-story home on Rockdale Avenue, kept his daughters in nice clothing, and put ample food on the table. He loved the downtown neighborhoods he patrolled and felt personally responsible for everyone's safety. On this particular day, he had already been instructed to be near downtown to assist as the racers arrived.

"There will be crowds and exhausted drivers coming to the finish line all too close together," said his lieutenant the day before.

"Mary and I are going into town, Father," Kathleen said as she walked into the kitchen and smiled at him sitting at the table.

"Ah, Katie, you're not going to watch that silly race," he said. "It's going to cause a lot of commotion and all sorts of people will be there—lots of crowds and noise." He sipped his tea from the cup's saucer and looked at her with a frown. "You know I don't like it when you girls go to town by yourselves."

She gave him her best smile and took a seat in the wooden chair next to his. "We're not going by ourselves. Lizzie Hannah and her brother are going to be there. We're taking her new Ford, and Corry Martindale is coming. And besides," she squeezed his bicep in a loving way, "you'll be on duty about the time the first racers are supposed to hit Public Square."

Chester James thought to himself, *well that's good company to be in for sure.* He knew the discussion was over and that he had lost. The Hannahs and the Martindales were two of Cleveland's most prominent families.

For his daughters to be seen with them would elevate his entire family's status in the eyes of other Clevelanders.

"Well," he smiled, "I suppose if you're going to be part of that group it will be fine. But you know the route I walk if you need me."

Kathleen smiled at him as she rose to leave. "Oceans of love Daddy," she said.

"Where does that phrase come from, my dear?"

"I think it's biblical," she answered. "Love as deep and broad as the ocean—like Jesus had. I'd like to see the ocean sometime!"

✳✳✳

As the town's clock struck one, the first of the racers came roaring down Euclid Avenue into Cleveland's historic Public Square. Harry Kern was not among the first of these drivers to finish, but he was far from the last. The drive had been almost a straight shot from its Mentor start. It was a test of speed and fuel consumption, but Harry thought his run had been a fair test of his vehicle and his race theory. It had been a long pull though, and Harry felt the strain of the day throughout his body. His face was covered in dust, except for where the goggles covered his eyes. His throat was parched from a lack of water over the last hour-and-a-half, and his right foot ached from the tension it had placed on the gas pedal. He was pleased with his effort but also relieved the race was run.

Kathleen and her friends had lunched not far from where the race would end, and their excited talk centered on the morning's newspaper article and the fact that this Harry Kern seemed to have a knack for racing, which was a bit unusual considering his upbringing.

Corry Martindale was of another opinion. "Don't you know, farmers need to be good at many things they do. They can't just call a repairman in from town."

"I hadn't thought of that," Kathleen said smiling. "He's probably very good with his hands." She blushed deeply and the girls all giggled. "Perhaps we should finish here and walk down to the square. We want to get a good seat or at least good standing room for when the winners are announced."

"Daddy said we could watch the finish from the mezzanine balcony of the Hannah Building," said Lizzie. "It's just across from where the race ends and only one floor up from the street."

"That's perfect," said Kathleen. "We'll see all the activity."

"You mean you'll be able to get a good look at Harry Kern," her sister Mary said icily, then smiled at Lizzie's brother Jack.

Harry came to a stop just past the official's viewing stand and jumped down to the brick street. Kathleen had been correct about their ability to get a good look at Harry and his vehicle from the Hannah balcony. She admired the confident way he seemed to smile to himself despite being in an environment so different from what she assumed he was used to. She recalled that same smile from the picture in the morning's paper. He walked toward the race marshal's review stand to turn in his stopwatch. A marshal took his name and noted where he had parked "Number 3."

Having the best race time overall as well as the least gasoline consumption was all Harry could write home about following his win. He included the photo from *The Plain Dealer* with his letter, and as his father read it aloud, Mam studied her son's jubilant face in the black-and-white image.

"Guess he's grown up now," Pap mumbled after setting the letter down. "He's the first to leave us."

Mam took her husband's hand. "But he can always come home. The boy knows the farm's always here."

"As long as we can make the bank payments and have some of them boys here to work it. The longer he's gone the more some of the others will want to go too. Sure hope Cleveland's hard on him," Pap said with a smile, then walked to the barn.

But it was not. In fact, Harry's life in the city began to miraculously fall into place the moment his results were posted. All the race sponsors and promoters were anxious to get a look at the cobbled-together pile of metal this country boy had constructed. The other thing Harry mentioned in the letter home was his meeting some awfully nice people, especially Kathleen James of Cleveland. Had his race time not been the best, he would have been embarrassed by the way he looked when the smiling Miss James boldly introduced herself that afternoon. He assumed she was somehow connected to the race sponsors and his accomplishment that day was the cause of her attention. He saw she was with "fancy" people, but she seemed only interested in him at the moment, which added to both his joy and awkwardness.

"Congratulations Mr. Kern," she began, smiling broadly. "You appear to be the man of the moment. I'm Kathleen James."

Harry did not know whether to shake her outstretched hand or bow. He did manage to remember to take off his cap. She was so very pretty!

"Yes, I guess I am." He proffered a smile and felt a bit out of place taking the hand of this young beauty. He took his eyes off her for a moment and noticed the people she was with, particularly the men, who were dressed so well.

"Do all of you live here in Cleveland?" he ventured, then felt foolish; of course they did.

"Yes, we do, more or less," she answered. "This is my sister Mary. This is Lizzie Hannah, Bruce Scofield, Corry Martindale and Lizzie's brother Jack. Lizzie and Jack's parents recently built a home in Bratenahl. It's a new streetcar suburb on the lake and technically not part of the city."

"How do you like Cleveland so far, Harry?" Jack Hannah asked with a smile. His sister and Corry were looking at him and smiling too.

Harry turned his head from looking at Kathleen. "Time will tell," he said. "What little I've seen is just wonderful. A grand city, progressive."

"Will you be staying here then?" Kathleen asked.

"I have no plans at the moment," Harry managed, feeling at a loss before such grand people. "I'll be here at least for the night and likely a day or so longer. Like to find a job if possible."

The group talked for a while before Harry was sought out by race officials for more photographs and the awarding of prize money. He was to spend the next several nights as the guest at Cleveland's grand Wade Park Hotel, with full access to its restaurants and amenities. He had never been in such an elegant place. His room, with a bathroom right inside, overlooked the art museum and symphony hall. He wondered what they would be like. His first meal in the hotel dining room was just a wonder, and the food was very good. *Perhaps I'll invite the lovely James ladies for supper one night,* he thought, then wondered how he'd get in touch with them.

CHAPTER SIX

Mr. Thomas White, owner of White Motor Company, found the young Mr. Kern to be an exceptionally promising young man from what he read and saw on race day. White Motor Company started producing steam-powered automobiles in 1905 and in fact was selling more steamers than its biggest competitor, Stanley. The morning following the race, Harry received a note from White inquiring if he would be amenable to accompanying him on a tour of his automotive plant in the next day or so. Harry jotted a quick note in return that he would be more than interested.

The next morning, when the plant on Canal Street opened, Harry stood at the gate. Their first stop was the machine lathe department. Overhead were what seemed to Harry miles of leather belting, like the one he had used to power his racing machine, all running a multitude of machinery as skilled operators turned out metal gasoline engine cylinders.

"I didn't begin in the automobile business, you know," White said as they walked through the plant. "Started out making sewing machines and roller skates—not at all related to automobiles. It was my oldest son, Rollin, who talked me into setting aside an area in the factory so he could tinker around with building an automobile. Then his two younger brothers got the itch and joined in, and I had to construct this building. Rollin built a revolutionary steam engine to power a car in 1909."

Harry was full of questions, and White was happy to take whatever time was necessary to answer them. The precision of the lathe work appealed to Harry, as well as the attitude of the men working the machines. *These are skillful operators,* he thought to himself, and hoped he could one day join their ranks.

"Steamers have had their day," said White as they walked along a line of new White Model 30, gasoline-powered automobiles. "Don't get me wrong, we had a good run with them. We won many races with Whistling Billy in oh-seven and later, but gasoline is the future—just ask Mr. Rockefeller—and we plan to play a major role in that."

Harry's eyes were everywhere; he loved the plant's atmosphere, the smells of rubber, leather, oil, and gasoline.

"Rollin wants to get into tractors and trucks," White continued. "You know about tractors I suppose. Most of your racer's parts probably came from them. You showed great ingenuity with that racer. The country is keen for a luxury automobile that can run on dirt roads as well as on pavement. The Model Thirty here," he waved his right arm at the line of autos, "is our answer, son. Old man Ford lit the fuse of the future. I think you could be part of it, Harry. You seem to have a natural knack for understanding machinery and making things work."

Harry and White spent most of the morning on their tour, talking with workers and watching them fit parts all made within the facility itself into finished automobiles. White seemed to know most of his employees by name, and there were quite a few! Harry enjoyed the way White was interested in the men who worked for him. Finally, White turned to face him.

"I'd like to offer you a job here. What do you say? Going to pay better and more regular than farm work, and to get you started, you can have a room in a house I own just down the street. Run by my wife's widowed sister. She's a fine cook!"

Harry was dumbfounded. He looked at Thomas White and around the plant buzzing with energy, his head swimming. "I'd love that sir," he finally said and shook White's hand.

☆☆☆

Harry began working two days after accepting White's offer. The Motor Works was located in an area of Cleveland known as the Flats, a gray, industrial area home to a myriad of manufacturing enterprises near the lake. His first weeks were spent with the plant's head foreman, observing the company's operations sequentially by department. He wanted to learn everything there was to know about automobiles. Then, for six months Harry apprenticed at every stage of assembly. He was most keenly interested in the workings of the gasoline engines and how the shop made its parts. Cutting rubber gaskets was satisfying work for him, fitting them into the engine's metal parts. Working six days a week, he was quick to understand the processes and quicker still to think of ways in which assembly might be made more efficient. Everyone agreed he was a natural!

The boarding house belonging to Mr. White was on Holyoke Road, just a couple blocks from the plant. The room he was given was on a corner, small with a single bed and a very comfortable overstuffed chair. A bathroom was just down the hall. During his evenings, Harry wrote home twice a week. He read back issues of *Mechanic Monthly*, as well as works of American literature he found in the first-floor library to improve his vocabulary and expand his limited views. With a bit of his winnings, he purchased clothing he thought suitable for social life in the city. He was so pleased with them, far finer than any he had ever owned before. He kept them pressed and neatly hung in his room's closet, amusing himself by wondering what his brothers would think of the city slicker he was trying to become.

☆☆☆

Kathleen James was a stunning young woman, a bit taller than Harry, which somehow made her more attractive to him than her facial features alone. She was lithe—that was the way he described her. Her hair was a light golden color and curled around her head and neck, and her eyes were bright blue. She did not laugh a lot out loud, though there was a merriness she exuded that infected those around her, including Harry.

Her courtship of Mr. Kern began innocently enough with a light picnic supper she organized two weeks after the race. Kathleen suggested a spot in the city park where other groups gathered with the same idea and where, she knew, her father would pass on his way home. She was all smiles, as were her friends, but Harry felt distinctly out of place. The chilled wine helped, and he came to terms with the little crustless white-bread sandwiches with slices of cucumber inside. There were no fried chicken drumsticks or hot cobs of corn to pass, but it was a city picnic after all. Lizzie and Jack Hannah were there, as was Mary James and a friend of hers from school, Margaret Hamilton.

"Margaret's family recently moved to Bratenahl," Mary said to Lizzie and Jack, "probably not too far from your parents' home."

"Lots of building going on there," Jack quipped. "Just as long as it's below the railroad tracks, they'll be in great shape."

"We're not beach front," Margaret said, "but we're glad to escape the congestion of downtown."

"Can't blame you there," Jack answered. "Didn't I see you last season in a production at the Cleveland Playhouse?"

Margaret blushed, "it was just a small part, but I do so enjoy the escape being in theater brings."

"Margaret's been in several productions at school," Mary offered. "Perhaps a part in each of the plays we've done over the past two years."

"Is that right?" Lizzie interjected, trying to draw the conversation away from being between Jack and Margaret. "I sometimes think drama is overrated. Real life is dramatic enough."

"Well said!" Kathleen agreed. "Just read the headlines in *The Plain Dealer* and you'll get a sense of the dramatic moments here and in the rest of the country."

Harry listened to all this back and forth and wondered how long it would take him to be conversant in what these people were saying. He had never been to a play and wondered why being in Bratenahl would beat living downtown near your job. Thirty minutes later Margaret excused herself to catch the streetcar home. Jack asked if he could walk her to the station, which Margaret graciously declined, and he said he hoped to see her on stage in the coming year.

"Oh, my goodness," Kathleen exclaimed when Margret was out of sight. "I just can't believe she wants to be a movie star in Hollywood! With her looks the only part she could get would be that of…a witch!"

Mary James pushed at her sister. "You're being unusually mean-spirited. Margaret's a lovely person who's dedicated to her art and I hope she flourishes in an acting career."

Jack Hannah agreed. "It's sure better than being in the iron ore business, though probably not as financially rewarding. Dad just bought land in Georgia, someplace called Thomasville, I think. It's as far south as the railroad line goes. They're calling it a plantation, of all things!" He turned to face Harry. "How are you liking the car business, Harry? I think that would be exciting, fitting all those parts together to make something so useful."

"Oh, I enjoy being there very much. Rollin is just great to work for, and I'm learning so very much. I'm embarrassed now thinking of old Number 3!"

"Don't think that way Harry," Kathleen said. "You built something from scratch, and it won a race. The number three is lucky. I've always thought of having three children after I'm married!"

Mary groaned. "Such a planner! Down to the last detail. Let's call it a night folks. I'm tired and I'm sure Harry needs to be at work in the morning. Unlike the rest of us laggards."

The picnic led to Harry's being casually together with Kathleen at least one evening a week. Along with his new clothing, he had his hair cut in the style of his new friend, Jack Hannah. In no time Harry was dining with the James family an additional time each week, listening to Chester's tales of criminal intrigue in the city and the people living in the different neighborhoods on his beat. There was always laughter, and of course there was Kathleen to look at. While her parents enjoyed having Harry in their home, they were concerned the attachment between their daughter and an hourly wage earner was deepening. It was not what they had in mind.

CHAPTER SEVEN

1915

After his first year at White, Harry was promoted to assistant production manager and later began working with Rollin exclusively, designing tractors that could accomplish many operations farmers needed. He was also able to purchase a used White Model 30 Town Car, which he drove with precision and pride, particularly enjoying its reverse gear and practicing parallel parking on city streets. His new status at White came with an increase in earnings. He found an apartment near the James home, which Kathleen was only too happy to help him furnish with secondhand furniture, and he began saving money at a bank instead of in the shoebox under his bed.

Though he had not expressed the depth of his feelings to Kathleen or her father, he hoped they both understood his intentions were serious. He wished to make Kathleen his wife, though he felt his station in life currently was still well beneath hers. His savings were the beginning of a nest egg for their future. Eight months later, after a second promotion at White, he did express his intentions to Chester, whose approval was taken under advisement. Harry purchased an engagement ring and a year later finally proposed. It was during that year he and Kathleen made their first trip together to visit Pap, Mam, and the family Kern on the farm. His Model 30 made the trip much quicker than his racer, though speed was never its intent. Along the way Harry remembered points of interest from the race to Cleveland and regaled Kathleen with the story of his great adventure. Two hours later they arrived in Ashtabula and Harry stopped in front of Rainey's 5 Star Hardware, where he climbed out of the car and helped Kathleen out. Upon entering, Harry spotted Mr. Rainey behind the long counter talking to customers paying for supplies. It took several moments before the store owner noticed the smartly dressed couple near the entrance, and a few moments more before it came to him who the man was.

"Oh, my goodness, look here! It's Harry Kern," Rainey said as he came from behind the counter to welcome them. "You've gotten taller and look so grown up! And who's this lovely lady with you? She's not from around here."

Harry introduced Kathleen, who gave Rainey a hug. "I wanted to show Kathleen where my oil can and goggles came from," he explained. "I keep them both on the shelf, along with the trophy I won. I thought of wearing the goggles today, but the Model 30 has a windscreen!"

They all laughed at that, and Rainey looked out his front window at the blue four-seater with red wheels. "That's a beautiful automobile Harry, no doubt about that. Pretty as Miss James here! This the first time you've been home since the race. Headed to see the folks?"

"Yes we are. Figured I needed to give Kathleen a chance to get used to all twelve of us. She may decide to back out of any serious discussions of matrimony."

Harry laughed and Kathleen blushed. Though they were less than sixty miles from Cleveland, the changes in locale were pronounced. It was a whole new world for Kathleen to experience and adjust to.

"Been great seeing you, Mr. Rainey. We've taken too much of your time here this afternoon. I think of your kindness to me all the time."

They all shook hands, and Rainey waved as they walked to the car. Harry put it in reverse to head to the farm.

"What a nice fellow," Kathleen said.

"Yes, and he probably knows most everyone around. Tomorrow we'll be news!"

Harry made the turn that would take them to the farm, remembering how rural the countryside was outside of Ashtabula—flat, with farms on either side of the road they traveled down. He wondered what Kathleen must think of all this, so different from the city where she was born and raised. *She's going to think I'm a real hayseed.* Twenty minutes later, Harry turned off the paved road onto a dirt one that led to the Kern farm.

A good hour before dusk they caught sight of the homestead's roofline.

"All the boys would sleep up there," Harry said softly. "No heat, two windows, no bathroom, and nine beds." He slowed the car and looked at Kathleen. "Maybe we shouldn't have come, it's all like out of a bad dream. I'm sorry."

"Oh, don't be Harry. I've wanted to meet your family and see where you grew up, especially where you built your racer. I'm looking forward to all of it!"

He stopped the car twenty feet or so from the porch that led to the kitchen door he knew so well and honked the horn twice. "You're a good sport," he said to her.

The kitchen door opened, and the Kern family all filed out, everyone's clothes clean and hair combed.

"They just keep coming," Kathleen giggled when Mam and Pap finally brought up the rear.

The boys circled the Model 30 and admired it greatly, then hugged Harry and shook hands with Kathleen.

"Just look at you Harry," said brother Graham. "You're a regular city slicker! Can't work the fields tomorrow in them clothes!"

Mary and Mam approached to greet Kathleen, who smiled and stepped forward to hug each of them.

"I'm so happy to meet you both. Harry talks about you all so often." She reached into the car's back seat for two small parcels and presented one to each of the ladies. "I wanted to bring something you'd remember me by."

The boxes contained Irish linen handkerchiefs from Cleveland's Higbee's department store, which brought a tear to Mam's eye.

"Never seen nothing so fine in my life," she said, hugging Kathleen again.

Harry was being jostled by his brothers, then turned to hug his father.

"Let me have a look at you, son! You're all grown and on your own in that big world of Cleveland, with an important job, making good money. And most importantly with a pretty young lady on your arm." He hugged Harry again and whispered, "Mighty proud of you."

They all filed back into the house, which seemed much smaller to Harry than he'd remembered, and had rhubarb pie and lemonade around the enormous kitchen table. That night Harry joined his brothers back in the attic—his bed made where he'd left it—and Mary got to have a roommate for the first time in her life!

After breakfast the following morning at six thirty, Harry spent most of the day showing Kathleen around the farm. She had brought clothing suitable for strolling through the countryside, and when they came to the pond, even dug a shovelful of earth in search of a worm or two for bait. The perch they caught were fried for lunch by Mam, along with okra and tomatoes.

"I've never eaten so much before dinner in my life," Kathleen laughed. "It must be the fresh air!"

Learning she had never been on a horse, Harry brought out Pap's new gelding named Star, put a bridle on him, and they both climbed on for a ride into the pasture to find the family's cow. The afternoon air was clear, sunshine mingling with leaves in the breeze. Kathleen held on to Harry's waist as Star ambled along. They both felt the weekend was going too quickly. The leisure they were enjoying would all too soon be replaced by the hubbub of Cleveland.

After dinner that night the men adjourned to wicker chairs outside. Harry had brought a box of cigars and offered one to each of his brothers. Pap didn't hold with tobacco himself. A couple of the boys tried them, but it was Harry who developed a fondness for the taste that lingered throughout his life. Mam, Mary, and Kathleen sat in the kitchen, where Mam delighted Kathleen with stories of Harry's life prior to leaving for the race. Great bursts of laughter could be heard by the men outside as the stars came out and the evening became night.

The next day, following another farm lunch, the Kern family again surrounded Harry's Model 30, where tears replaced Mam's happy laughter of the night before and promises of return trips to the farm were made. Harry felt a heaviness too, different than the one he had held upon leaving for the race just two years before. He thought his father looked older than he'd remembered, and some of his brothers mentioned their plans to leave the farm and go out on their own as Harry had done. He always knew some of his brothers would seek their own futures bigger than the farm and the lives they had known as children, but it saddened him and somehow made him feel guilty about going off himself. He wondered what paths the boys would follow, where they would travel to, if he would ever see them again. Kathleen put her arm through his and leaned as close to him as the car's seats would allow. The ride back to the city was decidedly quieter than the one they'd made two days before.

"I had a fine time with your family, Harry. Your mother is so very wise and strong. Love your sister Mary, we talked long into the night. I think she liked sharing her room! Your brothers admire you very much, you know. You can see it in the way they respond to things you say. You broaden their view of the world. And of course, your father is kind of," she paused, "a free spirit. Follows his own path I expect in most things. I respect that. I do wish they had indoor plumbing though!"

CHAPTER EIGHT

"You know, Kathy," Harry said, "I wonder sometimes if your father is ever going to come around to accepting me as a son-in-law. I know he was hoping for someone like Jack, with more stature and a future."

"Oh Harry, I think you have a bright future at White. You're practically running the truck and tractor division!"

"How you exaggerate, but I do enjoy working there, and I'm learning so much. Rollin wants to take us completely out of the automobile business and turn the company's attention to trucks, especially as it looks as if the country is moving closer to joining the European war. We're selling almost every truck we make to the French Army, and he's even arranged for my deferment from military service due, he says, to my importance to the potential White war effort."

"Well, that's wonderful news! See, you do have a future Daddy can appreciate. He can marry Mary off to a Hannah if he needs to make that connection. She's much better suited to be part of that dynasty anyway." Kathleen hugged Harry and kissed him on the cheek. "This apartment of yours will really be kind of small for the both of us, after the wedding.

I like it of course and it suits you perfectly now, but you know, I have a lot of things!"

Harry laughed, "I just bet you do."

✯✯✯

Pap, Graham, and Mary came for the wedding. Mam felt she couldn't leave the farm and did not wish to experience Cleveland. They came by train, which neither of Harry's siblings had ever ridden. Harry met them at Lakefront Station and housed them at Mr. White's boarding house, with Mary getting his old room. His brother and sister were enthralled by everything they saw during the three days they spent with Harry and Kathleen. Pap was another story but largely kept his mistrust of the city to himself. As he was to serve as Harry's best man, Harry suggested he get him a new white shirt and bow tie and have his suit cleaned and pressed. Pap seemed to enjoy this attention, though he thought the price Harry paid for the articles was excessive.

"We've been invited to have dinner with Kathleen's family this evening," Harry said. "Mrs. James is a fine cook, and I know you'll all enjoy meeting Kathy's father and sister."

Harry's apartment was closer to the James home than was the boarding house, so he took them there to freshen up. Pap donned his new shirt and tie, Graham wore one of Harry's shirts and jackets, while Mary rearranged herself and looked lovely. Kathleen met them at the door when they arrived.

"Come in. It's so nice to have you here and meet my family. Graham, that shirt and coat fit you perfectly. He may just have to take that home," she said, winking at Harry. "And Pap, your shirt and striped tie make you so handsome!" She hugged Mary and whispered, "You're always so very pretty."

Kathleen introduced everyone to her mother and sister. Chester had not arrived home yet. He had taken the longer route of his beat tonight, thinking how, even at this late hour, he could prevent his daughter's marriage to this glorified automobile mechanic. He liked Harry well enough but had higher hopes for his number-two daughter who was so much like him. Harry's nails always had grease under them, and Chester felt the family was moving backward with this marriage. Fifteen minutes later, he entered the back door of his home, hung his pistol, handcuffs, and nightstick on wooden pegs, and joined his wife and daughters.

Harry noticed Chester first, moving his father across the room for the introduction. "Pap, this is Chester James, Kathleen's father."

The two men were physically, philosophically, and likely politically exact opposites. Chester extended his beefy hand to Pap and could feel the blisters of farm work, as he did again when meeting Graham. Pap felt Chester's hand was firm but somehow soft to the touch, though he gauged Chester very fit for his age and size.

"A pleasure to meet you, Mr. Kern," Chester said. "Seems we're about to be related."

A glass of sherry followed for those guests over eighteen, then dinner was served with quiet conversation. The Kern family returned by taxi to the boarding house, and Harry walked to his apartment.

After the wedding, the newlyweds lived with the James family for six months while Harry continued to save all he could from his salary, always sending a part of it to his parents on the farm. Shortly thereafter, the couple were able to purchase a modest house in a respectable neighborhood of Cleveland. Kathleen's family and friends provided enough housewarming gifts to get the couple well started. A few years later, they would be able to buy a larger home on Euclid Avenue, a much more fashionable address that greatly appealed to Kathleen.

CHAPTER NINE

By the war's end, Harry found himself increasingly involved in vehicle sales, especially to military procurers. While White tractors and trucks would form the backbone of the business, in the post-war era he found customers, especially returning veterans, wanting cars. Harry was good at sales; he understood the burgeoning marketplace and had a way of relating to his customers. He was Harry Kern after all, winner of the great Ashtabula/Cleveland Road Race.

The problem was the Whites were out of the automobile business, now producing only trucks. So Harry began thinking about selling automobiles on the side. During a trip with Rollin to Detroit, he met Frederick Hayes, the new president of the Dodge Motor Company. Hayes remembered the Cleveland race and knew from Rollin how Harry thrived at White. He was looking for a sales representative for Dodge in the Cleveland market, wanting to begin distribution slowly, and Harry seemed to him to be a promising fit. Harry agreed, and as he was working on truck design for White, neither party saw any conflicts. When the Detroit meeting concluded, Harry returned home in a blue, 1918 Dodge Model 30 Tourer.

"Oh Harry," Kathleen said. "Surely you didn't buy a second car so soon after signing our mortgage?"

"No, love, it's for me to sell and get a commission on, in addition to what I make at White. Rollin is completely agreeable. It's a honey though, isn't it? Much faster than our Model 30 and certainly more comfortable!"

The following day being a Saturday and only a half day of work for Harry, he spent the afternoon looking for vacant warehouse space he could use to sell the Dodge and perhaps other models. He found a small building near the White plant, rented it, and spent the next two weeks after working at White cleaning it out for use as the home of Kern Motor Sales.

✳✳✳

Harry Kern, Jr. was clearly the apple of his parents' eyes, the first child born to Harry and Kathleen some six years after the race and three years after they were married. He was a blond-haired, blue-eyed charmer from birth, and Kathleen always had an affinity for charming men. Called Sonny, he quickly learned just how far he could push his mother before she would invoke the wrath of his father. In her view, this was the ultimate punishment for boys not behaving as she thought they should. There had been no male children in the James family for a while, so Sonny was quite a hit, particularly with Papa Chester, who could not come home quickly enough from his daily beat to be with him. The boy's incessant activity was exhausting, and Kathleen sometimes just could not cope. By midday she was a frazzle, and Harry would not be home until much later. Still, Sonny had a way about him and could generally turn her head just enough to be spared physical punishment for unsuitable behavior. It wasn't too many years later that a second child was on the way, and Kathleen packed Son off to the farm that summer to stay with Pap and Mam. That year, and in subsequent years even with her daughters, she loved that quieter time.

And if Harry wasn't amorous during the nights of her month's bliss, she didn't begin subsequent autumns "in the family way."

While Sonny being at the farm offered a break to Kathleen, it provided him times of high adventure. It was magical, particularly those mornings when he would look out one of the second-floor windows into thick fog engulfing the ground and trees below. Sonny imagined all sorts of creatures lurking in the mist, and later, as the sun shown through, he scampered about looking for things they might have left behind. He spent most afternoons swimming in the pond or fishing in it, or climbing around in the barn, playing cops and robbers or new world explorer. Then there was a horse or even the cows to ride. Bringing in fresh eggs from the hens or milking the cows had not become chores yet. He enjoyed being with his grandparents and the freedom from life in a city.

Pap's horse, Star, was a favorite with Son, as he moved slowly and did not mind being ridden bareback. Typically, Star would be out in the large pasture in the mornings and allowed to graze most of the day. Near the end of his vacation one summer, as afternoon was beginning its slide toward evening, Son decided to hitch a ride from the lake to the barn. After being astride for a few moments, both horse and rider heard Pap strike the iron triangle that hung outside the kitchen door—a signal for the livestock to begin their trek back for feeding. Old Star must have been particularly hungry, as he took off at a gallop with Son holding on to his mane, attempting to keep from sliding off his wide back. The horse gained speed as they neared the barn. With Star showing no signs of slowing down and the barn door coming up fast—its top post only slightly higher than the horse's head—a couple dozen thoughts ran through Son's young mind, mostly about survival, how bad the pain would be if he hit the low beam, or if he would even survive. With only seconds to spare, Son grabbed the base of Star's neck and lowered his head as far as he could. He saw Pap as a blur as they sped by. Son could not understand what it was Pap was shouting when horse and rider galloped into the barn, finally coming to a sliding stop. Pap and Uncle Ben came into the barn at a run, the same moment Son slid down from the horse who sauntered over to a bucket of oats hung on his hook.

"Sure must be good eatin'!" Son said to them with a trembling walk and a sly grin. "Suppose I should try some?"

Pap and Ben looked down at the boy who had nearly been lost to them. "We're not going to tell your mother about this," Pap said. "It will be our secret. In fact," he added with a bit of a smile breaking through, "we're not going to tell Mam either."

CHAPTER TEN

Kern Motor Sales was doing well, with Harry able to sell everything he brought in from Dodge. His routine consumed the weekends when he needed a new vehicle—taking the train to Detroit after work on Saturday afternoon, picking up the automobile, and returning to Cleveland with it on Sunday, for a total distance of 170 miles. He'd be home for dinner with Kathleen, Sonny, Agnes, and little Nora, born in 1927, then he would wash off the new car. Early Monday morning he'd drive it into the sales office before work at White. It was a tiring schedule that was occurring more frequently it seemed.

Commissions were good, but not good enough to leave White and go out on his own. He needed to increase his inventory from one vehicle at a time and planned to talk with Fred Hayes about how to get that accomplished. The two men had become friends in the relatively short time they'd known one another. Hayes always met Harry on his Sunday morning pick-ups, and before the return trip to Cleveland, would show him the newest Dodge engine designs, especially for racing. Harry called him a day or two later after finishing at White.

"Hello Harry. I trust you had a good return trip in the DD6 Coupe? Thanks again for the cigar! Smoked it yesterday afternoon."

"Yes sir. I made good time and arrived home for supper with Kathleen and the kids. Have the coupe shined up and sitting here in the garage where customers can see it through the window. Don't think it will be here long."

"Excellent! You must come to my home for dinner on your next trip—might even find you a bedroom for the night."

"Oh, that would be very gracious of you! So, Fred, I was wanting to talk to you about increasing my inventory here. The garage I'm using could hold at least three vehicles, and the building next to it is coming up for lease. As yet, I can't afford to purchase more than one or maybe two from you, but I was hoping we could work out an arrangement where I purchase what I can afford and you float me one or two additional vehicles, on which your financial return would be more than what you make on the cars I buy at fifty percent."

There was a pause as Fred Hayes thought Harry's proposition over— long enough to make Harry wonder if he'd asked too much of his reasonably new friend.

"Harry, I believe we can work something out between us," Hayes said finally. "You've got a Dodge there now that you own at half price, and I can send you a Plymouth and a DeSoto at say a seventy percent return to the plant, to see what the market is like for those models. As you know, they're basically the same vehicle as the Dodge, the DeSoto's just a little fancier while the Plymouth is a step or two down. One's a bit more money, one a bit less. Let me just run this by the brass at Chrysler, but I don't anticipate a problem as I'm recommending the deal. Since they bought Dodge from the brothers two years ago, I just need to make sure they're in the loop. I can get the additional vehicles to you first of next week if that would be enough time to allow you to freshen up your garage and add signage and advertising for the new lines of cars."

"Can we make it the week after next, please? I'm still working at White six days a week and I want time to provide the very best showroom space I can."

"Let me see if we can help with that too. Did I hear you say a building next to the one you're using now will soon be available? Perhaps the boys at Chrysler would give me the okay to lease it for you and make it presentable as an additional showroom. We'd work out some modest financial arrangement that would maybe add a percentage or two to the seventy percent return I've mentioned and relieve you of leasing an additional space. Perhaps we could even relieve you of the rental on your current space and maybe, if sales increase with the addition of the two new lines, you might consider leaving White and going into business for yourself!"

There it was, the conundrum Harry had wrestled with since the first of the new year. He was making a good wage at White, but working there meant he had little time for selling automobiles, which he was good at and enjoyed. Doing both also limited his time with Kathleen and his children. It would be a gamble for certain, and he could not escape a feeling of betrayal in leaving White, but his heart was no longer in trucks. He wondered how Kathleen would feel about his dealership thoughts; he had not mentioned anything to her. She loved their new home, and Harry had never missed a mortgage payment. Could she make a leap of faith and trust in his abilities?

At that the telephone rang. "Kern Motor Sales."

"Harry, it's Jack Hannah. Bruce and I are leaving work and wondered if you had that new Dodge in your shop that Kathleen mentioned you were bringing down over the weekend. We had a swell dinner party Saturday, and she said you had gone to Detroit."

"Yes, sir, I'm sitting here looking at her. She's a DD6 Business Coupe in a deep red."

"Could Bruce and I pop over and have a look at her? We could be there in say, fifteen minutes."

The arrangement was made, and the men arrived in good form. After looking over the coupe the three of them took it out for a spin, and upon their return Bruce bought it with cash. Harry had been correct in his boast to Fred Hayes that the Dodge would not be in his shop long, but he had no idea the sale would happen that quickly. Alone again in the sales office, Harry put the cash in an envelope and the envelope in his coat pocket, not wanting to leave it in the building. Having driven the coupe to the office that morning he called for a cab to get home. *I can't count on this kind of a chance sale every time I have inventory,* Harry thought. *This was nothing but a coincidence. But what if I could sell one or two a week? Those boys have friends out there in Bratenahl...just maybe the business would work out. Need to speak to Kathleen though.*

✢✢✢

Though the stock market crash caused financial tremors leading to the Great Depression, Walter Chrysler's business grew, in large part due to his Plymouth automobile. It was well built but nothing fancy, and Americans who could afford an automobile turned to it for its reliability and affordability. Harry sold a lot of them from his dealership the Chrysler Corporation helped him expand and renovate. In the face of the Depression, Harry left White and went out on his own. Fred Hayes began shipping a sampling of Chrysler automobiles to Harry in 1931, including the newly developed Dodge with a straight eight-cylinder motor. Kathleen, initially stressed by Harry's decision, grew more comfortable with his decision as sales did not lessen.

With a nearly full Dodge line of automobiles, Harry felt increasingly confident as his first full year in business came to an end. As before, he was selling more Plymouths than any of the others, but he did sell a Chrysler to Jack Hannah's dad, Howard. It was the first automobile he'd ever owned, and as fall approached, Hannah had it shipped by train to his Georgia home for hunting season. Harry could only imagine "riding the hounds" in October and November and quail shooting closer to Thanksgiving. *Another world,* he thought.

As the financial downturn was not hitting Cleveland as hard as other northern cities, his sales remained stable, and midway through his second year, his earnings were a bit more than he had made in his last year at White. Harry was happy, Fred was happy, and even Kathleen was happy.

During the summer of that second year of business, when sales seemed to drop off just a bit, Harry and his growing brood decided to make a trip to the farm. He sold his White Model 30 and purchased from himself a new 1931 Dodge straight-eight sedan—tan body with brown fenders. The eight-cylinder engine had come out in Dodge cars that year, and the temptation to own one was just too great! Sonny had just turned eleven and was eager to get to the farm. His mother packed him a bag just in case Pap and Mam asked him to stay awhile. Agnes and baby Nora had never been to visit their Kern grandparents. Harry enjoyed the sound of his children in the voluminous back seat, as well as the purr of the engine. He still sent his parents money every month to help support the farm. Four of the other boys had left since Son's last summer trip, and the absence of Pap's free labor supply, Harry hoped, had not been a hardship on his parents' health and physical abilities. Apparently sister Mary had a serious gentleman caller. Harry wondered how Mam would cope with the possible loss of her only female offspring. This visit would likely not be as lighthearted as the last one they made. His parents were the first two Kerns out the kitchen door, followed by Mary and a nice-looking young man who must have been her beau, then Graham, Melvin, Charlie, and Ben. Except for Mary, they all looked somewhat older, Harry thought, especially Pap, who now walked using a cane. The car doors opened, and Son and Agnes burst forth, then Kathleen with Nora, and finally Harry.

"Hello everyone," he offered as his brothers gravitated to the new Dodge, which was at least twice the size of the Model 30. "Sure is grand to be here with you all."

Kathleen and Nora were enveloped by Mam and Mary, Mam taking a sleeping Nora into her arms. Pap hugged his "Cleveland" son, then led them all to chairs arranged under the shade of the maple trees Pap had planted twenty years earlier. Sonny, not interested in sitting, took Agnes on a tour.

"Mind where you're going Son, and be careful," Harry said to their backs as they ran toward the barn.

✼✼✼

Over the next two days there was talk about the past on the farm, as well as the struggles Pap and Mam continued to face making ends meet. A few of the other boys who left occasionally sent money home, but nothing like Harry did. Pap had hurt his left leg the previous winter when he slipped on a patch of ice and twisted it badly at the knee. Being housebound in winter was not all that bad, he'd said. He was able to read and had especially enjoyed the biography of William B. Greene Ben had brought him from the library in Ashtabula.

"Greene was an absolute anarchist," he confided to Harry. "I much admired that as I did reading accounts of his time at Ripley's Brook Farm. Just wish I'd been there."

Mam and Mary outdid themselves, baking and cooking full meals three times a day, but to Kathleen's chagrin, there was still no inside toilet. That Sunday afternoon, Harry and Kathleen packed up their things, and with Agnes and Nora prepared for their return. Sonny wormed his way into staying two weeks longer than usual, promising to help with chores and catch fish from the pond when required. Kathleen, as always, was happy for the time alone with her girls, but wanted more for her son in life than the farm could offer. Graham said he would deliver Son home on the train so Harry would not need to take time from work and looked forward to a tour of the Kern Motor Sales showroom.

Arriving downtown bright and early the following Monday morning, Harry found five inquiries in the mailbox. He flipped the showroom's lights on, made a pot of coffee, lit a cigar, and began returning calls from potential customers. It was going to be a fine day!

CHAPTER ELEVEN

Kathleen was readying herself for a luncheon with her sister and Lizzie Hannah. Her mother would arrive shortly to stay with the girls while she was in town dining at La Cuisine in the Halle Building. Mary had not married into the Hannah family, but instead had recently become the second wife of criminal attorney and Assistant Cuyahoga County Prosecutor, Norman Minor. Once again, Chester James wondered what his first daughter was thinking to be involved with a divorced man. He was touted as Cleveland's best criminal attorney, which as a policeman Chester admired, but a divorced, black man was really too much. Not wanting to be the butt of jokes at the station, Chester put in for retirement just before the engagement was announced in *The Plain Dealer*.

The three women, seated at a comfortable corner table, ordered gin cocktails and perused the luncheon menu. Lizzie was still single and admitted to enjoying spending time with the single set in Thomasville, Georgia when there for hunting season.

"Daddy just loves that car he bought from Harry," she began. "Drives it all over down there and especially likes to take us to Tallahassee for an afternoon and dinner."

"That will make Harry very happy to hear, Liz! I think that is the first and only Chrysler he's sold since he's been in the business. The economy is more comfortable with Plymouths. What's life at the end of the railroad tracks like anyway?"

Lizzy folded her menu and placed it before her, indicating she had made her luncheon choices. "Well, it is so completely different from being here in Cleveland. Not up with the times at all, mostly dirt roads, except for the cute, tiny downtown strip. The people we associate with all live on large tracts of land as if they were still in the nineteenth century. There are still black servants, cooks, and nannies. Our set still ride horses, and, in the fall, they dress up as if they were in England, red outfits and all, then set their hounds loose to chase poor foxes through the countryside. Maybe twenty-five men and women on horseback, with a bugler leading the charge. I feel so bad for the poor little fox!"

"I would too," Mary said.

"There are these wagons with cages built in for the dogs. There's a lot of drinking before the crowd sets out, so spirits are high! Different hunts are arranged for different estates, but most of the same people are on every hunt. I must say, the men look so gallant and handsome in their red tunics, white britches, and black knee-high boots!" Their second cocktails arrived. "And, what about you, Mary, and Attorney Minor? You'll be Mary Minor!"

They all laughed at that.

"Norm is an awfully good man and is part of a fine criminal law firm. He's blazing a trail for black attorneys to come. 'Course our family's taken the interracial thing hard. Don't you think, Kath?"

"Daddy's the worst," Kathleen said. "Quit his job over it. Didn't know what his fellow officers would say about the marriage and didn't want to wait around to find out." The waiter brought their salads. "I think Mother is getting used to the idea," Kathleen continued. "I don't want to appear as being ugly, Mary, but I think it's a blessing Norman and his first wife did not have children. I think that would have pushed Daddy over the edge."

They all laughed.

"I know," Mary said. "I sometimes just want to tell him that once you try black you'll never go back! But I'm sure his heart wouldn't take that, and I'd be responsible."

The three of them laughed over Mary's little rhyme.

"He'd be lynched in Thomasville," Lizzy said with a very straight face. "I wouldn't take the train south, Mary."

"Fortunately there are plenty of criminals here in Cleveland to keep him busy. Oh, his current case against this Willie The Mad Butcher Johnson fellow is just beyond reason! When Norman convicts him of murdering twelve women, maybe he'll be Harry's next Chrysler buyer," Mary said, turning to her sister.

"What colors does he like?" Katherine asked without pausing.

"Say," Lizzie said, "I want to have you two meet a new couple in the community. I'm thinking of having a lady's lunch at the house in Bratenahl for Cynthia Coats Clarke, whose husband Clark is a new string musician with the symphony."

"Wait," Kathleen interrupted, "his first name is Clark, and his last name is Clarke?"

"Yes, isn't that a scream?" Lizzy laughed. "I don't think he has a middle name, or if he does he doesn't use it. He's very handsome, and she's quite attractive too. She descends from the Coats thread people in Scotland, very wealthy. They live on her income! He is the new first viola."

"I'm in," said Kathleen, "though it's crazy for people to have names all beginning with the letter C. I just can't imagine how confusing that must be! Be good to have some artistic friends."

✵✵✵

Harry was having a very good day too. He sold two autos before noon to new clients who had left notes while he was at the farm, and used the Dodge dealer sales brochure to select specific colors and options for a third customer, from whom he took a fifty-percent deposit up front. Afterward, he turned his attention to thinking over an advertising opportunity presented to him by Cleveland Indians baseball promoters. Games were played at League Park and were all day games as lighting had not been installed there for evening or night games. Games were broadcast by radio, and business sponsors were touted in twenty-second spots throughout each broadcast. Harry talked the Indians promoters into allowing him to park one of his cars outside the park's entrance at no additional cost. He enjoyed baseball, so it was no inconvenience to sponsor a Sunday game, go to the game with Son in a new Plymouth sedan, and return it to the showroom afterwards. Kathleen felt the baseball crowd was too rough for her and the girls and was only too happy for Son to have a bit of time with his father. Of course Harry made the most of it with his boy!

Parking one of the Kern autos outside the park was at least as successful as the twenty-second radio spots. Harry always found folks looking the auto over and engaged in conversation with them. He passed out his business cards to people who seemed most interested and generally would sell a car or two during the two-week period after a game. He thought about offering first place prize money for winners of the stock-car races that took place quarterly at the Akron-Cleveland Speedway. He also considered talking with Fred Hayes about sending him a specially modified Plymouth outfitted with the Dodge straight-eight engine to enter in a race if he could find someone to drive it.

Closing the sales office at six Monday evening, Harry drove home for dinner with Kathleen, Son, and the girls. There was a breeze off the lake—the temperature must have fallen ten degrees—and he was looking forward to being home. Agnes greeted him as he parked the Dodge in the detached garage and pulled him inside to show off the new artwork she'd made while spending the afternoon with Nana James.

"Hello," he said softly in case Nora was napping. Instead, he found her quietly playing in her basinet while Kathleen was napping in a chair next to her. He could smell a chicken roasting in the oven and looked forward to having a scotch and soda beforehand. He reached down for Kathleen's hand, kissing it softly, which woke her.

"I really just sat down. Had lunch with Mary and Lizzie and quite possibly one too many gin cocktails."

"And how are your sisters-in-crime?" Harry asked. "I guess I can't use that phrase anymore now that Mary's married to Norman! How are the ladies?"

"Oh, they're both just as fine as frog hair. Mary's really taken a leap with her marriage, though. I'm just not sure how ready Cleveland is for an interracial couple at that level. I'm glad he gets excellent marks from the newspaper and he wins his cases. Lizzie, well you know, she's still the same Lizzie, bitchy as ever."

"You mean full of crap?"

"Now, don't be ugly, she means well, just a bit of a flibbertigibbet." Kathleen got out of her chair to make Harry's drink while he grabbed up Nora. "Seems she's taken in new friends she wants to introduce around. I expect we'll be invited to a party on Lake Shore Boulevard in a few weeks."

"That's good, I love talking with all those wealthy, potential clients. Who are her newcomers?"

"Well, you are not going to believe their names! You'll be meeting Clark and Cynthia Coates Clarke."

Harry thought that through a moment. "He's Clark Clarke?"

"That's correct, all their names begin with the letter C. He's a new string musician at the symphony, and she's just wealthy, from the Coats and Clark families in Scotland. Guess she just couldn't help herself when she found a man whose last name so reminded her of her ancestry!"

"Goodness," Harry said with a smile. "That's just too funny. What were his parents thinking?"

"Hard to imagine, but I do hope we like him at least. I've been thinking about music lessons for Son. He needs a bit of culture and he'll be twelve on his next birthday."

"I'll bet Pap knows a fiddler or two he might recommend!" Harry was pulling her leg of course, but wanted to see her reaction.

"Really? I want Son to begin to appreciate some of the finer things in life."

"I know honey, I was only teasing. But somehow I just can't see Son with a violin under his chin. He'll think we're turning him into a sissy."

"Maybe there are other types of string instruments that might be of interest. Let's wait and see."

Fred Hayes thought the notion of putting a Dodge straight-eight into a Plymouth body and hitting the stock car circuit was a wonderful idea, and Harry pursued having Dodge Motors Inc. and Kern Motor Sales sponsor at least two races over the racing season. There was only one problem. Stock car racing was predicated on the automobiles in a race being "stock" cars that could be purchased from a dealer. A Plymouth with a Dodge engine could not be purchased off a dealer's lot.

"Fred, we're going to have to race a Dodge Eight if we want into this venture, which is a shame because Dodge is a heavier car."

"We've started thinking about putting an eight-cylinder engine in the Business Coupe model and will likely start production in the fall," Fred said. "That would give us a lighter auto with a bigger engine that will be a stock item first of the new year. I can have one of those made up and sent down to you for publicity purposes."

The deal was done. Harry set about looking for a team of three drivers who could be engaged by Dodge in 1932. Secretly, he wanted to drive in a future race himself, but put that thought out of his head as

Kathleen's reaction to such an idea would be to take to their bed, slamming the door behind her.

CHAPTER TWELVE

A few days later Kathleen received an invitation from Lizzie to lunch at Otto Moser's restaurant to meet Cynthia Coats Clarke, and a week later, an invitation to meet both Clarkes at the Hannah estate in Bratenahl.

"She's a rich bitch," she informed Harry the evening after they had lunch. "Honestly, she never let the other ladies get a word in. Overdressed, which I can attribute to, and perhaps forgive, not having been at Moser's before, but I expect she enjoys having people look at her."

"What type of car did she arrive in? Maybe she'd like to trade up?"

"Oh hell, Harry, honestly!"

"It's how I make my living, my dear, which I'll point out is getting better, even in these lousy economic times!"

✵✵✵

The Bratenahl event began at six with cocktails. The girls and Son were delivered to the James' home at five and were to stay the night, which suited both the children and grandparents very well. It was a beautiful, warm, late spring evening, and Harry chose to drive a black 1932 DeSoto

Coupe that had just arrived at the dealership. It was a handsome vehicle, with the new models featuring a streamlined body. The interior was white leather, and under the hood was a Dodge straight-eight. He and Kathleen made a splendid entrance pulling up the long Hannah driveway. Letting Kathleen out at the estate's front door, Harry found a conspicuous place to park the DeSoto so it could be admired.

Lizzie met Kathleen at the door and led her to where Mary, Norman Minor, Cory Martindale, her brother Jack, and his new bride Nancy were already conversing with Mr. and Mrs. Clarke. Clark Clarke was, Kathleen immediately thought, a magnificent specimen! He was tall, blonde, well-built for a musician, and extremely well-spoken. As she and Lizzie joined the group, Norman was answering a few questions concerning the forthcoming Willie Johnson trial. *Why do people seem to dwell on and enjoy hearing about violence?* Kathleen thought. Apparently, Cynthia had brought the subject up upon meeting Norman and just had to know as many grizzly details as he could provide in mixed company. Clark seemed to be drifting from the conversation, she thought, hoping the subject would soon change.

"Oh, Norman, that's quite enough about all of that. I am sure you have everything in hand," Kathleen said. "Clark, tell us about Severance Hall and the mysterious Nicolai Sokoloff."

His focus seemed to drift back to reality and he looked at Kathleen as if he had only now seen her.

"Ah, Nicky! You know those Russians! He's a string musician like me, a great fellow! Very innovative and encouraging to all of us. He was the first conductor at his last post out west to hire female players and pay them the same wage as the men in his charge. Rumors are he will leave Cleveland after this season. I hope not though. The hall? Well it's the best money can provide, puts Cleveland on the musical map."

Kathleen felt as if Clark were talking to only her, though it was certainly not the case, and as the group continued to talk, she felt a special attachment to him she had not expected.

"You and your husband should come to a rehearsal sometime," he said to her as the group dispersed to mingle with others. "I'd be happy to let you know our schedule for the next few weeks."

Kathleen said she would like that very much and didn't know if her husband Harry would join her. She found Harry an hour or so later talking with a group of men about baseball and Cleveland's chance at a pennant race this year. He seemed happy talking easily to men he hardly knew. *That is his gift. It's what makes him good at sales, and I am grateful for that, but heavens, his preoccupation with cars and business can be so tiresome.* Her eye followed Clark as he and Cynthia moved onto the wide stone patio.

"Having a nice time?" she asked Harry.

He smiled and winked at her. "I am! Love these parties at Lizzie's—they're good for business! Sold the DeSoto just now. Where have you been anyway? Lizzie taken you away?"

"Well yes, she did actually. We were on the other side of the house with the group, meeting the Clarkes. Clark has invited us to attend a symphony rehearsal some time. I thought that would be nice. We could bring Son along, but the girls are too young."

"Well unless they rehearse in the evenings, I'll have to take a pass. Can't afford to close the dealership in the middle of the day. But you go and take Son. It'd be good for him, something very different from the farm!"

They toured through the mansion's rooms for a while, then waved at Lizzie who had just come back in from the patio area with the Clarkes. While sampling a few of the hors d'oeuvres, they found the Clarkes standing next to them.

"And is this Mr. Kern?" Cynthia Clarke asked of Kathleen.

"Yes, this is my husband, Harry."

Harry affected a slight bow, then put out his hand to Clark. "Welcome to Cleveland to you both. I trust you will find it as pleasant as I have over these past twenty years. Folks here are very friendly. Where are you living?"

"We're still looking over areas," Clark replied. "Currently we're in fine quarters at the Wade Park Hotel, a very nice suite of rooms on the fifth floor. We understand the Wade family is planning to develop a residential area on the remainder of the land they own, which would be very nice for me, getting to Severance. But I think Cynthia would like to be somewhere outside the city proper, maybe in Shaker or Lakewood Heights."

"Shaker is very nice," Harry said. "I expect the lot sizes are a bit larger than those that the Wades might be laying out."

"Yes, I think that's true, and why I'd like us to be out there," Cynthia said, "though I'm not all that keen on taking the streetcar into town."

"They're very clean and airy, Cynthia," Kathleen replied. "And they can drop you off wherever you wish on their routes." Then turning to Clark she said, "It's so kind of you to invite us to one of the symphony's rehearsals, Clark. If I were to come to one, might I be able to bring our twelve-year-old son, Harry Jr.? I would love for him to take up a musical instrument and that would be a good introduction."

"Oh, yes it absolutely would. Any thoughts about what he might like to play?"

"No, we've really never talked with him about music lessons. It's really something I've been thinking about to expand his horizons."

"Music has that ability. I'll be sure to send you a note about rehearsal times and dates."

The two couples talked a bit longer before Mary and Norman joined them. Harry was impressed by the way it never seemed to bother Norman that he was generally the only minority in the room at the functions they attended.

"Good to see you Norm," Harry said. "Understand you're going to put that Johnson fellow away—maybe for the rest of his natural life."

"Our case against him is looking very good. When it's over and he's in prison, I can talk more freely. Terrible murders, all those poor women."

Mary turned to her husband and brother-in-law. "Time to go honey. Momma's getting bored."

Norman put his arm around his wife's waist and turned to Harry. "Looks like it will soon be time for a Chrysler, Harry. Bet you can get me a good deal on one!"

Mary kissed her sister's cheek as she and Norman turned to leave. "Kids with mom and dad?"

"Yes, for the night. I'm going to have a little more party and try to catch up with Jack and Nancy who've just returned from Georgia."

"Okey dokey then, sweet dreams!"

"Oceans of love!" Kathleen said.

CHAPTER THIRTEEN

Kathleen received a note from Clark Clarke with dates and times of symphony rehearsals she and Son could attend. She made a note of one on a Saturday a few weeks later. Son often went with his father on Saturdays to the dealership to wash vehicles or watch Harry fine-tune an engine. It would take some persistence, on both her and Harry's parts, to talk Son into giving up a day in the Flats. Kathleen found Clark's penmanship very handsome for a man's, and the notecard he used was thick and probably expensive, his name embossed at the top. She tucked it into her dresser drawer. She and Son would take the streetcar into town, she'd buy him lunch someplace fun, maybe the New York Spaghetti House on East Ninth, then on to Severance Hall. She wished Harry would teach her to drive an automobile; she'd asked him several times. It would be a good bit of advertising for him, she thought, but he put her requests off by changing the subject.

"Honey," he'd say jokingly, "you're not strong enough to turn the engine crank!"

✧✧✧

Friday morning of the next week, Harry, with his shirtsleeves rolled up and his tie tucked into his pants, was adjusting the idle of a Dodge Deluxe Six when Cynthia Clarke walked into the dealership. He waved at her, picked up a red rag to wipe off his hands, and pulled his tie loose.

"Well, good morning Mrs. Clarke, very nice to see you. Clark here too?"

"Please, call me Cynthia, and no, he's not here."

"Oh, well," he paused, "call me Harry then."

They shook hands and Harry escorted her to one of his comfortable client chairs across from his desk. "What brings you in Cynthia? How may I be of assistance?"

"Well," she smiled, "I've come to purchase an automobile of course!"

"Oh?"

"We've recently purchased a lot in Shaker Heights. I'm interviewing architects—there are only a few that the suburb will allow to design there—and I need to meet with the principals of the firms. I really am not the streetcar type!"

"Do you know how to drive an automobile?"

"Oh, of course. My father taught me in my teens. I understand the industry has made some improvements since then, but I'm sure I'll catch on quickly."

"What make were you thinking about then? I have access to all Dodge and Chrysler lines. A coupe, a convertible, a sedan? I only have four automobiles on the floor at the moment, but I'm due for a delivery the middle of next week."

"I'm thinking a convertible actually. What would you suggest?"

"Dodge makes great-looking convertibles, as does DeSoto and of course, Chrysler. I just recently received this new brochure, let's see if any of these catch your fancy."

Cynthia looked through the pages and asked Harry questions about what she saw. She finally indicated what she really wanted was an automobile with style, in a mid-blue color with a white top.

"I can certainly see to that," Harry said. "I have some color samples here, as well as samples of interior fabrics."

"Leather only, Harry!"

He opened his desk drawer for an order pad and began making notes. Cynthia turned the pages of several other brochures of Chrysler products and finally decided she wanted a 1932 GC Imperial LeBron Custom Eight rumble-seat roadster in electric blue, with white leather seats and an ivory-colored top. Harry reviewed all the options of the car with her, including the new Chrysler automatic starter. The car could be delivered in three weeks and would cost $3,575.00. Cynthia didn't flinch and asked him to put the order through.

"Very happy to, Cynthia. Do you need to speak to Clark at all before we proceed? I'll be here in the shop all day tomorrow."

"Certainly not Harry—I'm the money in our family. I suppose my situation is a bit unusual. I'm an heiress. How much would you like down to begin the process?"

Harry cleared his throat. "Typically we like fifty percent, but I'd be happy with twenty-five."

"Nonsense." she pulled a checkbook and fountain pen from her purse, wrote a check for $1,787.00, and handed it over to him. "All right then, here you are. I look forward to visiting you again when the car arrives. Three weeks you say?"

"Yes. You'll be exceedingly pleased with it. I'll get the specs to Detroit this afternoon."

Cynthia rose, as did Harry, shook his hand, and turned to walk to the showroom door. "Very nice doing business with you, Mr. Kern. I expect you don't get many women in here buying cars. Times are changing!"

"Yes, I suppose they are. Anything the car needs—tune-ups, oil changes, whatever else—I can do here in the shop. Just call for an appointment!"

He waved as Cynthia Clarke left. Then he turned to call the Chrysler factory in Detroit; his contact there was named Walter.

CHAPTER FOURTEEN

Sonny Kern continued to spend at least a month each summer on the farm. It provided him with exercise, broadening his shoulders and strengthening muscles in his arms and legs. Pap had finally conceded to a tractor, an eight-year-old White model Harry had found and paid for. No more walking behind Star with a plow to break the soil, and happily Son was there to give his grandfather technical advice on the new machine. The sun would bleach his hair and tan his body; the air was clear, and the fish were plentiful. Two more of his uncles had decided to leave and strike out on their own, leaving only four sons to work the farm. Mary had married her young man, moved closer to Ashtabula, and had recently announced the two of them would be three by Christmas.

With the onset of the new school year, Son would enter the junior high in the city's west end. He was a good student, particularly in mathematics, which was attributed to his father. Returning from the farm that August, he continued to spend most Saturdays at Kern Motors, where he learned to work on engines, assisted with moving new cars into showroom spaces from transport trucks, and generally helped with whatever needed doing. On the Saturday of the symphony rehearsal, however,

Kathleen insisted he change his plans, promising lunch at the Spaghetti House beforehand. Harry said they'd go to the Indians game that the business was sponsoring on Sunday.

Lunch was fun; he enjoyed being out with his mother without his sisters along. Nothing could have prepared Son for the enormity of Severance Hall and the sounds emanating from the stage as musicians tuned their instruments. They took seats in the middle of the hall, where other attendees were seated. Son admired the wonderful tile work on the ceiling and the gigantic light fixtures overhead. He was trying to gauge the number of seats the hall held on the first floor when a tall dark-headed man walked to the front of the musicians, mounted a low platform, and produced a white baton from his pocket. It was Rudolf Ringwall, the orchestra's associate conductor. A man near the conductor began playing a single note on his violin while the rest of the instruments attempted to match its tone and pitch. Ringwall lifted his arms, and at once the music began! Son was enthralled and hugged his mother's arm. Several times during the two hours the Kerns were there, Ringwall would stop the music to give specific instruction to one of the musicians, then they'd begin exactly where they left off. While Son found he enjoyed tuning an eight-cylinder engine maybe a bit more, he did come to realize both activities—engine tuning and making music—relied on attaining a certain sound.

Afterward, Kathleen introduced Son to Clark Clarke and the three of them talked about Clark providing music lessons for the young man. They could be done after school at the Kern home for an hour a week, and if Son seemed to like them after a month, Clark would discuss a modest fee for his time. It was agreed that Kathleen and Son would talk about an instrument choice, and she would call Clark in a week or two after the new school year began. This she did after seeing Son was adjusting well to the seventh grade. However, they could not decide which string instrument to consider. Harry was no help at all, teasing Son and Kathleen about the violin. There was talk about perhaps learning the cello, but when she called Clark, he suggested the steel guitar. He happened to

own a console steel he had not played in some time and would be happy
to leave it with Son to practice on between his weekly lessons.

CHAPTER FIFTEEN

Three weeks to the day, an automotive delivery truck pulled up to the front of Kern Motor Sales. It contained the most beautiful car Harry had ever seen, soon to belong to Cynthia Clarke. Under its long hood was an in-line eight-cylinder engine producing 130 horsepower on a 125-inch chassis. The blue color she had selected, along with the white leather interior were a perfect combination, he thought, and hoped she'd be as delighted with it as he was. It was the only car on the truck. After the driver pulled it onto the street, Harry lowered the top and backed it into his front showroom, then sat in it for at least twenty minutes, playing with all the interior features. In the glove box he found a note from Walter Chrysler himself addressed to Mrs. Clarke. *Now, that's something you don't see every day!* he thought, and placed it on the driver's seat where Cynthia would not miss it.

Walking to his office desk, he placed a call to Mrs. Clarke. It rang without being answered. He called every hour thereafter until she picked up around five thirty.

"Cynthia? Harry Kern calling. Your new automobile arrived this afternoon and it's a beauty!"

"Harry, hello. Thank you for the call."

"Absolutely! You may come for it tomorrow if you'd like. I'll be here all day."

"Tomorrow's a busy day for me, then I'm headed to Chicago for several days with girlfriends from college. It will be toward the end of next week before I can get by. Hope that's not an imposition for you."

"Not at all. I won't get tired of looking at her, and it will give me time to make sure she's perfectly tuned. May I get you on my calendar?"

They set a date for her arrival and rang off. *Perhaps I can take her by Mary and Norman's,* Harry thought to himself. *Use her as bait to catch a county prosecutor!*

✧✧✧

Clark Clarke delivered the console steel to Son as promised and provided the first lesson, showing him how the steel was used in one hand while strings were plucked with the other. The instrument was enjoying an upsurge in popularity, particularly among country groups. It appealed to Son for that reason, and he found he enjoyed plucking away at its strings and experimenting with the sounds he could make. He also enjoyed Clark's lesson visits, as did his mother, who sat with them for the hour-long sessions. Kathleen served cucumber sandwiches on white bread and lemonade at the end of each lesson and chatted with Clark as Son practiced what he had learned that day. They all got on well and were typically joined by Agnes and Nora. Kathleen enjoyed these conversations with Clark, whose world experiences were much broader than her own, and certainly Harry's. Perhaps she was enjoying them a bit too much, as soon the very thought of an upcoming visit sent her into an emotional state she hoped she hid from her children. Harry was another matter! He could easily sense when something was causing his wife anxiety and by December had deduced her stress always peaked on the days of Son's music lessons.

"I would never have expected Son would take to music like he has," he said. "That goofy instrument of Clark's really appeals to him." Harry pulled out a chair in the kitchen. "Oatmeal smells great!"

"Oh, it's not goofy. Son can make interesting sounds. I think Clark's very impressed with him."

"That's good to hear, I wouldn't want Clark wasting his time. Does his being here upset you, Kathleen? You seem to get a bit nervous as Son's lesson days approach."

"Absolutely not. It's probably related to my time of the month. I'll make a point to ask Dr. Schneiderman about it when I take Nora in for her next checkup."

Harry looked over at her and smiled. "I think Norm's about ready to sign up for a Chrysler. Think he'll go for a sedan. I'll try to sell him on the new Imperial model."

"Busy day today, Harry?" she asked.

"Have a truckload of Dodge and Plymouth models coming in, probably mid-day. I may be a bit later getting home. Christmas is coming, and hopefully Santa will throw a few customers my way! Hey, maybe that would be a good holiday marketing promotion."

"How about teaching me to drive? I could be Mrs. Claus in your advertising," Kathleen suggested, hoping she had changed the subject from Clark's next visit.

"I've been thinking about that too," Harry said. "But let's wait for spring when the bad weather has passed. I'll even buy you a car! You'd be a cute Mrs. Claus though."

Harry finished his toast and left for work. Driving in, he thought about Kathleen's anxiety and again wondered why it seemed to be worse on the days of Son's music lessons.

✵✵✵

As Christmas Eve approached, Kathleen busied herself with decorating and for the holiday open house she and Harry always threw. The party was mostly for family and close friends, but at the last minute Kathleen invited Clark and Cynthia as well, despite knowing his presence would add to her stress. Son had promised to provide background music for the evening,

Harry stocked the bar and hired a bartender so he could mingle, and the girls decided they wanted to dress up like elves. The evening turned cold, with snow off Lake Erie, but these were Clevelanders who were used to the city's winters, so the night proceeded. Kathleen's parents arrived early with a large tray of Christmas cookies from her German mother's recipes. Chester asked for a bourbon old-fashioned from the bartender and took a handful of peanuts. He had come to terms with Mary's marriage and wished Norm a Merry Christmas upon their arrival. Lizzie arrived with her brother Jack and his wife, followed shortly by the Martindales, and even Rollin White came by with a bottle of twelve-year-old scotch.

Kathleen sat among her guests, listening to the music Son was making and watching her girls romp around in their costumes. Clark and Cynthia had not arrived, and her stomach was in knots. Then the front door blew open and Clark entered, snow on the shoulders of his topcoat, but no Cynthia. He shook his coat off, placing it in the parlor with the others, ran his fingers through his hair, and ordered a gin martini. He looked around the room, greeting the Hannahs and the few other people he knew, then turned to Kathleen who had now stood up and walked toward him.

"So sorry to be late. Cynthia has a holiday cold and took to her bed. I hear Son somewhere in the background. The music sounds good, a Hawaiian Christmas!"

"I'm so glad you came," Kathleen said. "I was beginning to think you weren't going to make it."

"I should have telephoned." The martini took the evening's cold from his face. "Where's Harry?"

"Around somewhere. Probably trying to sell someone a car. He's got some holiday specials."

"The car he sold Cynthia is certainly a beauty. She drives it too fast though."

"Harry says he's going to teach me to drive in the spring. Maybe she and I can race." They both laughed. "And you can announce the winner!"

Clark finished the last of his drink and placed the glass back on the bar table. "I should be leaving soon. Shouldn't leave Cynthia alone too long. Walk with me to get my coat."

Kathleen followed him into the parlor and helped him on with his overcoat. When he turned toward her, heading for the front door, she was holding a sprig of mistletoe over her head. He reached for her cheek as she turned her head and kissed him on the mouth for what seemed to her to be forever. They parted, only to see Harry staring at them from the hallway.

✳✳✳

It was not a kiss that launched a thousand ships, but it was the one that saved Son from becoming a steel guitar musician in a honky-tonk band. Harry was stunned as he watched his wife lay a Hollywood-style kiss on Clark, even raising one leg at the knee! Their expressions upon seeing Harry were equally traumatic. Clark made for the door, rushing past Harry, while Kathleen slowly sank to a parlor chair. Chester James had seen it too and quickly turned away toward the bar. For one of the few times in his life, Harry found he could not speak and turned away. Finding Son, he asked him to please stop playing. He then poured himself a glass of the scotch Rollin had brought, drinking it down in two gulps. Kathleen pulled herself together and left the parlor to join her yuletide guests but could not bring herself to look at her husband. Shortly after, Harry grabbed his two elves and took them upstairs to get them ready for bed. Upon his return there were only a few stragglers left in the living room talking casually to Kathleen, and soon they were gone as well. Snow was still coming down.

Kathleen sat in a chair facing her husband. "I'm so sorry."

"Are you in love with him?"

"No. Yes." She began to cry. "I don't know! I don't know what came over me tonight. It was like I was in this sad, romantic dream. I'm sure Clark was more surprised by my kissing him than you or Daddy or anyone else."

"Hopefully there was no one else!" Harry retorted, a bit of anger flaring in his tone. "I don't know what's going on here, Kathleen. I know I'm away from home too much and not spending enough time with you. But I can tell you this, there will be no more music lessons!"

"It wasn't Clark's fault," she whimpered. "Son shouldn't be punished because of my foolish daydreams!"

"I cannot, will not, have the two of you in our house together. I'll not play the sucker in some romantic fantasy the two of you are rehearsing. That guitar leaves this house the day after Christmas!"

Harry rose, checked that the doors were locked, unplugged the Christmas trees lights, and went to a bedroom near the one the girls used. An hour or so later he heard Kathleen in their room. Harry thought about Kathleen and Clark and the time they had shared with Son at his music lessons, pretending who knows what, and could not help getting angrier. The beautiful Kathleen James was the first and only woman he had ever coveted and loved. He listened as she prepared for bed and turned out the table lamp. He rose, entered their room, rolled her over, and with a passion he had not known before, made love to her. She did not resist, and in fact, found pleasure in his exuberance. They remained together through the night.

CHAPTER SIXTEEN

As 1933 began, the pace of sales at Kern Motors was far better than the year before. The Christmas specials Harry had organized had indeed sparked interest, particularly it seemed, with customers living in Bratenahl. Plymouth models also were doing well, leading Harry to begin thinking of adding other makes of cars within a similar price range. He'd had a number of inquiries about Chevrolets, particularly the Business Coupe. Fred Hayes had no problem with Harry adding a non-Chrysler line to his offerings. Harry planned a trip to Detroit when winter weather allowed to see Fred and meet William C. Durant, president of General Motors and business partner with Louis Chevrolet. Like Harry, Chevrolet enjoyed tinkering with and racing automobiles, winning his first race in 1905. With little or no formal education, also like Harry, he learned car design working for Buick, then owned by Durant. In 1909 he designed and built an overhead valve, six-cylinder engine in his Detroit machine shop.

Harry's meetings with Durant and Chevrolet were successful, so he ordered a Chevrolet Business Coupe in silver and a Chevrolet Master two-door in cream. He had dinner with Fred Hayes at his Detroit Club the evening before his return to Cleveland. Fred had arranged for Harry to have a bedroom at his club for the evening, a Romanesque Revival structure completed in 1891 with twenty-four suites. Harry wondered to himself what a boy from a farm near Ashtabula was doing there.

"Well," Fred asked, "how did you find Bill Durant?"

Harry gathered his thoughts. "Very charismatic. I understand he has big plans for the car business. Had to meet with Durant and Chevrolet separately as, I gather, they don't get along."

"That's putting it mildly," Fred said with a laugh. "I think Louis came to that conclusion early in their partnership."

"I liked Chevrolet. We have much in common, though he's done much more racing. But we think along the same lines and his engine design seems very practical."

"Watch out for Durant. He is either loved or hated around this city, but always seems to land on his feet. Spends money much too freely if you ask me. I think it will be his undoing in the long run. What did you drive up here in?"

"One of those new Dodge Eights you sent me last month. Rides like a magic carpet. Maybe I'll use that image in this spring's advertising!"

"Damn Harry, that is a great image and slogan: 'Drives Like a Magic Carpet!' I should get you up here to run our advertising department. Can we use it?"

The two men laughed and finished their dinners and brandies, then Harry turned in, thankful he did not have to leave the building.

The next morning, Harry had breakfast delivered to his room, showered, dressed, and was on the road by eight-thirty, arriving at his sales office by mid-afternoon. He checked through his mail, washed the Dodge Eight, gassed it, then started making notes on the magic carpet advertising campaign. He also thought through how he was going to announce the addition of Chevrolets to the public. The next day, he was scheduled to tune Cynthia Clarke's Imperial, the first time seeing her since the music lessons stopped last winter. He wondered if Clark had ever said anything to her about that.

He was glad to be home that evening. The weather had made an unusual warmer shift, with March coming in as a lamb. Son was outside throwing a baseball with a neighbor boy. He and Harry had snagged the ball the past summer at an Indians game. As he came in the back kitchen door, he could smell supper in the oven.

"Hello! I'm home!" Kathleen and the girls came into the room, giggling over something Nora had said.

"You look good for being in Detroit and driving back," Kathleen said. "How was Fred?"

"Fred's just fine, as always. Put me up at his club, very luxurious, and even paid for it. He's a great friend. I happened to make a remark about the Dodge Eight that he liked and wants to use in national advertising."

"You getting paid for it?"

"In a manner of speaking. He's giving us a bigger commission on cars we haven't purchased from him outright. Ordered two new Chevrolets while I was there. Those GM folks have a whole different sales philosophy than Chrysler, much more focused, seem driven to capture the entire marketplace. Not sure it's for me or our business here, but Chevy makes a good car that people seem to want."

The girls ran back through the kitchen playing tag, followed by Son, who was glad to see his father home.

"How was your trip Dad? I worry about you being all alone driving to Detroit. You ought to take me along. I could even drive some of the way if you wanted to nap!"

"Well, that's a nice offer, let me think on it! What do you think of my taking Son along Kath, if it's not during the school year?"

"Travel's broadening, I suppose," she admitted, "but not worth missing any school."

Kathleen brought dinner to the table and they all passed plates around for Harry to fill. Pork chops were one of his favorites and Kathleen had made potato salad and a tomato and cucumber salad. Harry looked across the table at his wife, whom he thought was beautiful as always. Perhaps a bit paler than usual. She had turned thirty-three on her last birthday. He thought early middle age seemed to agree with her, though he was smart enough not to mention her age in front of their children, or even when they were alone! After all the children had left the kitchen and they were alone he did gently ask how she was feeling.

"I have been feeling a bit sluggish, actually. Particularly in the mornings, I just want to lay in bed. The girls won't allow that though. Do you think Son will be going to the farm next summer? He's really not a bother since he's gotten older, but it would be something of a relief for me not to worry about where he was or what he's doing."

"Haven't talked to Pap about the summer yet, but was actually thinking I could use him at the shop and that he might like to help me there this year. He's got a good mind for mathematics and mechanical applications."

"I'm sure he'd enjoy that, and I wouldn't need to worry about him." She seated herself on a small kitchen stool she kept in a corner of the kitchen. "Maybe I'll go see Dr. Schneiderman sometime this week for a checkup."

Harry gave her a hug and said he'd be happy to take her if she'd like.

"Thanks," she said, "but I can take the streetcar and get Mary to meet me somewhere for an early or late lunch, depending on when he's available."

✧✧✧

The following morning at ten, Cynthia Clarke drove her GC Imperial into the service bay of Harry's shop. The white leather top was up and looked in good condition, as were the leather seats and the rich blue pearlescent exterior.

"She's a real beauty, Cynthia," Harry remarked as he helped her out of the car. He then raised both sides of the hood to help the engine cool before making any adjustments. "Have you and Clark been enjoying her smooth ride?"

"Clark doesn't get much of a chance to enjoy the car," she replied. "The orchestra's been on tour for the last month and a half, and besides that, he doesn't drive. His loss! I, however, have enjoyed the car quite a bit, especially the drive to Shaker to inspect the house construction. It's on Marshall Lake in the Malvern neighborhood, an English Tutor style. Looks like in another month or two we'll be in. Now I'm busy buying furniture, carpeting, draperies, kitchen appliances, so it's just as well he's away!"

Harry listened to her while changing the oil. "Must be lonely for you though, Clark being gone. The tour almost over?"

"No, another month to go, which should put him back in Cleveland by the time the house is finished and the furnishings are installed. I'll need to find a maid to clean. Know any good agencies I should contact?"

"Haven't had the need, actually. But I'm sure Lizzie Hannah could help you with that. Okey dokey, let me just put some gas in the tank and you'll be ready to go."

"How nice," she said, opening her purse. "What do I owe you?"

"Not a thing—first one's on the house!"

✵✵✵

Kathleen was able to get an appointment with Dr. Walter Schneiderman on Saturday following the good doctor's lunch break at one, his last appointment of the day. Mary was able to join her for an early lunch at Higbee's Silver Grille, and the two women happily chatted, both enjoying gin slings with their meals. Norman had decided to go back to his law firm full-time and give up working for the county by the beginning of summer. He would become a full partner in the new firm of Payne, Green, Minor and Perry—the largest African-American law firm in the state, maybe even the country.

"It's where the real money is," Mary said. "So, you seeing Walter for anything in particular, honey?"

"No, just a checkup. I've been feeling kind of droopy lately, probably need some vitamins. Not twenty-five anymore, you know."

"I certainly do," said her sister, who was two years older than Kathleen. "Time is our enemy!"

At one, Kathleen entered the office of Dr. Walter Schneiderman, who had been her attending physician since birth. In due course, his long-time nurse, Hazel, dressed in her starched white uniform and nurse's cap, escorted Kathleen into the exam room.

"Well now, my girl," Schneiderman said, "what seems to be bothering you?" He placed a thermometer under her tongue, produced a stethoscope from the deep side pocket of his white lab coat, and listened to her chest. "Deep breath!" Then her back, "Deep breath!" Then her stomach. Dr. Schneiderman rose to his full height, rubbed his chin, adjusted his glasses, and said, "Well my girl, I think I can safely diagnose your condition. You're pregnant—I'd say about three months. Congratulations!"

"I'm what?" Kathleen screamed. "That can't be! I've only ever wanted three children and I have them. I'm done!"

"Be that as it may Kathleen my dear, you are with child, and I expect to deliver the baby myself before retiring!"

He looked at Hazel, then at Kathleen and smiled. Ten minutes later, Kathleen called her husband at the sales office. He picked up on the third ring.

"Harry, while I'm in town, I'm going to do a little shopping. Do you think you could close the office early today and run the kids over to my parents' house? It's been a while since they've seen them, and we need some alone time."

As Kathleen asked, Harry closed shop an hour early, picked up the girls and delivered them to Chester and Mary James, who were delighted to have their company, even arranging for a sleepover. Son had already said he was spending the night at the home of a school friend. Harry stopped at a local grocery in the city's Italian neighborhood to pick up a bouquet of mixed flowers and a bottle of the white wine Kathleen preferred before heading home. He parked in the driveway, grabbed his purchases, and entered the house through the kitchen door. Putting the wine in the re-frigerator, Harry grabbed a vase from the pantry shelf for the flowers and headed into the living room to look for his wife. Surprisingly he found her already with a glass of wine in hand.

"Hello, my love," he said, placing the flowers on a table beside the chair Kathleen had taken. "I picked up some of your favorite wine, which I see you've already started on. Hold on while I get a glass to join you." He was quickly back with an empty glass and the newly opened bottle. "How was your day? The girls were happy to see their grandparents, they are planning to spend the night. Did you get a good report from Dr. Schneiderman?" Harry filled his glass and sat in the chair across from his wife, looking forward to a quiet evening.

"Well, you're certainly full of questions," she said finally. "I would say my day started out ordinarily. The girls were enjoying the early spring-like weather, and Son was good about watching them while I went to town to see Dr. Schneiderman."

"I hope he was well, must be getting close to retirement. I wonder how many children he's delivered over the years."

Kathleen finished the wine in her glass and poured another from the bottle Harry had purchased. "Quite a few, I'd imagine," she said, "in-cluding all of the James children and our three. Probably half the births in the city since the 1920s."

"And how was your exam? He have any thoughts about your drop in energy over the past couple weeks? I hope he recommended some over-the-counter vitamins."

Kathleen set her wine glass on the table with the flowers Harry had brought. Her face was flushed a bit from the wine, and she straightened herself in the chair.

"No vitamins needed as yet," she said. "He advised me to eat heathy food and get plenty of rest."

"Well, that's a prescription we all should follow." Harry grinned as he said it, the wine having its effect. "So, doesn't sound like there is any-thing really wrong—"

Kathleen cut him off. "Walter says I'm pregnant, Harry! Three months pregnant. I never wanted four children, only three!"

Harry finished the wine in his glass in one swallow. "Who's the father?"

At that her anger exploded and she hurled her wine glass in his direction, smashing it against a wooden bookcase.

"You are, you bastard!" she screamed. "You raped me! You must certainly remember, when you entered the bedroom and forced yourself on me Christmas Eve!"

"Seems to me to that was the same night I saw you kissing Clark Clarke in our parlor," he said, suddenly very serious. "How can I possibly trust your word on the paternity of this child?"

"I had a schoolgirl crush on Clark. It was silly and stupid—but it was nothing more. I couldn't help myself that night. It was Christmas, and he was leaving our party early. I grabbed the piece of mistletoe and—"

"Kissed him on the lips passionately! I saw the whole thing, as did your father. Really Kathleen, how can I or anyone else be sure who the baby's father is?"

Kathleen rose from the chair, her hands clenched together, the veins in her neck visible as she stared down at her husband. "I know who the father of this child is! This fourth child that I never wanted and will hate all my life! You've done this to me. I've always said that three was my limit. I can't have you on the same floor of this house at night or any other we may have in the future. Make a bedroom for yourself down here, in that office of yours."

At that she bolted from the living room and up the stairs. Harry heard their bedroom door slam and lock. He began picking up the remains of what had been Kathleen's wine glass. He then took a chair at their kitchen table and finished the bottle he had bought from the grocer and reviewed what had just transpired. He was going to be a father to another Kern child, no matter how it got there!

CHAPTER SEVENTEEN

Robert Kern was born in September, 1932 to little fanfare from Kathleen, who nursed the child as an infant but hired a nursemaid for everything else in his young life. Son and his sisters found the baby, who they all called Bobby, to be a disruption to their routines, and because of the age difference between them, the baby represented the beginning of a second family. Harry provided the child with the attention denied him by the other four. With business growing steadily, his time was limited to Sundays, when he would devote most of the day to his new son, which happily caused no resentment in Sonny. Bobby became the lonely child within the group, keeping to himself and trying to cope with his isolation. His salvation came in 1937 when he turned five and took over Son's annual farm visits with Pap and Mam, who delighted in having a boy around again.

Much had changed on the farm as eight of the nine Kern boys had left to seek lives away from Ashtabula. Harry continued to send money to his parents and urged his brothers to do the same. Sometimes they did, but often they did not or could not. Mam was feeling her age from birthing all those children and her own years of work on the farm. Not having to cook so much food and do laundry for so many people had given her increased amounts of leisure time, which she mainly used to worry about her grown children's lives. Harry would write brief notes to his parents when sending money, but nothing personal about his marriage or living arrangements. Kathleen stopped going along on trips to the farm when Bobby would leave in the summer or return in September. Harry wondered if his parents sensed the marital stress between them.

✳✳✳

1940

Harry had done well with Dodge and Plymouth models, but was glad he had decided to diversify his offerings with Chevrolets before the political climate in Washington forced manufacturers to stop automobile production and re-tool for the military. He had been able to put away enough money to purchase Chevy models outright, a welcome departure from his early days with Chrysler. He ordered a Business Coupe, a Special Deluxe Fleetline four-door and, deviating from his past offerings, a Special Deluxe Fleetline Station Wagon he hoped would appeal to affluent families with children.

Son helped at the dealership after his high school graduation in 1938, and two years later, Harry arranged for him to attend a newly established General Motors Technical program for three months in Detroit. The program was available only to sons of GM dealers and was limited to fifteen students per term. Students would participate in every facet of an automobile's construction—engines to upholstery—and after graduation would be able to remedy anything that might go wrong with a Chevy. Housing and meals were provided. With $300.00 in his pocket from his father, Son took the train north.

To her surprise, Kathleen missed her first-born more than she'd thought and wrote to him often, always signing her letters or cards "Oceans of Love, Mother." Her cursive handwriting was large, so she rarely wrote over two pages of news and said hardly anything about

Harry other than business was good, with cars spending little time in the showroom. Son was always heartened by comments like that, as he hoped to join his father in business at some future time. The technical school's operation allowed him and the other students to work alongside technicians and engineers to understand every phase of the current mechanics, as well as occasionally glimpsing what they thought the future might hold. Son found it all amazing and enjoyed the comradery of his classmates, even the one from Pittsburgh.

Son's Detroit schooling seemed to speed by. As a final exam, each student was to build an automobile on the assembly line by themselves, using line workers to help only with heavy items, such as finished engines, which they would also build. Each student was given a book of technical drawings for the model they would be building. Son's was an Oldsmobile Series 60 Club Coupe that would be painted a metallic mid-red. His engine was a "Rocket 8," which moved on an assembly line to be installed to the driveshaft through the transmission with ignition wiring to follow, then the steering assembly, seating, and other body parts. He loved every aspect of each day's adventure.

On the final day of assembly, Son followed his Oldsmobile to the end of the assembly line, polishing its newly waxed exterior along the way. He then filled its tank with five gallons of gasoline and handed the keys to the school's director. This was the supreme moment for Son and his fellow students, when their times "on the line" came. He watched the director enter the driver's seat, insert the ignition key, put the transmission in neutral and, giving Son an acknowledging look, turned the key. The engine fired immediately and the car was driven off the line. Son jumped up, punched his left hand with his right, and smiled brightly as the director cut the ignition and opened the car's massive front door.

"Congratulations Mr. Kern, you've built a beautiful automobile!" He handed Son the keys. "Here you are. Your father purchased this car for you, so you can drive it back to Cleveland tomorrow with our best wishes for a successful career in the automotive business. You've had the best training anyone could ask for, particularly for a GM dealer. It will serve you well. Plus you can come back every few years to see what our engineers are designing and how their improvements work and are repaired. Have a wonderful evening, Mr. Kern, and try not to park this beauty under a tree!"

Son returned to Cleveland the following afternoon and drove straight to the dealership to show off the Oldsmobile. Harry was glad to have him back and was astonished at the automobile, which the two examined in some detail. Finishing their perusals, Son parked the car on the street in front of the dealership. Some minutes later, father and son noticed it was drawing a growing crowd of admirers.

"Well, that's certainly good for business," Harry said, smiling at Son.

"Do you think we ought to sell it if someone comes in?" Son asked. "That's up to you, my boy, it's your car."

Later that afternoon, before it was time to close, a cash offer was made that was two hundred dollars over the Oldsmobile's suggested retail price, and Son sold the car. His first sale as an automotive dealer! Father and son drove home in a Chevy Master and had a beer in celebration.

CHAPTER EIGHTEEN

In August, Kathleen and her daughters decided they needed a month away from Cleveland on the shore of another state. After asking around for recommendations, Kathleen rented a cottage in Dunkirk, New York for September, on the eastern tip of Lake Erie. Harry could join them on weekends, she decided. It was the beginning of many trips away from Cleveland, where they were often joined by Mary and Norman for a week or brought friends of her girls to stay.

That first year, Son drove his mother, sisters, and brother to their rented cottage on a tree-lined street two blocks from the shore. Kathleen, dressed in long sleeves, lightweight beach slacks, and a large-brimmed straw hat, would take her daughters and nine-year-old Bobby to the beach every morning at ten, returning for lunch at the cottage by noon. Son would come and go as he pleased, but Kathleen, wanting to keep her daughters' skin lily white and to lessen wrinkling with age to enhance their prospects for finding suitable husbands, strictly adhered to no beach time in the afternoons. At the end of the first week Son drove back to Cleveland, leaving Robert with their mother and sisters. The following Friday Harry took a train to Dunkirk for a weekend visit, using the cottage's sleeping porch as a bedroom. Son stayed back to operate the dealership on Saturday and retrieve his father from the train station Sunday night, and so the month of September passed.

In January 1941, Son began taking classes at Case Western Reserve University on a limited basis. His goal was to find courses in general business that would be beneficial for him at the dealership, but his attraction to mathematics kept him taking at least one class a term in that area. As his father had foreseen, US automobile production ended in February, and manufacturers began producing vehicles for the war effort. Harry purchased some of the last vehicles in inventory, saving back a third of these for the war's conclusion and returning soldiers. Son turned twenty-one that year, and the family had nightly discussions about how he could best avoid the draft. Thousands of young men and women were needed once the United States joined in the war, which had been going on since 1939. Kathleen was beyond thinking clearly about how to keep Son home, to the point of advocating she chop off his trigger finger at the second joint! Harry gave much better advice, suggesting it might be better to join a military branch rather than letting the draft suck him in. He knew Son would be funneled into the war sooner than later, and at least if he joined he might be able to avoid the infantry.

Most of Son's friends were already in the various military branches and truthfully, he felt awkward not being in a uniform. Father and son both thought his mechanical abilities with automobiles might be of great value to the Army. He would likely be stationed in Europe, but at least away from the front lines of fighting. Kathleen finally came around to this thinking but was still distraught over the thought of her Sonny in the service.

By the end of 1941, Private Kern was sent to Camp Howze near Gainesville, Texas for basic training and evaluations to see if he possessed any skills that might prevent his becoming German bullet fodder. His aptitude in mathematics became apparent after the first series of tests, so along with the physical part of boot camp, Son continued to be tested three afternoons each week to determine the extent of his mathematical abilities. His results were shared with an officer who was specifically seeking recruits who tested well in mathematics. After his boot camp was complete, Son and three other men from Howze were sent to Texas A&M to study engineering. Col. Albert Copeland was looking to recruit an outfit of no more than ten men who could design and build pontoon bridges to help move troops and material on or near bodies of water. Son happily spent six months at A&M to the relief of his parents before Copeland and his recruits were shipped to Europe in late 1942 and Japan in 1944. None of Copeland's "boys," as he referred to them, were injured during their tours, and eight of the group became highly interested in the card game of bridge. Son was one of them.

✵✵✵

Harry spent a good part of these years working to connect his contacts at Chrysler and General Motors to the military's procurement needs, spending increasing periods of time in Washington, DC. Always the consummate salesman, he was able to extrapolate what the military most needed in its vehicles and relay the information to Detroit manufacturers. He was able to arrange handsome fees from manufacturers for his assistance in these efforts, which more than made up for not having inventory to sell back in Cleveland. Kathleen did not mind his being away from home more often, though it did not reconcile their sleeping arrangements when he was home.

Robert seemed to constantly be at odds with his mother while Harry was away. During one trip, she kept a list of his transgressions to give to Harry upon his return.

"You just wait until your father gets home," she scolded. "He'll tan your backside with his shoe brush."

True to her word, she gave Robert's list to Harry immediately upon his return and told him to "deal with your son over your knee!" Kathleen then retreated to her second-floor bedroom, slamming the door.

Harry took Robert into his bedroom. "Bob, this is quite a list of abuses your mother has catalogued. Did you really do all these things while I was away?"

"I guess so, but I really didn't mean to be trouble, not at all."

"I see," Harry said. "Tell you what. I've had a long week away, and well, when I hit my hand with the back of my hairbrush, you scream really loud. We'll do it six times—okey dokey?"

And so, justice was handed out, and Robert was sent to his bedroom until dinnertime.

When Kathleen and the girls returned to the first floor, they were dressed to go out. Kathleen explained they were dining with Mary, Lizzie, and at Lizzie's insistence, Cynthia Clarke, at Higbee's Silver Grille.

"There's a porterhouse steak in the refrigerator, potatoes for baking, and a fresh salad I made this afternoon for you boys. We won't be out late!"

Since Harry had taught his wife to drive, she found freedom behind the wheel. He wondered what she would have done with Robert had he not been home. She had begun talking about sending him off to military school when he was a bit older, thinking that would straighten him out, and had even begun writing to schools for informational brochures. All her choices were in other states, where Robert would be far from her view.

CHAPTER NINETEEN

With V-E Day in May of 1945 and V-J Day following four months later, the dreams of peace and returning veterans was soon at hand. Son's 1190 Engineering unit ended their service aboard a troop carrier far from Hiroshima, but did spend time on Japanese soil assisting American troops exiting the country upon the formal signing of surrender documents. While they saw no combat in either theaters of the war, the group was credited with capturing a small group of German soldiers willing and ready to be prisoners of American troops. Years later, Son would happen to sell a car to one of these fellows who immigrated to the United States and settled in Cleveland.

Son returned home having achieved the military rank of sergeant and begged his family and friends not to call him "Sarge." Never an overly demonstrative child or young man, his participation in the conflict left him subdued and introspective. Whatever feelings he'd had about organized religion and a loving God were rended from his soul; surely no merciful, loving God would have let that war or any conflict between men happen. The church and all its teachings and platitudes were a farce he'd concluded as he packed away all references to his time abroad.

Feeling his son was too slowly readjusting to civilian life, and with the oncoming Cleveland winter, Harry arranged for the family to take a two-week vacation in Florida. Resting in the sun would be good for them all, especially Son. Finding suitable accommodations in Flagler, the Kerns boarded a train from Union Terminal and made the trip in two days. Harry and his sons spent their days fishing off the surf, while Kathleen and her girls spent theirs shopping. The rental cottage squeezed everyone into bedrooms—Harry assigned to spend his nights with Robert, the girls in another bedroom, Son and Kathleen in their own bedrooms. Everyone was having a fine time, with Son responding well to this time in the sunshine, when a telegram arrived from Ashtabula saying Mam had died.

The return trip to Ohio was filled with memories of Mam, especially from Son, whose happy memories of his farm summers now seemed to have occurred to a boy in another lifetime. Harry added his own memories of sleeping in the attic with no heat in winter, farm chores, Mam's ample meals at lunch and dinner, her love and care of the family. He secretly wondered how his father would survive without her.

The funeral was a simple affair. Neighboring families brought food, a grave was dug for her near the pond below the house, the local pastor prayed over her body, and a few of her grown sons who were there refilled the earthen opening. Pap vowed that losing his wife and best friend would not get him down, but as time passed he began to let things on the farm go, though he did continue to look after his animals and even took in two stray kittens for company. Harry made a point to visit one weekend a month, sometimes with Son and Robert, sometimes alone. He always brought enough food for a week or two, the cold cellar being adequate to keep meat from spoiling before his next visit. Harry's brother Virgil had stayed on the farm and was some company for Pap, though he was the laziest of the boys and prone to drink at night. He would work on neighboring farms when a need arose, which accounted for the money he used to purchase liquor, Harry assumed. Overall, it seemed to him a sad life his brother and father were sharing, and he was always relieved to be driving back to Cleveland after each visit.

✵✵✵

Son decided to re-enroll at Case Western as a degree-seeking student under the GI Bill beginning in January 1946, focusing on business, while also working with his father at the dealership. Harry's prediction that returning GIs would want automobiles was accurate, and his business was booming once again. Harry established relationships with two local banks to assist returning vets with low-interest loans if they had not saved funds to purchase vehicles outright; he did the same with an insurance agency located in the Flats. Talking with manufacturing friends at both GM and Chrysler, he knew re-tooling after the war would take longer than his wartime inventory would last, so he purchased late-model vehicles to sell until the 1946 models became available.

CHAPTER TWENTY

Harry and Kathleen's daughters, now 21 and 19, had grown up largely under their mother's influence, attending the Laurel School in Shaker Heights as day students and enjoying outings with their mother, their Aunt Mary, and occasionally "Aunt" Lizzie. In their turn, Kathleen taught both her girls how to drive in the 1942 Chevrolet Special Deluxe Harry had provided. As automobile inventories began to grow, Kathleen received a 1946 Dodge Custom Town Sedan. After all, Harry reasoned, putting her in a car like that was good advertising!

Their oldest, Agnes, had developed physically by fourteen and had been interested in the opposite sex since then. She lost her virginity at sixteen to a neighborhood boy, a fact known only by her sister Nora, who was shocked at first, then titillated. Agnes found a box of condoms in one of her father's bureau drawers one Saturday when putting away laundry and tucked two into the pocket of her slacks. While she knew her parents didn't sleep in the same bedroom, she blushed at the thought of why her father might have a use for them. Perhaps they belonged to Son, who kept them in Harry's bureau so Kathleen wouldn't find them. Yes, she was sure that was what was going on, as her father would never...

Pocketing the condoms was the beginning of Agnes's lifelong interest in pilfering objects from shops or from homes of her mother's friends if she thought she could get away with it. She became very accomplished in her sleight-of-hand endeavors, always being careful to change her technique slightly and keeping the timing of her thieving episodes far apart. Her need for men was not far behind this interest, and with so many young men returning from the war, she had quite a wide field to choose from. Regularly, she dragged Nora to USO dances at the Aragon Ballroom on West 25th Street, where she parked her sister at a table for most of the evening while she prowled. She found she had a predilection for "bad boys" rather than college boys like her brother, often slipping outside with one to the Chevy's backseat.

At twenty-one, Agnes longed to be on her own, marry, have children, and live in her own home with the man of her dreams, who would hurry home to her and their family after a day at work. She would keep him happy in bed, which she thought was the key to keeping men content. By June, Agnes had identified her man. Tom Keck had served in the Navy during the war as an engine room technician, keeping the four oil-fired boilers and steam turbines moving in Pacific waters on his destroyer, the USS Kidd. Tom was the definition of tall, dark, and handsome, and was from Erie, Pennsylvania, just up the lake's coastline. He'd migrated to Cleveland looking for work in the shipping business and found a job at the American Shipbuilding Company, formally Cleveland Shipbuilding, before the war.

They met in a bar when she sat down beside him one early summer night after an Indians game. Tom liked baseball and a beer or two, not counting what he consumed during the game. It was another reason to like Cleveland, he thought. Agnes opened her purse for a cigarette, Tom obliged her by lighting it, and they began talking. She had been at League Park only because it was a game Kern Motors had sponsored and Harry needed someone to drive one of his Chevrolets to the ballpark and back to the dealership afterward. The Indians had won their game against Cincinnati, and Tom was relaxed and in a good mood. After about an hour, he walked Agnes to the park's entrance where the 1945 Chevy Coupe was parked.

"Nice car," he'd said, looking over the inside when she'd unlocked the door. "Low mileage too!"

"It's never been owned," she replied. "We're waiting for the '46 models to start rolling out from Detroit."

"We?" Tom asked, thinking he had been at a bar with someone's wife.

"My family," she said. "My dad is Harry Kern. His automotive dealership is downtown, probably near where you work."

"Well, nice meeting you Miss Kern. Hope to see you again. I'm leaving in the morning for a week's passage to Canada hauling whatever's in the hold, then I'll be back." He smiled at her, tipped the brim of his hat, and closed the car door after she'd settled herself behind the steering wheel.

"I hope so too, Mr. Keck," she said, slipping him her telephone number on the back of a ticket from the game. Then she eased the Chevy onto the street and drove off. Tom was duly impressed!

CHAPTER TWENTY-ONE

As the new year began, Kathleen was set to enroll Robert into the Staunton Military Academy in Virginia at thirteen years of age. Founded in 1881, the school had a distinguished history, a highly rated academic program, and was a good ten-hour drive from Cleveland, eight by train. Harry's "indiscretion," while not entirely mitigated, would be more than an arm's length away. She had talked about this eventuality often enough that its finally happening was not as shocking to Harry as it had once been. Bobby's public school career had been sordid at best; spending more time during the day in the principal's office than either parent would have wished. Kathleen convinced herself the discipline at Staunton would correct these tendencies and turn Robert into a civilized human. He was to begin school with the spring semester in March and stay until the following Christmas break. Harry planned to drive Robert there, which he figured would take two days each way, and would stay in Staunton two days getting him settled. He had arranged and paid for a private barracks room, hoping his son would make friends with cadets he'd like to room with in the years ahead. All things being equal, Bobby would graduate in 1952. Harry paid the tuition through the Christmas break, bought him two regular uniforms as well as a dress uniform with leather boots, and a wide Staunton Military leather belt with an embossed metal buckle.

As his room was not quite ready, father and son spent two nights at the Stonewall Jackson Hotel in town. They ate steaks both nights and explored the town together. Harry thought those two days were some of the best he had spent with his youngest son and wished he had not given into Kathleen's urging to send him away. She had no real reason to dislike Bobby as she did; for his merely being a fourth child was absurd. Making sure he had taken care of all his son's needs, Harry put two hundred dollars into his hand the following morning, and with a hug, the two parted for nine months. Harry promised to visit for Parents Weekend in September with or without Kathleen, and to write him every week.

Son happily skipped most of his classes the days Harry was away to keep the dealership open in the afternoon, when sales were most frequent. Still living at his parents' home, Son was anxious to be on his own, live a bit, find a wife, and get on with life. A part of that future, a result of the war he felt, was getting his teeth some attention. As the family didn't have a regular dentist, he made a call to Dr. Schneiderman for a referral.

Son soon made the acquaintance of Dr. Oliver Martin, DDS, whose office was on the top floor of the Higbee's Department Store downtown. Martin diagnosed Son's dental condition as a gum problem; they had gotten infected due to poor cleaning and the rations soldiers consumed while in Europe. Some teeth would have to come out, he would need to rinse his gums often with antibiotic wash, and he would need to come by weekly to check his progress. Morning appointments were subsequently made from March through May with the dentist's lovely receptionist, Miss Rosalee Mills.

✯✯✯

Tom Keck lost little time calling Agnes upon his return to Cleveland two weeks from the day he'd left for Canada. Kathleen answered the telephone, handing it over to her daughter with a wary look. The two talked for half an hour and made a date for dinner at the Harbor Inn, where Tom had met the restaurant's owner, Mike "the Russian," a month before.

"So, my girl," Kathleen began, "who's this Tom person? And more importantly, where does he work?"

"Oh mother." Agnes feigned indifference. "Tom's a guy I met when I stopped for a beer after a baseball game Dad sponsored last month. He's a Navy vet who moved here from Erie to work in the shipping industry with American Shipbuilding."

"He designs freighters then?"

"No, he works in their engine rooms, keeping them going across the lake. He's just back from Canada and has ten days off before his next trip. It's what he learned in the Navy, except the pay is better and there are days off."

"And a girl in every port," Kathleen said. "You're just one of many I'm sure, Agnes, that this Tom person has scattered around. And he's a laborer—your father and I want someone better for you than a beer-drinking lout."

"That's not fair, Mother. You know nothing about Tom!"

"You don't either, honey. That's my point. He'll leave you barefoot and pregnant and be off for a better job on Lake Superior."

"Tom's not that way, you'll see. He works hard. He has to or the cargo his ship carries won't be delivered, and large sums of money will be lost. Knowing how to run a turbine engine is not a small thing, and so what if he likes a few beers after work and an occasional baseball game. He's young, single, handsome, and I'm not getting any younger living my life here with you and Father."

With that Agnes left the house and drove into the city.

☆☆☆

By May Robert Kern was well-versed in life at Staunton Military. He found he enjoyed the routine of his days—up for reveille on The Asphalt at six, breakfast at six forty-five, and his classes beginning at seven. Lunch was at twelve thirty, then free time until two, followed by athletic activity, military drills or study time, dinner at six, and lights out at nine. Mary Baldwin College for female students was located not far from Staunton's main gate, and both schools sponsored monthly social functions and dances that were well attended.

The physical activity was making Robert stronger, and he grew taller, two uniform sizes by September. As promised, Harry wrote to his son weekly, describing the activities of each member of the family, most of which Harry only knew through Kathleen's relating. He knew the most about Son from their daily interaction, but was disinclined to dwell on Son's life at home when Robert was so far away. Once a month, Harry would include cash in his notes to cover an occasional outing away from campus or other unexpected needs. Robert was prompt at writing to his father in return, with the two becoming closer while further away. Throughout the month of August, Harry addressed his promise to visit Robert during Staunton's Parents Weekend at the end of September, using all his best sales techniques on Kathleen.

"Really Harry, he hasn't been gone all that long. Seems like he was just here, and then there's this romance Agnes is having with this Tom fellow, and what would Nora do if we went off?"

"We'll take her along. There ought to be plenty of young men there that would like to meet a pretty, young girl."

"Oh no! I won't chance losing another daughter to the military!"

And so the conversations about Staunton and Robert would swirl in the Kern household. Ultimately Harry and Son made the trip as Agnes's surprise engagement to Tom in September made Kathleen take to her bed.

CHAPTER TWENTY-TWO

Rosalee Mills finished her secretarial studies at the Griswald Institute in 1946. The program ran for forty-eight weeks, with her tuition coming from her father, whom she promised to pay back when she started to work. The Mills family lived in the Lakewood neighborhood of Cleveland just west of the city's limits, the city's first subdivision. Her father, a contractor, built their home in the Fourth Ward on Cove Street near the Detroit Avenue streetcar line. Her mother was a homemaker.

The advertisement that appeared in *The Plain Dealer* was just the type of first position she had been trained for at Griswald. After answering the ad and sending a resume of her abilities, Rosalee was granted an interview the following week. She and her mother visited Lakewood's business district and purchased a business suit for Rosalee with money her mother had been saving. On the appointed day, Rosalee took the streetcar to the Higbee's building on Public Square, arriving at Dr. Martin's office by eight. She was introduced to Martin briefly, but her interview was conducted by Martin's part-time business manager, a bookish woman who also worked for several other dentists with offices in the area.

After taking typing and shorthand tests and performing very well on both, Rosalee was offered the receptionist position at fifteen dollars a week and would begin the following morning. Thanking her interviewer for the opportunity, Rosalee left the dentist's office thrilled with her appointment and decided to celebrate by having coffee and a scone at Higbee's Silver Grille. Then it was back to her parent's home on Cove Avenue to give her mother the good news and create a weekly budget— making sure she repaid her father for her education at Griswald, purchasing another suit for work, and saving as much of what was left as she could. It was a month later that she formally met and made dental appointments for Richard Kern.

✸✸✸

Son and Harry arrived in Staunton in good time, both taking turns driving and admiring the change of season as they wound their way through the Shenandoah Valley and Appalachian Mountains. They took a large room at the Virginia Hotel upon arriving and hoped they could find Robert and all have dinner together. However, cadets were detained to barracks the evening prior to Parents Weekend, attending to room cleaning and inspection, making sure their dress uniforms were well pressed, boots polished, gloves mended, rifles oiled, and swords shining. There would be a dress parade on The Asphalt beginning at nine the next morning, after which cadets would be allowed to find their families. The school presented an annual ball during the weekend, inviting female students from Mary Baldwin. Cadets attending would be in their dress uniforms, the ladies in formal gowns.

The next morning, Harry and Son ate an early breakfast and drove to the school, finding good seats on bleachers brought in for the occasion. The bleachers afforded excellent views of the 450 young men who would be marching and performing drills for their parents, brothers, and sisters attending. At nine on the dot, a bell located in the tower of the main class building rang nine times, and the building's doors were opened by two men in resplendent uniforms. Through that portal marched the Corps of Cadets, with three bagpipers in the lead wearing leopard-skinned capes over their shoulders in striking contrast to the rich red of their dress uniforms. Behind these three were the sons of the assembled parents, who strained to see if they could identify their own from the mass of students who all looked alike. Harry and Son were no different from the other families in this effort, but could not find anyone who looked like the boy Harry had brought there the March before. The cadets' precision was flawless and wonderfully complex, Harry thought as he continued his search.

"Better than the Army I was in," Son remarked. "A thing to behold. I can't believe Robert's out there. I wish Mother was seeing this."

Those were Harry's sentiments exactly, but he said nothing.

Rifles were shot, a cannon fired, a small brass band played, and at ten, dress review concluded. The cadets broke ranks and were dismissed by the school's commandant. Harry and Son stood on their bleacher seats and waved their arms hoping to attract Robert. The man who waved back at them could not be Harry's son, Son's brother! He had to be at least six feet tall, and no longer the thinly built boy they had seen in swimming trunks on the beach in Dunkirk. Harry and Son descended the bleachers and stepped on The Asphalt where Robert awaited them. He was now taller than both his father and brother and built like a Notre Dame lineman.

"Is that really you?" Harry asked, looking up at his son.

"Last time I looked," Robert replied. "I've been working out! Lifting weights, and then there's the drilling. Sometimes I even find the time to study!"

The three Kerns all laughed at that.

"Bobby, you can borrow anything of mine anytime you'd like," Son said. "I'd be afraid to say no to you."

They laughed some more.

"Come on up to my room so I can change out of these dress reds. I'm off duty now until Monday morning at six, and Dad, I'd really like a thick steak for lunch—maybe dinner too!"

Son reached up to put his arm around his little brother's shoulder, and the three men went to Robert's room after he returned his rifle to the armory. Robert changed into civilian clothes and the three Kern men drove into town, choosing the Mill Street Grill for lunch, where beef cuts were plentiful.

"Are you attending the social event tonight?" Harry asked.

"Oh, you know, Dad, I don't pay much attention to girls, and I'd have to be in uniform. I'd rather be with you two and talk about home, how my sisters are, how the car business is, and of course how Mother is doing. Haven't heard much from her since I've been here, but sure do appreciate your letters, Dad. And Son, I want to know all about what you've been doing."

After lunch the three men walked up one side of Staunton's main street and down the other. It was a lovely early fall day in the mountains. Ending at the Virginia Hotel, Harry was able to get an extra room for Robert, and the three sat in wooden rocking chairs before dinner and talked about old times and the future.

CHAPTER TWENTY-THREE

Agnes became Mrs. Thomas Keck one Tuesday afternoon in November of 1946. They went to the Cleveland Courthouse to purchase a license the day before and were married by a municipal judge the following afternoon. Wanting her mother to get used to the idea before seeing her, they sent Kathleen and Harry a telegram from Erie, where they were going to spend the remainder of the week honeymooning. The telegram arrived just as Harry was pulling up the driveway, and he heard his wife's scream as he opened his car door in the garage. Fearing someone had died, he rushed into the kitchen and found her in tears with the telegram still in her hand. Nora ran down from the second floor to see what had happened.

"She married that drunken sailor," Kathleen sobbed. "I'll bet he's got her on her back right now in some seedy motel room taking her virginity."

Harry hugged her, but she was too mad to be comforted and pulled away.

"Momma," Nora began, trying to be comforting. "I think we both know Agnes lost her virginity years ago, probably before high school!" That set her mother off on another round of screaming, even though she knew it was probably true. It had not occurred to Harry before, but then he remembered the absence of the condoms from his bureau drawer. *Oh, goodness!* he thought to himself.

Some weeks before, Agnes had brought her young man by the house to meet her parents and have dinner. Tom was a good-looking fellow—tall, clean-shaven, trim—and he had interesting stories to tell about his work and his service during the war. Harry liked him well enough, though he had wished for someone with a college degree for his oldest daughter, and perhaps without a tattoo. But Agnes had always been an obstinate child, and he thought this was just one more example.

"I know neither of us would have wanted her to run off and marry Tom or someone else, but she's always known what she's wanted and had her way. Tom's a nice enough guy and I'm sure they'll be happy and settle into a nice life. In time have children..."

Talking of children set Kathleen off again, shrieking into a sofa cushion, "I'm too young to be a grandmother! Stop talking Harry, you're not helping here!"

He left the living room for his bedroom/study to review inventory figures and look over his office mail. Nora sat with her mother's head on her lap, rubbing her shoulder and humming as one might to comfort a baby.

The following Thursday morning Son had his first extraction appointment with Dr. Martin. Arriving a few minutes early, he took a seat in the waiting area, greeting Miss Mills as he sat in one of the leather chairs.

"Nice bright morning," Rosalee said with a smile. "Is it still cool out? We can have the longest winters here, Mr. Kern, don't you think?"

Son agreed and hoped she'd worn a woolen coat. "Might have a few flurries this evening. Do you have a car, or do you use the streetcar to get home after work?"

"Oh, the streetcar, can't afford a car. I've only recently begun working! Were you in the service, Mr. Kern?"

"Army Engineers, both theaters!"

"Doctor is seeing quite a few service men. It must have been just horrible in the war. I just can't imagine—"

Dr. Martin's nurse came through the door. "Mr. Kern, Doctor will see you now."

"Best of luck," Rosalee said as he walked past.

Son lost a back tooth that day to periodontitis. He was to come back in ten days' time and was told to gargle with warm salt water twice a day and to stop smoking. Forty minutes after he entered the dental office, he was again facing Miss Mills, this time with a mouth full of cotton swabbing where the tooth had come out. He paid a dollar fifty for the day's extraction, made a second appointment for ten days in the future, and wished Miss Mills a very pleasant day. *She smells of gardenias,* he thought.

✳✳✳

Fearing she had lost her oldest daughter, Kathleen decided she would begin paying more attention to her younger son, whom Harry had informed her was now nothing like the young boy he'd taken to Virginia. She began sending him a floral greeting card once or twice a month, adding very little to the greeting except "Oceans of Love, Mother." Robert found the cards' sudden arrivals quite amusing and wondered what sort of homecoming he should expect when the Academy shut down for Christmas break. He was to take the train back to Cleveland. Harry had booked him in a sleeping car, which he was looking forward to experiencing.

✳✳✳

On the Monday following her wedding, Agnes called her mother from the apartment Tom rented and where they both now lived. To her credit, Kathleen held her anger in check. Agnes asked if she could come by for some of her clothing and personal things while she was out that day, and they settled on two that afternoon. Nora heard her mother's end of the conversation and asked if she could be there as well, having missed her sister's company. Wanting to keep the visit as pleasant as possible, Kathleen agreed. Shortly after the living room clock struck two, Agnes drove up the driveway, coming into the house from the kitchen.

"Hello there," she said, slipping off her heavy beaver coat. "Wonderful to see you both."

Agnes kissed both women on their cheeks before her mother handed her a cup of tea.

"Well," said Kathleen, "here you are, Mrs. Keck. See much of Erie last week?"

"I'm sure she did Mother, though there's probably less to see there in November," Nora interjected, trying to take the sting out of her mother's question.

"Tom and I had a very nice few days. Our hotel room looked out over the lake. He told me what kinds of ships were moving on the water. We ate well and slept late. It was very pleasant," Agnes reported.

"And where is Mr. Keck this afternoon?" Kathleen asked.

"Shipped out this morning for Canada. Likely the last time this winter. He's due back Thursday, and I'm out house-hunting until then. We're looking for something with three bedrooms on a level lot with trees. Tom's been saving his money since the Navy, knowing he'd want to settle down after he found the "perfect woman." I'm not sure we'll even need a bank loan. How about coming along one afternoon, Mother? I'm sure I'd benefit from your practical advice."

Agnes knew how to work her mother, and this was a perfect offering to relieve some of her anger about the elopement.

✳✳✳

Staunton cadets were dismissed on December twenty-second at noon. Robert took a bus to Richmond and its Main Street Station for the overnight trip to Cleveland. He found it quite an adventure, almost like the Agatha Christie mystery he had recently read. Over dinner he watched the other passengers, giving them imaginary lives and making notes about them on the pages of a small notebook he'd begun to carry with him. While his grades at Staunton were largely above average, he found he excelled at writing both composition assignments and short articles he'd submit to the Academy's literary magazine. Writing about this trip and who might be on board with him was just too good to pass up!

His dinner, plus the gentle swaying of the cars, made him ready for bed earlier than he might have liked, but he gave into it and retired. The train was to arrive at Union Station at noon the following day, so he wanted to be up, shaved, and breakfasted well before that. Son had said he'd meet the train and drive him home, and Robert hoped it would just be Son in the car to have a bit more time to adjust to the thought of being in his mother's presence.

Son picked him up in one of the automobiles from the dealership, a 1946 Chevrolet Fleetmaster Sports Sedan, two-tone tan and white, which Robert admired inside and out.

"Looks as if we'll have a white Christmas this year," Son remarked, as it had snowed overnight.

"It's what Bing Crosby sings about. Nice to be in a big city again," Robert replied. "Staunton's a nice little town, but very insular. Are you enrolled at Case now?"

"Yes, in the business program. They gave me credit for the courses I was taking before enlisting, so I'm not in my first year there, but barely into my second. I'm helping Dad out a lot at the dealership. He has a real gift for selling cars. No pressure, lets the car sell itself. He's so good about service too. We have two factory-trained mechanics now, and I sometimes help, trying to remember what I learned at GM Tech." Son pulled up to the curb in front of the house on Clifton Street. "Well, here we are! All ashore that's going ashore."

The brothers entered their parents' home through the front door, Robert carrying his Staunton duffel containing the few ill-fitting civilian clothes he had taken with him the spring before. He hoped if he received any cash for Christmas, he could remedy his clothing situation before returning to Virginia in January. They found the living room empty and guessed their mother was either away or in her second-floor room. They repaired to the kitchen to see what the refrigerator might hold and were enjoying bologna, cheese, and onion sandwiches when they heard their Mother exclaim, "Son, who the heck is with you in the kitchen?"

At that Robert stood and turned toward her.

"Oh my God," she gasped. "Bobby, is that you?" She looked up at her youngest child who stood a good six inches above her. "Wait until Agnes and Nora get a look at you."

Robert bent to hug his mother, but was wary of her sudden change in attitude toward him.

"You look a lot like your father," she said, which Son mulled over later. He thought Robert did not look at all like Harry. "Take your things up to your room when the two of you have finished lunch. It's just as you left it."

Kathleen left the kitchen as quickly as she'd entered, making a telephone date with Agnes to look at several houses.

✹✹✹

During the war years, and especially when Son was serving, the Kern family deferred from hosting their Christmas Eve socials, preferring instead to listen to holiday specials airing on the radio. Harry would light a fire and the family would admire their Christmas tree and, in turn, empty the contents of their stockings hung on the mantel by their mother. This being the second Christmas after the war's end, and with Son safely back and Bobby home from school, there had been some talk about reviving the former festivities, but they all concluded quiet Christmas Eves were preferred.

The next morning, after gifts were exchanged and breakfast dishes cleared, Kathleen, Nora, and Robert began preparing for the evening's dinner. Kathleen's parents would be there, as would her sister, Mary, and Norman, and Agnes and Tom—eleven in all. Harry and Son made their way into the dining room to fit all the table extensions together. They then placed it in the center of the living room while Kathleen lamented not having a larger home.

During the lull before guests arrived, Robert slipped on his overcoat and went for a cold Christmas walk. The air felt good after being in the house and kitchen most of the day, and he was glad for the opportunity to be outside. He had grown accustomed to being alone in his life while in Cleveland, and oddly enough while at Staunton, even with 400 or so cadets around. Things with his mother were somewhat better than before, but still he really didn't feel those oceans to which she so often referred. He walked to the very end of Clifton, where the street climbed a hill and came to an abrupt end, looking out over the roads heading into the city. He remembered being warned as a boy never to go to the street's end because he might fall off the hill and always feeling deathly afraid of being at the exact spot where he now stood. As the winter sun began its descent into the lake, the city was bathed in a rich golden glow, which he took to be some sort of good omen for the year ahead. Then he turned from the vista and retraced his steps as the family began to gather.

✲✲✲

On Tuesday morning of the week between Christmas and New Year's, Harry was surprised by a visit to his office from Cynthia Clarke. As always, she was nicely dressed in what he surmised were outfits harkening back to her Scottish ancestry—leather boots to her knees, a wool plaid tartan skirt, and a heather-colored boiled wool jacket. Her GC Imperial was parked on the street just to the left of where his desk was placed. It still looked wonderful, not a scratch he could see, even down to its soft leather top.

"Happy New Year Cynthia! Hope you and Clark are having a good holiday. How's that Shaker Heights home now that you're properly settled? Sorry, I'm asking far too many questions. You've only just walked in. What may I do for you?"

"It's quite fine, Harry. It's nice to hear a male voice. As you may know, Clark and the symphony are again on tour—Austria, Norway, and

Venice. I could have gone along, I suppose, but well, let's just say my tolerance of symphony wives is very limited. The house is just what I wished for, thank you for asking, and because my husband is away, my holiday season is, well, boring. That's why I've dropped by this morning. I want to trade the wonderful car you sold me for something newer!"

He looked at her, a smile still on his face, wondering why on earth she would trade in one of the most beautiful automobiles Walter Chrysler had ever made. *But,* he thought, *the customer is always correct!*

"Well Cynthia, you've come to the right place. Just sit right down here and take a look at some of these automobile pamphlets while I go out and get some information from the GC's odometer. Key in your purse?"

It was, and Harry was outside slipping into the driver's seat a second later. The engine fired immediately, as he knew it would. The beauty had been driven only 12,200 miles, and a quick look at the upholstery showed nothing amiss. He turned the engine off, got out, and opened the trunk. The spare was where it should be and looked as new as the day it arrived from Detroit, and the tires had never even been rotated. Still a wonder!

"Anything of particular interest?" he asked as he walked back in and settled in his desk chair. "Are you wanting to stick with Chrysler or try something from GM?"

"I'll stick with Chrysler. This Town and Country convertible is cute. I could see myself driving something like that."

Harry picked up the brochure. The model was new for 1947, with real wooden panels starting at the front doors and flowing to the back fenders.

"Yes indeed, that's something new. Let me just do a bit of figuring." He pulled her file from a cabinet. She'd paid almost $3,800.00 for the GC, a 1941 model in excellent condition. He could offer her $900.00 for it. The dealer cost of the Town and Country was $2,500 with a suggested selling price of $5,000. If he sold it to her for $3,100, he'd make $600 on the deal.

"Cynthia, the retail cost for this automobile is $5,000. With the trade on the GC, I can get it for you for an even $4,000 if that's agreeable."

"What colors does it come in?"

She picked light yellow with a white top and sidewalls. Harry promised to have it delivered to the dealership early the next week.

"I'll give you a call as soon as it's off the truck and we've cleaned it all up," he said.

"You've made my day!" She kissed him on the cheek. "How's Kathleen by the way? I haven't seen her in so long."

"Yes, well, she's fine, was terribly withdrawn during the years our son Richard was in the war. But he's home now, taking courses at Case and helping out here in his off time. Then there was Agnes's marriage that kept her occupied—always something with kids!"

"Yes, I suppose so," Cynthia responded and turned to leave.

"Be careful this week with the GC. It technically belongs to the dealership now!"

"Why don't I just leave it here with you and I'll get a cab home. I'm headed off to Miami in the morning, back in a week!"

With that and a wave she was out the door. She had left a check for $4,000.00 and the order was placed. *Nice bit of work this morning,* Harry thought, feeling the GC's keys still in his coat pocket. He buzzed into the service room. "Johnny, when you get a chance, Mrs. Clark's GC that we've just taken in on trade is on the street. How about rotating the tires and changing the oil on her, and wash her up, please. I think I've just bought myself a new car!"

CHAPTER TWENTY-FOUR

Robert returned to Staunton a day after New Year's, again by train. He had made plans with two other cadets to move from his single room and join them in a three-bed room, which he hoped would assist in reducing his social deficiencies. Sipping a ginger ale in the club car, he thought over the semester break and how it all now seemed to him. His father was still his best friend on the homefront, he concluded, though Son was much warmer toward him now, which he credited to his being taller and broader through the shoulders than his brother. Kathleen seemed a bit warmer as well, though not loving in the way she was with the other three. Tom Keck and Agnes seemed happy enough, having just recently purchased a three-bedroom home on Woodland Avenue. He hadn't taken time to see it as Agnes was not his favorite and had told him to wait until she had it properly furnished. Nora was her quiet self, still living at home with no particular direction to follow except, he imagined, to marry into money and make babies.

A lot had changed, and a lot had not. It seemed to him Son was the most in turmoil, lacking direction and purpose. He wanted to assist their father but did not wish to be a burden; he wanted to find a girl but didn't mention any prospects; he wanted to get a college degree but lacked the drive to finish his schooling. For the first time in his life Robert felt sorry for his older brother.

✡✡✡

Dutifully, Son had followed Dr. Martin's direction about the care of his mouth—brushing, flossing, saltwater rinsing, and he stopped smoking. As the day approached for his third appointment, he began thinking of Rosalee Mills, hoping she had had a pleasant holiday and wondering about her situation. She wore no engagement or wedding ring, lived at home, and was working. She seemed to have her life going in a forward direction. Then he remembered, as he had bent forward to make his next appointment, how wonderfully she had smelled.

On the way to his appointment Son stopped at a florist near Higbee's and purchased a small gardenia plant in a celadon-colored ceramic bowl. Initially feeling good about the gift, he began to have doubts about it on the elevator ride up to Dr. Martin's office. Was he being too presumptuous? Too forward? At least he thought his breath smelled better than the only other time they'd been together. *Damn Son,* he thought, *this was a very bad idea*. When the elevator door opened, he stood there for a good three minutes before deciding to go in. Miss Mills would either think it was a nice surprise from a young man or she would think him too bold, and perhaps reckless. He walked through the frosted-glass-and-wood door holding the plant to his left side.

"I thought your desk looked as if it could use some cheering up," he said, placing the gardenia plant where it would get sunlight from the adjacent window. "Happy New Year!"

"Oh, Mr. Kern, how very thoughtful. It's my favorite flower. Happy New Year to you too."

Her smile caught him off guard. He smiled back at her as she twisted the plant around to enjoy its best angle.

"How lovely of you. The nurse should be right out for you."

Son sat in the same leather chair he'd chosen on his second visit, and within a few moments he was called in. Returning to the waiting room forty-five minutes later, Nurse Ash followed him to record his next appointment ten days hence.

"Rosalee's on her lunch break," she said, "so I'm doing double duty."

Son smiled at Nurse Ash but was disappointed not to see Rosalee there. The woman handed him an appointment card.

"See you then, Mr. Kern. Keep that saltwater rinse going!"

✵✵✵

Harry settled into his desk chair after lunch. It had been a good day so far—three different prospective clients had been in prior to Cynthia Clarke, looking at cars in the showroom. The GC Imperial was again parked in the street on the other side of his showroom window. He loved that car, but he'd sell it for the right price. Early afternoon was always a slow time, so he opened his leather case to review the dealership mail he'd received. There were several ads from after-market parts manufacturers, a notice from the Indians' management about slight fee increases for game sponsorships, an invitation to the upcoming Detroit Automotive Show, and a letter from David Wallace, Chrysler's GM. He had met David years ago, before he had risen through the ranks to his current position. He would typically send an annual greeting to his dealers at year's end, but this letter didn't look like that type of message to Harry. It was a personal letter.

Dear Harry,

My best wishes to you as a new year begins
in the automobile business. I look forward to
seeing you next month in Detroit and to
share with you some of our newest models and
technical advances. As I hope you know, our
relationship with Kern Motors is one that we value

and is one of our longest. After talking with
my counterpart at GM, it has been decided that by
the beginning of 1949, all of our respective dealerships must select one automotive company to represent.
In your case we hope you will stay with Chrysler
but will certainly understand if
you believe GM would provide a better fit for your
clientele. Additionally, by 1950, should you
stay with Chrysler, we will require that your business
be housed in a new, state-of-the-art sales building
with an increased inventory of our latest
models. These changes have been discussed and
agreed upon by our top management team, and we
believe will be good for the corporation as well as
for our individual dealers. Similar
guidelines will also be mandated by GM to
their dealers nationwide.

So, there is quite a bit for you to consider, and I am
always available to discuss these options with you
in person at your convenience. Nothing is due to change
for at least a year, so there is no need for a quick decision on your part. Until then, we are more than happy to
keep our relationship as it has been, and congratulations
on selling one of our new Town and Country models!

As always, my best wishes Harry, and I look forward
to seeing you in January.

David Wallace
General Manager
Chrysler Corporation

Harry read through David's letter two more times, each time feeling as if his world was beginning to come apart. He found it hard to believe the major manufacturers would think an all-or-nothing approach would be good for people wanting to purchase automobiles, having to go from one dealership to another to look and compare. As it stood, at least at Kern, a customer could compare models in the same building. It just didn't make good sense! Plus a new building and increased inventory. *The debt I will be forced to take on,* he thought. *The sales volume will have to increase by who knows how much. I'll be forced to hire salespeople and more maintenance employees. The personal touch I have made such a priority since going out on my own will be greatly weakened.* Harry was shaken thinking of the pressure he'd be under in this new relationship with either of the two manufacturers he had worked so well with thus far.

He folded the letter and placed it in his desk drawer. He had not planned to attend the Detroit show this year but now was thinking twice about it, not that he expected he could get an exemption to the new business decisions. He decided to begin running the potential numbers for expansion over the weekend. For now he poured a glass of water from the cooler and fished in his briefcase for the Alka-Seltzer he knew were there.

CHAPTER TWENTY-FIVE

Tom Keck had been saving money since his Navy years. The house he and Agnes purchased cost $2,500, of which he put $1,500 down in cash, then made a contract with the home's seller to pay the remainder in monthly increments of $41.70 over two years. Average monthly rent at the time being $35.00, the seller, a local bank, was only too happy to make the deal. The house came with a newly equipped kitchen Agnes liked but hoped she would not be expected to use much. They would need furniture throughout, which was why Tom had decided not to pay the full price up front.

"You know, honey, I'm going to leave the furnishings and decorating to you. It will give you something to do while I'm working. Maybe Nora and your mother will help, but don't do any painting or papering yourself. We can afford to hire that out. Besides I don't want you black and blue in places that only I can see!"

Agnes laughed mischievously and opened two bottles of beer.

When he returned from his week away, Tom found everything moved from his former apartment to the new house, and Agnes was making a list of additional furniture to be acquired.

"Nora and I moved most of it," she said, smiling. "I did hire a couple fellows from the dealership to move the bed, dresser, and other heavy things."

There were paint samples taped to walls on the first floor and fabric swatches draped over chairs for the curtains she was considering. Tom was impressed with the progress she had made.

"And," Agnes said, "I'm not black and blue anywhere!"

"Well," Tom smiled, "we'll just have to see about that!"

After a welcome home romp in their second-floor bedroom, Agnes and Tom left for dinner at Otto Moser's downtown. Located in the heart of Cleveland's theater district, the restaurant had been providing ample food and drink to patrons and entertainers since the nineteenth century's end. Prior to Tom being in her life, Agnes and her female friends would only eat there for lunch, before the evening patrons arrived for dinner and drinks and got too out of hand. Now she figured Tom could take care of her, and it was fun to see who might come in, especially with the Opera House just across the street.

They were seated in a narrow booth overlooking the bar and were finishing another beer when their waitress dropped by for their dinner order.

"Hi there, Tom," Norma Bonner said seductively. "What are you two thinking about?" She looked at Agnes and smirked. "Or are you two taking a break from that?"

"I'll have a reuben," Agnes said, trying to ignore the joke Norma had made at her expense.

"Make that two, Norma," Tom replied. "And a couple more beers."

Norma wrote the order down and left their booth.

"I suppose you know her from sometime before you met me?" Agnes inquired.

Tom smiled slowly. "Norma's worked here for a while. I'd come in with friends and always seemed to sit at a table she was working. She'd flirt with all of us. We'd eat, drink a bit, and then leave, always before her shift was over."

"So none of you boys ever checked her out for black and blues?"

"Of course not. That would have ruined the fun of coming in and seeing if she was working the table we chose, which as I said seemed to always happen. I'm thinking she just likes Navy guys."

Norma came by with the beers in tall glass tumblers.

"You going to introduce me to this lovely lady?"

"You bet," Tom said. "I'd like to introduce my new bride, Agnes."

"Gracious, I had no idea. Never figured you for the marrying kind, Tom. Guess I was mistaken." Then, turning to Agnes, "Pleased to meet you, Agnes. How in the world did you talk this guy into settling down?"

"Animal magnetism," was Agnes's response.

"Yes, I can see that. You from around here?"

"Born and bred. Before Tom, I'd only come in for an occasional lunch."

"Feel safe now?" Norma asked.

"Wouldn't you? I mean look at this guy's big arms and shoulders. He's just big all over," Agnes smiled at her husband, "if you know what I mean."

Norma looked daggers at her and walked off.

Tom laughed. "I never thought I'd hear a comment like that come out of the mouth of a Laurel School girl."

"I just loved anatomy," Agnes replied.

Norma brought their sandwiches, first placing Tom's hot plate in front of him, then turning to Agnes with the other plate in her hand, dropped the sandwich on her lap.

"Oh, I'm so sorry," Norma said. "The sandwich just slipped off." The cheese and corned beef covered Agnes's dress from her chest to her lap.

"You bitch!" Agnes roared. "You did that on purpose, I saw you."

Agnes jumped out of the booth with such force it knocked Norma to the floor. Holding what was left of her dinner, Agnes pushed it into the waitress's face.

"Looks good on you too," she snarled. "We're out of here, Tom. Grab what's left of your sandwich."

Agnes left the restaurant, wiping the remains of her dinner onto one of the cloth napkins with "Moser's" printed across the top and laughing at the scene she had left behind. They were still laughing when they got into the car, Tom behind the wheel.

"Call it a night? You smell good," he said pulling the car into the street. "Bet you taste good too!"

✻✻✻

The following Thursday was Son's day to return to Dr. Martin to have a third and final tooth pulled. The anxiety he felt approaching Higbee's was less about the tooth than it was about how Rosalee would greet him when he entered the office. He brought along with him a thin box containing two pair of silk stockings, which had been hard to find stateside since the war. He and a couple of his engineer buddies had liberated three pairs each from a bombed-out shop in Paris. As with the gardenia plant before, he suddenly feared this gift was too personal. He felt he had lost his GI bravado and again was waffling in the hallway in front of Dr. Martin's door. He shoved the thin cardboard box under his shirt and entered.

He first noticed the gardenia had grown two new blooms and was still on Rosalee's desk. She waved at him and gave him a big smile. He was intentionally early for the extraction, hoping to have a bit of time with her alone.

"I'm so glad to see you, Mr. Kern," she said. "I don't think I was here after your last appointment. As you can see, your gardenia plant is thriving."

The flower's scent was glorious and seemed to fill the room the closer he got to it and Rosalee.

"You're well?" he managed to say, struck by her clear skin and dark hair.

"Oh yes, thanks for asking! You are too, I hope, except for being here for another extraction. But I understand this may be the last. I'll miss seeing you when you're all fixed up!"

It was just the remark he needed to give him the courage to fish the box of nylons from under his shirt and place them on her desk. "These are from a shop in Paris. I hope you like them."

She admired the thin box with French writing across the top and opened it. "Are these real silk stockings? Oh, Mr. Kern, thank you." She rose and kissed his cheek. "You can't find these anywhere. They're so sheer," she said, holding one to the light. "I'll save them for a very special occasion, they're much too nice to wear to work!"

Nurse Ash entered and led Son from the reception area. Forty-five minutes later, he again had a mouth full of cotton swabbing as he re-entered the reception area.

"He's to come back in ten days Rosalee," Nurse Ash said and closed the door behind her.

Son waved at Rosalee. "More cotton," he mumbled.

She smiled and handed him an appointment card, which he took, trying to smile back at her, but worried bloody drool would sneak out between his lips. He absently flipped the card to its back side and saw she had written a telephone number on it.

"Call me if you'd like—when your mouth heals a bit!"

CHAPTER TWENTY-SIX

Of the two sisters, Nora was considered by one and all the sweet one, and some would say the prettier one. Where Agnes's facial features were sharp, Nora's were round; where Agnes tended to sometimes push her life to extremes, Nora was happy-go-lucky. Nora had been pleased when her sister met Tom because it took Agnes's mind off besting her at most turns in their lives. When they married, Nora was happy for her, but even happier to have the bedroom they'd shared from birth to herself! She had been two school years behind Agnes at Laurel, and as a non-boarding student sometimes felt a bit estranged from the boarding girls, whereas Agnes fell right in with them. Nora enjoyed classes in literature and fine art and participated in the school's dramatic productions. She often made her own dresses, working with her mother in the second-floor bedroom that served as a sewing room.

Unlike her sister, Nora did not gravitate toward bad boys, but gentlemen from within their social circle, especially those who attended University School, the all-male equivalent of Laurel. After Agnes and Tom were married, Nora enjoyed the freedom of living in her parents' home, listening to her father's stories, helping her mother prepare meals, and lunching out with her and her Bratenahl friends. With Agnes gone, she became her own woman at last.

✹✹✹

Though his gum was hurting from where Dr. Martin had pulled a back molar, Son began considering a plan for making a date with Miss Mills. Giving her those silk stockings had broken the ice! He didn't want to wait too long to call her, but with his current condition he thought should wait a day to two for his gum to heal. *So, I'll call her tomorrow and make a dinner date for Friday. I could meet her after work, and we could have dinner at the Silver Grille in the same building as Martin's office. Or perhaps she'd prefer Saturday night. Yes, Saturday would be better, more relaxed.*

He drove through downtown to his father's dealership and parked the 1946 Chevy Fleetmaster on the street. An auto transport truck was parked opposite, and he could see several cars his father had ordered, including the '47 Chrysler Town and Country Mrs. Clarke had purchased. *It's a beauty,* he thought. The wooden sides against the pale-yellow paint was a splendid combination. Son's father came out when he saw him, and both men admired what was the second most expensive automobile the dealer had ever sold. Harry didn't expect Cynthia back from Florida until mid-week, which would give his garage guy time to get the car washed and polished. They watched as the car came off the truck, and the driver handed Harry the keys and an invoice sheet indicating he'd taken delivery. While two other vehicles were unloaded, Harry and Son got into the Chrysler and drove it into one of the wash bays, marveling at the car's interior improvements.

"Cynthia's going to be the envy of her Shaker neighbors," Harry said. "Maybe she'll help us sell a few more."

Son thought he detected an unusual bit of sadness in his father's voice. "Everything okay, Dad?"

Harry looked over with a grin. "Oh sure, just a long day, and the winter weather is getting to me a bit!"

✳✳✳

The following evening Son called Rosalee, and they made a dinner date for Saturday. They decided on The Harbor Inn. Son would make a reservation for six and would pick her up at five fifteen. Rosalee gave him her parents' address (he thought it kind of sweet that they both still lived with their parents), and he wished her a good night. He went into his bedroom, looked through his closet, and concluded he did not have anything suitable to wear for a Saturday night with Rosalee Mills. After his class the following day, he visited the Men's Department at Higbee's and purchased everything he thought he'd need: a couple nice shirts, a couple ties, a tweed sport coat, slacks, a new pair of shoes, and a wool camel-colored overcoat.

"Do you have a young man, then?" Mildred Mills asked her daughter. "He sounded very nice when I answered the phone."

"We'll see," Rosalee answered. "He's a patient I met when he was in to have some dental work done a couple months ago. His name is Richard Kern, an Army veteran. That's about all I know about him except where he lives, and that he seems very kind. Brought me a gardenia plant when he came for his second appointment, said he thought my desk looked lonely."

"Kern, you say? Does his father sell automobiles? I think that's the name. They sponsor baseball games down at League Park. Your father and I went to one last summer. I'm pretty sure that was the name of the sponsor."

"Don't know about any of that," Rosalee said, "but you'll get to meet him Saturday night!"

✳✳✳

Harry spent several evenings that week in his home office thinking about the letter David Wallace had sent him and estimating potential costs he would incur should he conform to the industry's new guidelines. The numbers seemed staggering to him—the cost of a newer, bigger building, the number of units he would be expected to purchase, the added personnel. He could bring Son into the business, and perhaps Robert when he was finished at Staunton, but he'd still have to pay them, plus several mechanics and office staff. It would be a gigantic enterprise, nothing like he was used to. At forty-two he was too young to retire, and while he'd put money aside for the future, it wasn't enough to last an additional forty years or so of life. When the time came, he would just have to sell the business if a buyer could be found. He did have a very full client list; his business was good, and he had an excellent credit rating at his bank. He wondered what he could sell the business for and who he could consult on that matter. His current location, while perfect for how he ran his business, was not large enough for a new structure with an adjoining lot, so the current building would not be of much value to a potential buyer. Still, the land would be worth something because of its downtown location. He went back and forth on the issue, keeping it all to himself for the time being.

✵✵✵

Saturday at noon, Son and Harry locked up the dealership and had lunch together at the New York Spaghetti House on East Ninth. They discussed the morning's business; a Chevy coupe had been sold, and Cynthia Clarke came in, tanned and smiling, to pick up her Town and Country. It had been a good four hours and caused Harry to reassess his future options. However, it was currently Son who was talking, telling him about his evening ahead with a beautiful woman and dinner at The Harbor Inn.

"You're going on a date, with a woman?" Harry asked, as if coming back from another world.

"I am. She's the receptionist at my dentist's office in the Higbee's building. Her name is Rosalee."

"Well Son, that's just fine. Your mother and I have sort of been hoping you'd start to get out more. Does she live in town?"

"No in Middle Lakewood. Lives with her parents. She's awfully pretty, has a secretarial degree from Griswald. You'd approve I think."

"I hope you have a wonderful time. Need any cash?" Harry handed Son a twenty-dollar bill. "You earned it today on that Chevy sale. We need to talk about your future and what kind of salary I should pay you if you'd like to officially join me at the dealership."

"You bet, Dad. I thought that was the reason you sent me to GM Tech. I can still take classes for my degree at night."

Harry smiled at his son. "So does Rosalee have a last name?"

After lunch Son went back to the dealership to wash the GC convertible his father offered for this first date. Even fifteen years old, it was still a beautiful automobile—solid and rode well, even in winter. When he got home, he entered through the kitchen, whistling to himself.

"Well," Nora said, "you're certainly in a good mood."

Son smiled at his sister but kept walking toward the living room and the staircase beyond.

"What's your hurry?" she asked as he passed her.

"Got things to do upstairs. I'm going out tonight!"

He took the stairs to the second floor two at a time and shut his bedroom door. Opening his closet, he laid out the clothing he had purchased and decided which shirt and tie looked the best with the sport coat. Then he took an unusually long, hot shower, shaved when the steam evaporated from the mirror, combed his hair, and went back to his bedroom to see if he still liked the shirt and tie choices he made. It was only four in the afternoon, and he did not want to be too early or appear overly anxious. He sat in the stuffed chair in his room and tried to be calm and meditate as Colonel Copeland had attempted to teach his platoon. It felt good now that bullets weren't whizzing overhead. *Too good,* he thought. *Just what I need, to sleep through my date!* He opened a window and let the winter air swirl around him, then rose and walked to his desk and the mathematics workbook for his current class. *Nothing like a little trig to keep you awake.*

At four forty-five, Son dressed, put the twenty his father had given him in his wallet, grabbed the GC's keys and, again whistling, bounded down the stairs. His parents were seated in the living room, Harry having told Kathleen about the events of the evening.

"New clothes?" Kathleen asked, looking him over. "Nice looking. New shoes too, I see. Very stylish. Your young lady should be impressed."

"Thanks Mom. I hope she will be, but I've got to get going. I looked her address up on the street map at the dealership. I didn't realize Lakewood is the first suburb going west. Don't think I've ever been there. I probably won't be out too late, but I have my house keys, so feel free to turn in anytime."

As he walked through the kitchen again, Nora gave him a wolf whistle, and he was gone.

✳✳✳

The steamer Tom Keck crewed did not get back to Cleveland until Saturday morning, and he was off the following week. With a couple of his mates, Tom headed straight for Otto Moser's. He had told Agnes he'd be home in the middle of the afternoon and was sure she'd have a list of honey-dos for him, so being able to blow off some steam with his shipmates was a welcome, if brief, diversion. As the restaurant wasn't crowded yet, Tom and his friends chose a large round table in the back. Seated, they began looking over the menus and low and behold, there was Norma Bonner to get their drink orders and make small talk.

"How's that bitch of a wife, Tom? Next time she comes in here I'm going to show her a thing or two!"

"Oooohhh!" his crewmates all said in unison.

"Better be careful Tom," one of them warned mockingly. "Norma sounds like she's got a grudge."

"St. Claires all around Norma," Tom directed. "First round's on me!"

She hurried off to fill her tray with tankards of the English ale. The table consumed several more before getting around to ordering food, and most of them had another with their meal. Tom was feeling just fine. A few of the fellows began to leave, but Tom was not ready to depart. He thought he might have one more St. Claire after he expelled what he'd already consumed and headed for the bathroom. Afterward, he washed his hands and stepped through the door, only to find Norma standing in the hallway. She grabbed his arm and pulled him into an adjacent storage room.

"Bladder feel better Tommy boy? I thought I'd give you a little something before you head home to the wife."

With that she unzipped his pants and reached her warm right hand inside. Then she got on her knees for fifteen seconds until the desired result was achieved.

"Bet Wifey hasn't given you that kind of satisfaction," Norma said and left the room.

CHAPTER TWENTY-SEVEN

As he drove downtown, then west toward Lakewood, Son was flooded with anxiety. He felt excited about the date he was about to have; he felt apprehensive; he felt scared. It was sort of like being in the war again, he admitted to himself. Rosalee had given him good directions, and he soon pulled up to her parents' home on Cove Avenue. It sat on a bit of a hill with cement stairs leading to the front door from the driveway. A light was on by the door. Son made his way up and rang the bell. In less than fifteen seconds it opened, with Rosalee smiling inside. She had her coat on and was ready to leave, which Son appreciated, and he led her to his still-warm automobile. She inched her way toward him when she got in—not too close, but not against the passenger door either. Son had noticed as he held the door for her that she was wearing a pair of the silk stockings.

Driving back into town, they talked easily. He was interested in knowing more about Griswald, which led to her talking about working for Dr. Martin. Son pulled the car up to the restaurant's door where valet parking was available. The attendant helped Rosalee out. Son asked him to be careful parking the Imperial, then walked Rosalee into The Harbor

Inn. They were greeted and seated by the owner in a cozy, made-for-two booth after checking their coats.

Though he was not much of a drinker, Son ordered two glasses of pink champagne, which he found, after a couple sips, had a warming effect. Rosalee wore a fitted black dress that accentuated her fair skin and red lipstick. Son told her amusing stories about his time in the service and the gang of men Colonel Copeland had assembled. She had an easy laugh and seemed to be enjoying his company. The evening flew by with good food and conversation.

After sharing a tin roof sundae, Son paid the bill and tipped the coat-check attendant and valet, and he and Rosalee drove back to her parents' home. The ride back was noticeably quieter than the earlier trip into town, with both parties wondering to themselves about the proper protocol once they returned to Cove Street. Rosalee's mother had encouraged her to bring the young man into the house afterward, but Rosalee was sure her father would be up waiting for them. Son knew he would walk her to the front door, but should he try to kiss her? It was a quandary. He wanted to very badly, but would she find it offensive on a first date? The silence was deafening as Son pulled the car to the curb.

"Thank you so very much for a delightful evening," she said. "I had a wonderful time at dinner and with you."

The front porch light was on, as were some lights throughout the house.

"Perhaps we can go out again," Son said. "There are a lot of restaurants in Cleveland I haven't tried."

"I think that would be lovely. Perhaps next weekend?" she suggested, then turned her head quickly and kissed him. With that she opened her car door, sprinted up the steps to the front stoop, waved, and let herself in.

After leaving Moser's, Tom Keck was reluctant to return home to Agnes and whatever chores she might have lined up. He had enjoyed the sex act Norma performed. It was true Agnes had never offered, and he had never suggested it during their frequent love-making. He spent the better part of the afternoon thinking through this situation over beers at several neighborhood taverns, finally arriving at their house on foot and a bit sloshed. The front door was unlocked, for which he was thankful as he had forgotten his house key when leaving for the ship the Sunday afternoon before.

Agnes had spent the day repainting the kitchen cabinets. She first was concerned Tom had not arrived at home after having a few beers with his crewmates that morning, then worried he had not called for a ride home, and finally angered that it was late afternoon when she heard the front door close.

"Hello," Tom said as he sat in a living room chair. "Your husband's home. I'm sorry it's so late in the day. Let's go out for dinner in a bit. What do you say, Ag?"

A moment later he heard her footsteps on the stairs.

"Well," she said, looking over to where he was sitting, "I both see and smell that you're drunk. How good of you to come home!"

"I said I was sorry. We had a rough couple of days last week with storms on the lake, and several of us thought we deserved a square meal and a beer or two once on shore."

"I see," she replied, visibly not pleased with his explanation. "And that took all morning and most of the afternoon? I suppose you made your first port of call Otto Moser's and you were the last man standing. I'm sure Norma was glad to see you and your thirsty mates!"

"Now Ag."

"Don't you 'now Ag' me, you drunken sailor. Did she fuck you for dessert? A fuck for you and one for me!"

"It wasn't like that at all, though she did wait on our table."

"Yep, I'm quite sure of that. She gets more of your time than I do." Agnes looked down at him as a bit of spittle drained from the corner of his mouth. "I was just headed out to visit my mother. Why don't you shower and get some sleep. I'll be back in the morning sometime—and you'd better be here!"

Agnes turned and walked out the door. Tom heard her car start and drive away. He sat quietly, finally falling into a troubled sleep in the living room.

Agnes had called her mother that afternoon when she finally tired of waiting for her husband's return.

"Sure hon," Kathleen had said, "come on over and we'll go out somewhere and have supper. Your father and brother are at a game the dealership's sponsoring. We can have a girls' night out and include Nora!"

By the time Agnes arrived, her mother and sister were drinking gin rickeys from a pitcher Kathleen had made. Agnes poured herself one and joined them.

"Bad day?" Kathleen asked.

"How's that song go? Something about what do you do with a drunken sailor?" Agnes took a gulp of her cocktail. "Tom has a good heart. I think there is just too much in his life that comes before his wife and home. Sure would like to get him into some other type of work; his current job is too much like the Navy in all respects."

"Maybe you should get pregnant," Kathleen suggested. "Having a child might provide an inducement for returning home after a week away and would give him someone to play with during his shore time."

"A dog would be less work," Agnes replied, which Nora found very funny, either because it was or because of the gin. Agnes shot her a look.

"You dating anyone?" she asked her sister.

"Lighten up, Agnes," Kathleen said. "Nora's dating several men, just taking her time selecting one. Besides, with your father and Son busy most days, Nora's good company for her old mother."

"What's this I hear about Son having a steady girl?" Agnes asked, changing the subject. "Either of you met her?"

"Not yet," her mother answered. "They've had a couple dinners out now and I told Son he should bring her by to meet his family."

"That likely scared him," Nora said with a giggle.

"He met her at his dentist's office," Kathleen continued. "She's the receptionist there, a business school graduate. Lives with her parents in Lakewood, her father's a contractor. That's about all we know."

"Working girl, huh?" Agnes tried to develop an image of the girl her brother was dating. "Great way to meet men I should think!"

"We'll see, I suppose. Maybe the three of us should take her to lunch."

"Son's too smart to let that happen," Agnes said. "He knows we'd be unforgiving."

"Let's go get some food before these rickeys add me to the list of drunken sailors. Silver Grille agreeable?"

CHAPTER TWENTY-EIGHT

After Son's fourth dinner date, Kathleen was determined to meet this Rosalee Mills he was spending time with. Of her children, he was definitely her favorite. She also knew he would inherit the dealership. It had grown considerably since Harry had gone out on his own, and he was recognized in the Cleveland business community as well as the automobile industry in nearby Detroit. Kathleen thought even if Miss Mills was a nice, educated girl, Son should be setting his sights on young women with addresses in Bratenahl, or at least Shaker Heights.

That evening at dinner, Son threw her a bit of a curveball. "Rosalee and I have been thinking it would be nice for you and Dad to have dinner with us this coming Saturday night. I've made a reservation at the Silver Grille, which I can change if you two have other plans. If not, we could meet you there at six. What do you think?"

Harry looked across the kitchen table at his wife. He knew she didn't like making quick decisions unless they were hers, but he hoped she would give Son's invitation a chance. He for one would like to meet Rosalee, as Son talked about her often at the shop, and she sounded like a sensible young woman.

"Well Son," Kathleen began, "that's a very nice offer. Let me look at our calendar tonight and I'll let you know in the morning. Are you needing to leave early for some class you're taking?"

"Not tomorrow. I'll be going in with Dad to tune an engine and wash a couple new cars that came in yesterday. Why?"

"I just didn't want to miss you so you'll know about the dinner reservation."

"I suppose you're all for going on Saturday?" Kathleen said to Harry after Son had returned to his room.

"Sounds good to me. I'd like to meet Son's girl. The way he talks about her, she seems like a very nice young woman."

"She's from Lakewood, Harry!" she snapped. "Son should be seeing women of a better class, a girl whose family has money!"

"You didn't," Harry retorted and left for the living room and the evening newspaper.

He was right, and she silently fumed. As she finished the dishes, she noticed Harry had left the living room for his office. Drying her hands on a dish towel, she walked into the hallway connecting the kitchen to the dining room where the telephone sat on a shelf in the wall. As quietly as she could, she dialed Agnes's phone number, and her daughter answered on the third ring.

"Take you away from anything important?" Kathleen asked, her voice lowered. "I need to ask your advice."

"Sure Mom. What's with the hushed voice?"

"I don't want your father to hear. Listen, over dinner tonight Son invited your father and me to have dinner with him and his Rosalee Saturday night."

"Woo! Son must be cashing in his Army money for a night on the town. Or did he want you and Dad to pay?"

"The question is, should we go at all? They've only had a few dates, maybe three, and I'm wondering if it's too soon for the parental dinner. What do you think?"

Agnes paused before answering. "Times have changed from when you and Dad began seeing each other. The war's done that to boys like Son who saw soldiers killed before they were old enough to vote. I think you and Dad should meet this woman. If Son picked her out she must have something going for her. At least you can gauge how the two of them act together, how serious they seem. If she's not up to snuff, well then you can plan some way to disinterest him. What would it hurt?"

"Your father thinks we should go. He's anxious to get to know the girl. You know your father, never met a person he didn't like."

"He didn't like Clark Clarke much."

"You would have to bring that up, Agnes!"

"Was Nora there during all this?"

"No, she was out with some friends tonight, so I haven't been able to get her advice."

"She'll agree with Dad—I'd bet on it."

"Yes, you're right. They are a lot alike in that way. All right then, we'll go. I don't intend to be too critical of her, but will certainly watch how they act together. I just want the best for Son, and the best doesn't live in Lakewood!"

Kathleen gently put the receiver back on the telephone and turned out the kitchen lights. Harry was bent over his desk working on something when she passed by.

"I'm going up," she said. "See you at breakfast."

He looked up at her standing in the doorway. "You bet. Thanks for dinner."

"As good as we'll get at Silver Grille?"

"I should think so," he said.

Kathleen climbed the staircase and walked down the hallway to Son's bedroom and looked in at him.

"Book good?"

"Mom, it's an economics textbook. How good could it be?"

"Yes, I suppose. So, your father and I have checked our schedules and we're available for dinner on Saturday."

"Great!" he said, slamming his book shut. "You and Dad are both going to like Rosalee. She's pretty, smart, and very kind."

"You like her a lot then? Haven't known her very long."

"Sometimes you don't need to. Anyway, I've known her three months now, since when I first went to see Dr. Martin. I think I fell for her right away!"

Kathleen smiled, bid her son good night, and walked to her room.

CHAPTER TWENTY-NINE

On very special occasions Rosalee would have lunch at the Silver Grille, enjoying the Welsh rarebit sandwich, one of their specialties, but she had never been there for dinner. The Grille's interior was built out in an Art Deco design, featuring aluminum tables with black marble tops, green walls, bronze light fixtures, and floor-to-ceiling columns in off-white. The room's focus, however, was a red marble fountain in its center with goldfish swimming in the base. There was often a band playing for the enjoyment of evening guests, as well as a polished dance floor for those diners who were so inclined.

Rosalee worried how she would come across to Son's parents, particularly his mother, knowing the attachment most mothers have to their sons. Earlier in the week she had shopped for a new dress and light jacket to wear, and Saturday morning had booked time with her neighborhood hairdresser.

Son worked half a day at the dealership with his father. There was better than normal customer traffic, so the two were kept busy. On their drive in that morning, Harry was discussing how he intended to form a small corporation for tax purposes and wanted to make Son vice-president, with Kathleen serving as secretary. The prospect of officially working for the dealership and being paid a salary was welcome news for Son. He could quit taking college classes, be of more help to his father, and perhaps consider taking an apartment somewhere and leaving his parents' home.

He was thinking through all these things as he parked the GC in front of Rosalee's parents' house. Bounding up the cement stairs, he found she was waiting for him just inside the glass door. He thought she looked wonderful in her new dress.

"I love that dress," he managed.

She put the jacket over her shoulders and stepped out. "How are your parents this evening?" she asked.

"Oh, they're both well, thanks for asking. They're generally early eaters, then they listen to the radio for a while before bed. You know, early to bed and early to rise."

"Sounds like a healthy philosophy. I'd have a bit of trouble with the early to rise piece of it though."

He opened the car door and she slid inside. "Got lots to tell you on the way."

By the time they arrived, Son had told Rosalee about joining his father at the dealership and the impact it would have on his life. She was thrilled for him and knew he would do well. Taking his arm, they walked through the department store to the elevator that would take them directly to the tenth floor. They arrived laughing and were seated at a table for four. Son's parents were not there yet, so they ordered gin rickies, talking quieter now. Fifteen minutes later, Kathleen and Harry walked to the table from coat check, both smiling at the young couple as they neared.

"Hello Rosalee," Harry began. "It's so nice to meet you. I'm Harry, and this is Kathleen."

Hands were extended by the three of them and they were all seated.

"Whatever that is you two are drinking looks very good!" Kathleen said, and two more rickeys were ordered.

Kathleen was on her best behavior and the drinks helped ease her apprehension about the relationship between Son and Rosalee. In fact, to Son it seemed an unusually pleasant evening with his mother. Dinner was very good, his father talked and laughed easily with Rosalee, and Kathleen was happily civil.

After the foursome broke up, Son and Rosalee went to her parents' home where he was teaching her the game of bridge. Harry and Kathleen returned home.

"I liked her," Harry said as they drove home. "She's bright, is well-spoken, has a good sense of humor, and is very pretty!"

"You like everyone, Harry," Kathleen said humorlessly. "That's why you're such a good salesman. She's just not right for Son, not up to his potential in life. I'll give it six months or so."

She was quiet the remainder of the drive, and upon entering their home she said good night and went to her room, leaving Harry alone on the first floor. Close to midnight, Son returned to find his father still reading in the living room.

"Hello," Harry said. "How'd the bridge instruction go?"

Son sat in a chair opposite his father. "I think she's getting the hang of it. The bidding's still a bit confusing, but she seems to enjoy it and even bought a book on the game."

"I'm sure she'll do well. She seems very bright and interested in learning new things. I enjoyed the evening and meeting her."

"And Mother?"

"Well, you know your mother. If Rosalee were a princess she would have a tough time accepting her for her Sonny boy! Are you two getting serious?"

"I think so, Dad. We haven't made any plans yet, except to be together as often as we can. Let's see what the summer brings. Perhaps we can take a weekend at Dunkirk when the family's there."

Harry offered to repay Son for the dinner bill, but Son refused. Patting his father's shoulder, he went to up to his room. Harry watched him climb the stairs and headed for his first-floor bedroom.

✿✿✿

Son and Rosalee were married the following December. Kathleen was less than pleased, Nora was non-committal, and Agnes—well, she hated the whole thing. Robert, who was home for most of the previous summer, got to meet Rosalee while at Dunkirk. They joked and enjoyed their time together. Son was pleased that at least Robert liked being with her. Harry and Rosalee's father Carl hit it off well, both enjoying baseball and auto-mobiles. Harry made him a good deal on a used Chevy pickup truck and hired him to rehab another garage he'd purchased that fall as a second mechanic's bay. Rather than renting an apartment, the couple purchased a nice-sized double occupancy home in Cleveland Heights, living in one side and renting out the other. Rosalee continued working for Dr. Martin while Harry and Son prepared for the new year, 1949, at the dealership.

✿✿✿

Harry always preferred years that ended in even numbers. He didn't know what caused this quirk in his personality—perhaps something Pap had once said—but there was a reason he was less cheerful this New Year's Eve than he'd been the year before. It was time to decide what product line he would offer, as well as build a new building to house the business. He would also have to purchase a sizable inventory of all Chrysler models (if he stayed with Chrysler) upfront. Even at half price, Harry, and now Son, would be on the hook for a great deal of money. More employees would be required both in the showroom and in the servicing area. Salesmen would work on commission, but the service employees would not. Automotive parts would also need to be purchased upfront and stored on the premises, which meant there would be an employee or two needed there, along with a bookkeeper and an accountant to ensure all transactions were properly tracked.

No matter how many times Harry and Son worked the numbers, the prospect of continuing seemed insurmountable. Harry thought about selling only used vehicles, but he knew his past clients wanted new models and generally purchased without trading in an existing car. A few clients did want to trade in for something older or more exotic—like Cynthia Clark and her GC that Harry bought for himself—but they were rare. If, after all the years he had invested in his business, he decided to sell out to someone, he wondered how to establish an asking price. The buildings he had cobbled together were not worth much, but his twenty-year book of business was certainly worth something, as were the fifteen vehicles he currently owned in the company's inventory. Harry, Son, and eventually Kathleen spent evenings talking through the selling option. Any decision they made would be new to them and, because of that, was worrisome. It seemed especially so to Kathleen, who enjoyed the life Harry provided.

Robert was another reason Harry was not enjoying the new, odd-numbered year. He had done well at Staunton, rising to the rank of captain, overseeing his own company of cadets. He also had developed a strong interest in the Air Force, intending to enlist upon graduation the following spring. Harry, Son, and Robert followed the rumblings of a potential conflict in Korea. The Chinese and Soviet governments seemed to be actively pursuing political influence in the north, while the United States and lesser former Allied partners from the second world war were attaching themselves to the government in the south. Should conflict break out, Harry reasoned the Air Force would be in the thick of the fighting.

Because of the family's estrangement, Robert had largely gone his own way in life, and his Staunton years were no exception. He had survived and indeed flourished there largely on his own terms, with sporadic advice from his father and none whatsoever from his mother, who still only tolerated him when forced to during his infrequent Cleveland visits.

That spring, the entire Kern family made the trip to Virginia. Perhaps it was just an excuse to get away from Ohio, but Kathleen, Agnes and Tom, Son and Rosalee, and Nora made the trip south with Harry in a Chevy Suburban that had recently come into inventory. The Suburban was just large enough for all of them, with luggage in a rack on its roof. Harry, Kathleen, and Nora were in the vehicle's front seat, Agnes and Tom in the second row, and Son and Rosalee in the third. They spent one night in Morgantown, West Virginia, and all agreed they should have taken the train!

Little had changed in the town of Staunton since Harry and Son's visit at the conclusion of Robert's first summer there. Three rooms had been reserved at the Stonewall Jackson Hotel, all with bathrooms, and that first evening they settled themselves into rocking chairs on the hotel's broad porch. Robert would meet them in the morning on campus, as his cadets were involved in the pageantry planned for the graduating class. They arrived after most of the shops along the main street that Harry, Son, and Robert once walked had closed for the day, giving Kathleen no excuse to explore on her own.

While they rocked, the men sipping bourbons and branch, the women sherry, a wispy fog began to roll down and into the Shenandoah Valley, as it did often at this time of the year. Its very sight chilled Kathleen, and she pulled her red fox stole up around her neck. The fog rolled deeper into the valley and, while Harry knew it was natural this time of the year, he saw it as an incarnation of his current mental state in dealing with the future.

✲✲✲

The following morning was bright and clear as they drove up to the academy, and even Kathleen seemed to be in better spirits. The sleeping arrangements had been a challenge since Harry and Kathleen were in the same room, but there was a couch and he made do. Robert had his cadets on The Asphalt at six that morning for a final practice, and most were in their rooms changing into parade uniforms when the Kern contingent arrived. From the window in his room overlooking the parade ground he watched them through binoculars he had recently purchased.

Kathleen, he thought, was typically overdressed, wearing the fox stole Harry had given her the Christmas before, a reddish-colored felt-brimmed hat that covered her eyes, and a white, boiled-wool coat. The remainder of the entourage were at least appropriately attired. He could see Agnes and Tom jostling one another as they walked toward the bleachers, and Son and Rosalee seemed happy together. He had enjoyed meeting Rosalee the summer before in Dunkirk when she and Son had come for a long weekend. She was kind and laughed at the short list of jokes he'd committed to memory, even if she did not find them all that funny. She didn't seem to take anything for granted in her life or in her relationship with Son or the larger Kern family. He hoped the women in his family would not turn on her now that she and Son were married, and that Son would take her side when the inevitable frictions occurred. He put down the binoculars, looked at his watch, grabbed his hat and white gloves, and joined his cadets.

The parading and graduation ceremonies went on for an hour and a half. At its conclusion, Robert became a senior cadet with rank and privileges. He dismissed his platoon, shaking hands with each of them and wishing them well over the summer, then walked to where his family was waiting. Nora seemed to almost swoon as he came nearer. He had grown at least another inch since the summer before, and the uniform, along with the ivory-handled sword he wore, made him an impressive sight.

He shook hands with his father, kissed Kathleen on the cheek, and hugged each of his sisters and new sister-in-law. "I'm sorry I couldn't get to your wedding," he said to Son and Rosalee. "I'm taking classes in aerial navigation next year and had to take some tests here to see if I would qualify for the program. I'm sure it was a very happy day. Hope the family behaved!" He laughed.

"They were on their best behavior," Son said with a smile, one arm around Rosalee. "Will you be coming back to Cleveland in the summer then? It's becoming an increasingly interesting place to live and work. I think you'd be happy there."

"Perhaps for a time in August. If I'm accepted into the program there will be one or two courses I'll be required to complete over the summer."

"Air Force, huh? Don't you think you're a bit too tall to fit into one of those things?" Son teased.

"Guess we'll have to see," Robert said with a smile, and hugged Rosalee a second time.

A luncheon for rising seniors and their families followed the graduation ceremonies, and Robert herded the family into the dining hall, where all eight of them were seated at a long table, four on one side facing four on the other, alongside other rising seniors and their families. At the head of the room, several chairs were set next to a speaker's lectern for remarks from the school's commandant and dean of students following dinner. Kathleen wanted her hat checked, but kept the fox around her shoulders. Harry returned from the coat room to find Rosalee seated between he and Kathleen, with Son on his mother's other side. Robert, Tom, Agnes, and Nora faced them. Son could tell Agnes was not comfortable with Rosalee being seated next to her father. However, the meal was served, which distracted her.

A friend of Robert's was seated next to Nora, who was glowing at his attention. Harry was engaged in conversation with Rosalee, and Kathleen was attempting to strike an appropriate pose while navigating her plate. Son and Robert attempted to converse with Agnes and Tom, who finished their meatloaf, green beans, and salad well ahead of the others. During the dessert course, the academy's dean rose from his seat and walked to the podium. He rang a small but unusually loud bell, drawing the attention of the assembly.

"Ladies and gentlemen, while you are finishing your desserts, I would like to welcome you to Staunton Military and to this gathering of rising senior cadets and their families and loved ones. I am pleased so many of you stayed after the stirring graduation ceremony to be here. The men who graduated today, and your sons who will graduate in another year's time, take their places as our nation is again being tested by the people of other countries who would see our country fail in its desire to live peacefully on this earth. It is the intention of this school to prepare our students, who may decide to enter the military upon graduation, enroll in universities, or return to their home states, to take leadership positions in the endeavors they so choose, and to be critical thinkers in all facets of their lives. As dean, that is my promise to my students and their parents. What they assimilate here at Staunton will guide the rest of their lives." The dean paused looking out over his audience. "It is now my great pleasure to introduce to you the commandant of Staunton Military, General Malloy Nash."

Applause followed as the sixty-something general rose from his seat at the dining table to take the speaker's position. Nash was tall and fit, his face tanned, his uniform crisp and spotless. There were three stars on his shoulder boards and a vast array of metals on the left side of his chest. His gray hair was closely cropped. He looked capable of walking through a brick wall and immediately drew Kathleen's rapt attention. The welcoming applause continued until he raised his arm to draw it to a close.

"Thank you, Dean Olmstead. I appreciate your kind introduction to these fine young men and their families."

The cadets were all still standing as was the custom of the school whenever they were in the presence of the General, and he asked them to be seated.

"This is always a very happy time at Staunton, as another group of seniors goes off to further their lives and we welcome the men of the next graduating class. For sixty-five years, the academy has prepared men for their roles in life. We lost some of these men in both of the world wars, but console ourselves with the knowledge that they fought bravely and did not die in vain. We are now just four years past the last great war, one in which I, and I'm sure some of you, fought in to free the world of totalitarian regimes in Germany and Italy. We pray events like these prior confrontations never occur again, but we must prepare ourselves for that possibility, because I do not believe human minds across our world can long sustain peaceful ambitions. Even now we hear of growing tensions between the peoples of Korea half a continent away. Should hostilities develop there, the United States has pledged to defend the south. Once again, Staunton graduates may find themselves caught up in this struggle, as we know a large percentage of our graduating class today have made plans to join one of our nation's military branches. The rhetoric of the leaders in North Korea suggests a confrontation is inevitable. If that is the case, the sheer number of North Korean troops, with the possibly of additional Chinese fighters, will surely overrun southern forces, even with American troops on the ground to advise and defend. Our Air Force will have a much larger role in the defense of the south, and bombers will be key to the struggle's end. I sincerely hope I am seeing a future through aging military eyes and that the politicians on both sides will work things out to avoid conflict. However, if not, be assured that Staunton Military graduates will serve proudly. Thank you, ladies and gentlemen, and God bless you all."

As the General finished, one could hear a pin drop on the mess hall's wooden floor. Then, en masse, the new senior cadets rose in applause, followed by their families. It was noted by the school's comptroller that a significant rise in contributions to the school was received that summer, and the school's board extended the general's contract by another five years.

✡✡✡

That afternoon, Kathleen, Agnes, and Nora left the hotel to do some shopping in Staunton and invited Rosalee to join their outing. Harry, Son, Tom, and Robert took up positions in the rocking chairs at the Jackson Hotel, where a discussion about the general's remarks was quick to ensue.

"Damn," said Son, "we just fought and finished a war. Just doesn't seem right that another may be coming. Surely it won't involve us too deeply."

"The general didn't make that sound very likely," Harry said. "It could put Bobby here right in the thick of it. Especially if you're serious about learning navigation. You'd be a sitting duck up there!"

"Using air technology of the past, you'd be right, Dad. But I'll be learning the navigation protocols of the newly redesigned B-twenty-nines—the Superfortress. It is generations away from the B-twenty-nines used in the last war. They're designed specifically for high-altitude strategic bombing, flying at over thirty-one thousand feet, an altitude fighters can't get to. And at three-hundred fifty miles per hour, they couldn't keep up even if they could get that high. It has four machine gun turrets sighted by periscopes from a centrally located position just behind the pilot. It's fully pressurized front and back and carries a ten-man crew. I think it would be pretty exciting!"

"That's because you're young, Bob," Tom interjected. "Your brother and I have both been in war and I can tell you there's nothing exciting about any of it." He drained the last of his beer. "There ain't even any pretty girls to see over there, certainly none around the base when you land."

"Well now," Robert said with a smile, "there's a disadvantage I hadn't considered."

The four men laughed, but Harry knew his second son went his own way on most things, and this part of his life would be no exception.

CHAPTER THIRTY

All summer Harry and Son debated the dealership question. It was, of course, complicated. Son and Rosalee were expecting their first child, Kathleen was wanting a larger house, Nora was now dating a young man from Pittsburgh of all places, and Agnes was pressuring her father to find a job for Tom at the dealership, which could not support three salesmen. Harry queried business friends who had taken or were about to take the leap into the new GM business model. He had a good idea of building costs, the number of vehicles the corporation expected each dealer to have on hand and their to-the-dealer-costs, the number of monthly sales required to satisfy bank loans, and the number of employees required to sell those vehicles.

The Cleveland bankers he talked with were only too anxious to make loans for a proposed new expansion, but the monthly stress of his cash-flow position was causing Harry sleepless nights. He had always hoped he could provide Son a decent living from the business he had grown the same way it had for him. But that dream, he knew, was quickly slipping away. His current sales were good with his limited inventory, but his time was running out and he owed David Wallace a response. He asked

Kathleen to prepare dinner Friday evening and invited Son and Rosalee. The Wednesday afternoon before, he telephoned David in Detroit.

"David, it's Harry Kern calling. I want to talk with you about the changes Chrysler is making after the first of the year. Can we arrange a convenient time and date for this conversation? I'm at your disposal!"

"Harry, it's always good to hear from you. I trust Kathleen and the family are well. Your monthly numbers, as always, are very good. Actually, I've got an hour right now if you'd like. Tell me what direction you're leaning."

"I've been so very lucky in my life so far, David," Harry began. "Winning the automobile race that brought me to Cleveland, finding a job at White in those early years, meeting Kathleen, raising a family, and with friends like you, starting my own dealership. I've loved every moment of all of it, but I must admit to loving the work most of all! I have done my due diligence, talked with colleagues who expanded their operations in anticipation of the new decade, and have really learned quite a bit. I'll turn fifty next year. I'm in good health physically and mentally, and David, I'd like to stay that way. I just cannot see how that's going to happen if I take on the obligation the future seems to hold. At the same time, I have no idea how to value my operation here or if it's even possible to sell my business to another dealer."

"I understand your dilemma and concerns, Harry. I really do, and you're not alone out there. I wish we could continue to do business with small dealers like you. They're all over the country, mostly in smaller towns, not like your location in a growing city. What's developing is a new model where a single dealer establishes operations in multiple cities. Because of the diversity of locations, they're able to satisfy their monthly obligations by juggling expenses and revenue between their dealerships."

"Gosh, David, that makes my head swim."

"Yep, mine too sometimes. If I may, I'd like to give your name to one of these new business owners with dealerships in Detroit and Pittsburgh who wants to get into the Cleveland market very badly. His name is Don Massey. I think he may be the right guy in the right place at the right time. Is that okay with you? He's a fair person to do business with, and as I say, really wants a presence in Cleveland."

Harry agreed and thanked his friend for the hour he'd been given that was rapidly coming to an end.

✳✳✳

The following morning, an early Indian summer day broke out in Cleveland, its golden haze adding a warming glow to everything Harry saw driving into town. His conversation the afternoon before with David Wallace played in his memory throughout the evening to such an extent that he couldn't remember half the things Kathleen and Nora talked about over dinner.

Nora's new boyfriend, Samuel Price, was from Pittsburgh, and Harry wondered if he bought cars from the Massey dealership there. Kathleen was interested in who this young man's family was, what he did for a living, and how he and Nora had met. Harry figured that was the natural questioning of a mother and let the two women prattle on. His recollection in the morning was Samuel had some connection to Westinghouse Electric through his father's family and he was employed there. How the two had met was part of their conversation he could not remember, his mind being occupied with how or when a conversation with this Don Massey might occur.

He didn't have to wait very long. Harry was reviewing the advertising proof sheets for *The Plain Dealer* weekend edition when his phone rang.

"Kern Motor Sales, Harry Kern speaking."

"Mr. Kern, I admire a man who answers his own telephone. This is Don Massey calling from Detroit. I hope I'm finding you well this morning."

Harry straightened in his chair. "Yes sir, good morning to you. I hope the weather in Detroit is as fine as it is here in Cleveland. I think we're having a bit of Indian summer today."

"Well, you know, Harry—if I may call you by your first name—the weather in Motor City is not often clear; manufacturing takes a toll. I try to spend as little time here as I can, or I'd forget what sunshine looked like." They both laughed. "As David's likely already mentioned to you, I am looking to put a Buick dealership in Cleveland. I've always liked the city and a location there makes sense for us logistically. I've had an opportunity to review your sales records over your twenty years there with both GM and Chrysler and I must say, they are very impressive. The number of clients you've made and kept in Bratenahl alone makes my head spin! Your clients buy from you knowing your business stands behind the sale. They're in effect buying a part of you when they come through the door. That is just so special, Harry! When word gets out you're thinking of selling, you're going to get a lot of calls like mine. That's why I'm calling a day after we both spoke to Wallace. I'm trying to get ahead of the rush."

"David speaks very highly of you, Don. He and I go way back, before he was GM's general manager. Don't see him as much as I used to when my business was new, which I miss, but I always thought he was watching out for me."

"Harry, let me get right to the point. I would love to purchase your business outright—buildings, land, client list, and current inventory— right now, today! I'll give you one million dollars cash and even throw in a 1949 Buick Roadmaster from the inventory in Pittsburgh if you like blue."

Harry was stunned. Not in his wildest imagination had he ever thought his business was worth that kind of money.

"I'm sorry Don, did I hear your clearly? Did you say one million dollars?"

"In cash or a cashier's check delivered to you in person Monday morning, along with the Roadmaster! Now I understand if you'd like to noodle this around for a while, and I hope you talk it over with people there or with David, but—"

"Don," Harry interrupted, "I accept your offer. Congratulations, you've just bought yourself a Cleveland presence!"

The two men talked together for another half an hour, Massey assuring Harry that when he opened Monday morning, the funds, the car, and the contract paperwork would be delivered. He also advised Harry to get his lawyer involved as soon as possible to ensure a smooth transition. After the sale was announced publicly, he hoped he could sponsor a Massey corporate event there to meet some of Harry's better clients.

The telephone call concluded, Harry rose from his desk and walked across the showroom floor and locked the front door. He placed his "Closed" sign on the door, turned off the lights illuminating the Chevy Styleline Coupe in the dealership's windows, and reclaimed his desk chair. *I do like blue,* he thought and almost said aloud. Harry called Norman Minor to arrange a meeting between the two the next morning at the dealership. Harry indicated the meeting was business and he wished to be billed as a client for the meeting and subsequent legal services. He then located all documents related to the business from its beginning, reading through each folder to assure himself all was in order. He finished this work near six and decided to have a scotch in celebration of the day and his future. He then drove home and acted as if he'd had a quiet day, deciding to wait to deliver the news the next evening at dinner when Son and Rosalee would be there.

The next morning, Norman arrived at the appointed time and was greeted by his brother-in-law, given coffee, and seated in a chair opposite Harry. Norman noticed Harry had locked the showroom door after he'd entered and had not taken down the "Closed" sign.

"Well then Harry, what may I do for you this morning?"

Harry smiled and folded his hands in front of him. "Has attorney-client privilege begun?"

"Yes, and you're on the clock!"

"Yesterday afternoon I sold this business to an out-of-town dealer wanting a Cleveland presence. He comes very highly recommended to me from David Wallace, GM's general manager."

Norman was stunned. "You sold the business you've grown practically since your adolescence? Who will I buy a car from?"

"You haven't purchased a car since you bought the Chrysler from me fifteen years ago. If you like Buicks, you can buy one from Mr. Massey. He has dealerships in Detroit and Pittsburgh, and next year he'll have one under construction here."

"Does Kathleen know about this? If she does she hasn't breathed a word of it to Mary. I'd know if she had!"

"Besides Mr. Massey, you are the only other person who knows, and I'm relying on the confidence between attorney and client to keep it that way—at least for another eight hours."

"You held out for a good price?"

"What's your hourly rate, Norm?"

"I'm billing out at twenty-five an hour currently."

"Yes, a very good price," Harry confirmed.

The two discussed the documents needed by the following Monday morning. Harry finally told Norman the selling price and watched him gulp and almost spit out the last of his now-cold coffee.

"That's going to make you one of the wealthiest men in Cleveland, Harry. I can't believe my brother-in-law's a millionaire!"

They finished what had to be done at Harry's office, and Norman got up to go to his own.

"Likely this will take some time tomorrow as well, Harry," Norman said over his shoulder. "Saturday work bills out at thirty-five an hour, plus fifteen for my secretary."

Harry shook his head and waved him out the door. Then he took the "Closed" sign down, turned on the showroom lights, and hoped he might sell a car or two in the afternoon and Saturday morning while the business was still his.

Kathleen prepared Son's favorite meal for dinner that night: a baked ham, her special potato salad, green beans, and a two-layer chocolate cake. As she puttered around her kitchen she considered Rosalee and the baby she and Son would be having. By the way she was carrying the child, Kathleen was sure it was going to be a boy, which was, she was also sure, what Son wanted. Rosalee had said the sex of the child did not matter to her as long as it was healthy. Kathleen thought that was a good answer and credited her daughter-in-law with having more sense than she'd given her credit for. Son seemed happy, and the duplex they had purchased was clean, tidy, and decorated well when she and Harry visited. Harry had phoned saying he might be a little later than normal; he had a customer who had just purchased a Chevy pickup. She made herself a gin rickey and turned her attention to Nora. If their relationship was serious, this Sam fellow would have to find a job in Cleveland. No daughter of hers was going to live away from her, especially in Pittsburgh! Nora said he had a job at Westinghouse Electric where his grandfather had been an original shareholder. Perhaps he could get on at GE. She shrugged as the gin took effect. Nora and a girlfriend were in Pittsburgh for the weekend to be with Sam and a friend, so Nora would miss this wonderful dinner.

Kathleen heard a car pull up to the front of the house; it was Son and Rosalee. She took off her apron, pinched her cheeks for a bit of color, and went to the front door to greet them. Since she'd last seen Rosalee, her baby bump had grown considerably.

"Hello Kathleen," Rosalee said with a smile. "I'd hug you, but this bundle won't let me get that close!"

The two women laughed, and Son said he'd hug his mother for both of them.

"Dad not home yet?"

"No, but I think shortly. He found a buyer for that truck he brought into inventory last spring and is finishing the paperwork."

"That's Dad for ya, never lets one get away! I'll bet he didn't take much off it either."

"That's between your father and his conscience," Kathleen said. "I never ask as long as he provides money!"

"And other things," Son added. "Like the new carpet here. What do they call this kind of rug?"

"Oriental. It's hand made." Kathleen had bought it recently and was quite pleased with it.

"It's huge," Son offered as he navigated Rosalee across it to what looked like a new chair. "I don't remember this either." Rosalee sank into its cushions, remarking on its comfort. "Dad must be working overtime!" The sound of a car came up the driveway. "Dad's home!"

They gathered in the living room with alcoholic drinks, except for the expectant mother who had soda water. The bubbles must have tickled the baby as it began moving around, which everyone had to feel.

"Hey Pop," Son began, "Gus Noland said he happened to drive by the shop yesterday afternoon and the "Closed" sign was on the door and the showroom lights were off. Everything okay down there?"

"Yes, right as rain. I had a bit of business to take care of, a couple of telephone calls to make, and I didn't want to be disturbed."

"That's not like you, Harry," Kathleen said. "I can't imagine what would be so important that you'd close the shop."

She got up to refill the drink glasses. Rosalee declined more soda and asked Son to help her out of her chair so she could use the bathroom.

"Sorry," she said as she got to her feet. "I seem to need a bathroom much more often than I used to!"

"Hurry back!" Harry said with a grin.

The gin tasted good, Harry thought, and the smell of the ham Kathleen had baked brought a smile to his face. *I think I'm going to enjoy retirement. There'll be time to do things I've never had time for before.*

Rosalee made her way back into the living room, but before she re-seated herself Kathleen said, "Anyone ready for dinner?" and the four of them went into the kitchen. Plates of food were passed around the table, everyone helping themselves. Rosalee was constantly feeling full but managed to take small portions of everything. Son rubbed her arm and winked at her as he took another spoonful of his mother's potato salad.

"Honey, you're going to need to know how to make this—if Mother will divulge her secret recipe!"

"Sure I will," Kathleen replied. "I'll write it out this evening for you." She smiled at her son. "Glad you still like the dish." Kathleen took another bite of ham and a sip of the wine she had poured herself and looked across the table at her husband. "So, Harry, what important business did you have that necessitated your closing the shop in the middle of the afternoon? I'm sure we'd all like to know!"

He looked across the table at her, smiled, and finished the bite he had just taken.

"I thought you'd never ask," he said with a smile. "I sold the business Thursday morning!"

Everyone stopped chewing and a sudden silence claimed the kitchen.

Finally, a good forty-five seconds later, Kathleen said, "What? You did what? To whom? When does all this take place? I can't believe it!"

"I'll bet!" He winked at her. "Kind of a shock, huh? As of Monday afternoon the Kern Motor Company will no longer exist."

"Are you serious Dad?" Son said. "You're joking with us, right? That business has been your life!"

"Times are changing Son. We've talked about this future that's coming. Small businesses like ours are being asked to take on tremendous expansion and risk. I've been looking at the anticipated numbers all year and there's just no way I'm comfortable taking on that kind of debt to satisfy the manufacturers. So I had a conversation with David Wallace Tuesday to see if there was any change in GM's position, and sadly there was not. He suggested talking with a dealer in Detroit who was interested in having a presence here and highly recommended this person. First thing Thursday morning this gentleman called. He was very complimentary about what we've accomplished."

"I bet," Kathleen said with a sneer.

"After we talked a while longer, he offered to purchase the business, buildings, land, inventory, everything, and I agreed. He's having a cashier's check hand-delivered to the dealership Monday morning when we open. I had Norman to the dealership to go over all the details and prepare the paperwork for the sale, which he will have to us Monday, along with a notary from his firm. By noon everything should be settled. Maybe we can all go somewhere nice for lunch. He's also giving me a new Buick Roadmaster as a gift!"

The kitchen was again silent as the shock began to settle over the other three people seated around the table.

Finally, Kathleen asked, "How much did you sell the business for, Harry? Do I need to find a job?"

Again, Harry smiled at her, Son, and Rosalee. "One million dollars. Don't think you'll need to be working anywhere, my dear!"

Everyone in the kitchen was still as the enormity of the amount of money sank in.

"Did you say one million dollars, Harry? Six zeros after a one?"

"Yes, that's correct!"

Kathleen looked at her husband, then at her son, then stood up and screamed, "We're millionaires! Bratenahl here we come!"

The following Monday morning, the entire Kern family arrived at the dealership, including Mary and Norman Minor. Norman had indeed worked Saturday on documents relating to the sale of Kern Motors, and now everything was ready. At precisely nine o'clock, a blue Buick Roadmaster two-door coupe came to a stop by the dealership's front door. Two smartly dressed men exited the Buick and entered the building, one of them carrying a leather briefcase.

"Hello," the one without the briefcase began. "Mr. Kern?" Harry left his family and shook the man's hand. "I'm Billy Massey, very nice to meet you. My father is Don and I manage the Pittsburgh business."

He turned to one side to introduce the man with him. "This is Howard Prescott, our company accountant and business manager."

Harry shook Prescott's hand and led them to what had been his desk, but was now void of any reminders of that past.

"Gentlemen, this is Norman Minor, my attorney, who has spent the best part of his weekend making sure all the contracts and legal issues are up to date so the sale of my life's work can be consummated."

Prescott smiled at Norman. "You've got quite a reputation, Mr. Minor. It's nice to make your acquaintance. I'm sure now there will be no issues to hinder this sale."

"Mr. Kern," Billy said, "my father is sorry he could not be here himself this morning. He sent me over because, well, the Roadmaster was in Pittsburgh. Oh, here are the keys. Howard here is the important one anyway. And who are these folks?" He turned to acknowledge the Kern family trying to blend in with the walls.

Harry introduced Kathleen, Son, Agnes, Nora, and Mary, who all smiled at the out-of-towners. Nora mentioned she'd just spent the weekend in Pittsburgh and even saw a Pirates baseball game. Introductions concluded, Harry, Billy, and Howard sat around the desk to review Norman's work, which took less than thirty minutes. Harry and Howard signed the sale documents, and a few moments later Don Massey owned Kern Auto Sales.

"Excellent," Howard said. "That was the easiest sale I've ever had! Thank you, counselor, your good work is most appreciated. And Mr. Kern, I have just one more bit of business that you'll be most interested in." He reached into his briefcase and removed a white business-sized envelope with Harry's name written across the front. "Don't spend it all in one place!"

Harry opened the envelope and there was the cashier's check for one million dollars. "My goodness," Harry said and sat down in his chair.

"Let me hold it, Harry," Kathleen said and hurried over to where the three men had just conducted the transaction. "Look at all those zeros! I can't believe I'm holding this much money in my hands."

Harry stood. Time's up, my dear." He slipped the check from her hand. "Our attorney's already opened a new interest-bearing checking account at Cleveland Trust for us and, after the check is endorsed, is going to make the deposit." Harry gave Billy Massey a set of keys to each of the dealership's buildings.

"Don't feel like you have to clear things out of the buildings in a rush, Harry," Billy said. "We aren't doing much here before spring. I'll send a truck down to pick up your automobile inventory, perhaps by week's end. Howard has all the keys. Which one would you like to drive back to Pittsburgh this afternoon, Howard?"

They settled on the Chrysler Windsor Sedan in the second showroom. Harry endorsed the check and turned it over to Norman for deposit. Son filled the Chrysler's gas tank, and the Pittsburghers were off with a wave. The Kern family filed out and Harry locked the door.

"I'll have my desk and office chairs put in storage until we decide what we're going to do with them," he said almost to himself. Quite unlike her, Kathleen decided she'd fix everyone lunch at home. It had been a very big, emotional day already, she said.

The following morning, Norman brought the deposit receipt to Harry at the house rather than the dealership. It was a surprisingly unsettling experience for both of them.

"Thank you Norm for bringing this out."

"The checks for the account won't be ready for a week. I'd hide them if I were you."

They both chuckled as Kathleen walked in from the kitchen.

"I heard that Norman! Under the circumstances, I think I'm behaving very well. I have started a list though."

"Oh boy. Your sister's started one for you too!"

"Does it have a new house at its top? Mine does, a big one. It doesn't really need to be in Bratenahl, Shaker Heights would be fine too. In fact, the Heights might be the better choice as I want some land around the house, with a long driveway from the street to the front door. What do you think, Harry?"

"Yes, it would be very nice to have a wooded lot." He decided to humor her in the wake of their new fortune. "There's just the two of us though. I'm not sure anything of an appropriate size is in Shaker."

"I think we need a much bigger house than this one. We need a place to properly entertain in, and there's the family to consider! I'm going to begin looking later this week with a realty firm that specializes in that community. I have a good feeling about it!"

✧✧✧

"Quite an exciting day yesterday," Rosalee said to Son as she set their kitchen table for breakfast.

"An exciting weekend too, with Dad's dinner table announcement and all. I really thought Mother would swallow her tongue when Dad finally said the sale amount out loud. She's always so, I don't know, scheming about things, trying to guess what's going on in the family and who's at fault. The girls have had it much easier than poor Bob. He was a surprise you know, the result of a 'gift' from Dad one Christmas Eve years ago. She banished him from her bedroom after learning of the baby's existence and has never really forgiven him or Bobby."

"Oh, how awful. Poor Bobby! Is that why he was sent off to school?"

"That's what I think, though I've never heard it said. Mother claims she thought it would be good for his character, would make a man of him. Well, she got that right. He was a scrawny little kid when he first went there all those years ago and, well, you saw him last spring. He's huge and done very well for himself on his own. When I was a kid, Mother would send me off to the Kern farm for most of the month of August. I enjoyed that time but was always ready to return to Cleveland. Bobby, on the other hand, loved it there when his time came. He was like Tom Sawyer spending his days fishing in Pap's lake or just wandering around the farm. Anyway, soon he'll likely go off to Korea as a navigator on one of those planes he's excited about—again alone. Sorry honey, I didn't mean to carry on so."

Rosalee gave her husband a hug and brought them each a two-min-ute egg.

"With the business closed, what kind of work do you imagine doing? Should I see about going back to the dental office?"

"You sweet thing," Son said with a smile. "You'll do no such thing! But you're an angel to offer. No, as Mr. Massey and I were walking out to where the Chrysler was parked, he gave me his business card and asked me to call the first of the week. I think I'll likely be working for Massey Buick in some form or fashion. He said he'd need someone here to take care of their new business interests and that I looked like an excellent candidate, especially after I mentioned being at GM Tech several years ago. The rent we collect from Mrs. Jenkins for her half of the duplex will pay our bank loan on the house and I'll get a check from Dad for this month. I expect we'll make it through until I can talk with Mr. Massey. And, after Dad and Mother are gone, I expect each of their children will come into a quarter million. So, I think our financial future is set, unless my parents blow it all!"

✵✵✵

Kathleen was doing her best to do just that. Within the month she had found a spec house in Shaker Heights with property and large enough for her needs. Painters were called in, hardwood floors were laid, fabrics were selected for curtains and bedspreads. A stone patio was installed in the property's backyard and a concrete driveway was laid from Newburn Avenue to the three garage bays at the house's side. A Mr. Andre St. Simon, manager of Higbee's furniture department, was engaged to assist Kathleen with furnishings. Nothing from their former home was suitable to go into the new house, she decreed, except for the Oriental rug, and would be giv-en to whichever of the children spoke up first. That, of course, was Agnes, who took the greatest number of things. Nora, still unmarried, thought good enough about her relationship with Sam to arrange for storage of several items, leaving Son and Rosalee the kitchen table and chairs and a few table lamps.

Kathleen's tastes in furniture, guided by Mr. St. Simon, was running to eighteenth century French designs in Normandy oak. Console tables, sofas with velvet upholstery, a dining room table that sat sixteen, crystal chandeliers everywhere, as well as Pier mirrors—hardly a square foot of floor space was empty. There were white marble statues of naked women scattered throughout the living and dining rooms and heavy silver candlesticks and cigarette lighters. Harry's dealership desk and chairs would be located in a bedroom turned into an office he claimed for himself that adjoined his actual bedroom on the first floor. Kathleen would occupy a suite of rooms on the second floor, one of which would become a walk-in closet. A small bedroom with an adjoining bath on the third floor was set aside for Robert should he return to Cleveland after Staunton, with Nora taking one of the two-bedroom suites on the second floor. The Cleveland home would be sold after the new year. The new house, decorating and furnishings cost Harry $20,000; he hoped he might get $1,000 for the old place if it were thoroughly cleaned and repainted over the winter.

Kathleen set about planning her annual Christmas Eve party, this year extending it into an open house for their new neighbors and Bratenahl friends. The house's living room with its twelve-foot ceiling would easily accommodate a ten-foot tree. She hired an interior decorator to trim it with hundreds of small, white lights GE had recently developed and put on the market, as well as holiday decorations for the house's exterior. As an early Christmas gift to herself, she made a detour from furnishings to the fur department at Higbee's to purchase a full-length mink coat. It was December after all, and it was getting cold! Harry said nothing, hoping it all was a pent-up blast of extravagance that would run its course.

✵✵✵

Son was indeed offered a position with Massey Automotive after spending two days with Billy and Don in Detroit. He would be making twice the salary he made working for his father, but it came with much responsibility. First, he was to find a contractor to tear down and cart away the rubble that was once Kern Motor Sales, then find a realtor to sell off the land. Working with Billy and area redevelopment people from the city, they would identify areas of urban growth where the new Massey Buick dealership could be built. Once that was accomplished, he would oversee the Massey architectural consultants designing the new showroom and service and parts departments of the planned facility, as well as learn the Massey way of doing business. It was a big plateful, but he was hungry and ready to go.

Additionally, he would spend two days each week with Billy in Pittsburgh, getting a feel for how that operation was handled. This amounted to a four-hour trip each way, which ordinarily would not have concerned Son, but Rosalee was now eight months pregnant. While she was doing well according to her doctor, it was still a worry. He was grateful her mother was nearby. To make these Pittsburgh trips and for everyday driving, Son was given a 1950 model Buick Special, a two-door fastback with automatic Dyna-flow transmission. The car was new to Cleveland and drew a crowd when parked anywhere in the city. He had a sign made to fit in one of the rear passenger windows that proclaimed the future arrival of Massey Buick – Cleveland in early 1951. An article in *The Plain Dealer* noted the former Kern Motor Sales was about to be torn down and the property sold as a "green grass" series of lots. Then, news that long-time automotive dealer Harry Kern (winner of the famed Ashtabula-to-Cleveland automobile race), had sold his business and retired to Shaker Heights became public. Shortly after, Harry was deluged with investment opportunities and other business proposals to consider. He'd been asked to sign a non-compete agreement by Massey, which barred him from entering into any future automobile business in the area for ten years. So any automotive opportunities were off the table for a decade.

✿✿✿

Work on their former home in Cleveland was completed that December. Harry walked through the house, noting how good it was looking with the refresh and wondered how much more than his original estimate he could sell it for. It had plenty of room for the average-sized family and the location was still sought after. Then he thought about Son, Rosalee, and the baby about to come, and wondered if they would have an interest in buying the home Son had grown up in. After discussing this notion with Kathleen, the subject was broached with the parents-to-be. For Harry it was a perfect solution for the house that held so many mostly happy memories for him. Son and Rosalee were thrilled with the offer, and a below-market price was agreed upon. Son had no trouble acquiring a bank loan and was able to find a suitable tenant for their half of the duplex, which they decided to keep as a rental property. The couple moved into the family home just two weeks before bringing a handsome baby boy into the world.

Harry was enjoying his first months of retirement, not having to rise early for work, having a leisurely breakfast with Nora if she was there, futzing around with the Buick he'd been given in his new, heated three-car garage (he had been allowed to take many of the dealership shop tools with him), and smelling the clean, country air. He remembered growing up on the farm and wondered if the town council would allow him to have a few chickens in the backyard. He thought about Pap and his brother Virgil, who had never married and stayed on the farm. Perhaps he'd drive out if the weather was not too bad this winter and see them and his sister Mary, who now had children of her own. If he gave Pap the money to put a bathroom in the house, perhaps even Kathleen would go along. He built a fire in his office fireplace, enjoying the warmth and memories of his family and the farm.

Robert would be joining them for a week at Christmas, before joining the Air Force and flying over Korea in what was now being called a conflict, not a war. Harry was pretty sure Sam Price was going to ask for

Nora's hand in marriage, which was going to cause Kathleen emotional distress if they moved to Pittsburgh. Agnes and Tom had had a child a year and a half earlier, making Tom decide to leave his shipping job to work at GE and be home every day. There would be a holiday houseful, and Harry figured this was what Kathleen was referring to when she said they would need a much larger house than the one they had lived in for so long. August to December now seemed like a whirl of activity he hoped would slow in the new year—though he was anticipating Nora's springtime wedding. Maybe not!

CHAPTER THIRTY-ONE

Kathleen had ideas about the new year as well. With the exception of trips to the farm, Staunton, Florida, and Dunkirk, she had never been far from home. It was a deficiency she decided to remedy that spring with ten days in Cuba. A stream of Cleveland's "first families" began making the island a fashionable destination shortly after the second world war's conclusion, drawn by its exotic nature, warm climate, and fast living.

Lizzie Hannah was, of course, the first of Kathleen's friends to spend a month in Havana in early 1949, returning with a wonderful tan and stories of her adventures with two other Bratenahl friends. They had flown to Miami and ferried to Havana from Key West, putting up at the Hotel Ambos Mundos in Old Havana. In the mid 1930s it had been a favorite residence of Ernest Hemmingway, where he finished his novel *Death in the Afternoon*, began *The New Green Hills of Africa,* and held court in the El Floridita Bar just off the hotel's lobby. His room there, number 551, was just down the hall from the three-bedroom suite Lizzie and her friends had procured.

The three ladies had immediately walked out on their balcony looking over the city and regaled in the sunshine and fresh, sea air Cleveland in winter could just not replicate.

"Oh," Lizzie had exclaimed, "I just might want to move here! I wonder what the summers are like and if they have air-conditioning. Let's call down for a pitcher of margaritas while we unpack!"

And so, their month's stay had begun. On their third night they had ventured to the Tropicana nightclub for dinner and entertainment. Owned by an American, Martin Fox, the Tropicana provided dinner, dancing, gambling, and the famous and infamous both in equal measure. American movie stars and entertainers frequented the club, as well as members of organized crime. The city was wide open—anything could be had if one knew who to ask—and the Cleveland visitors had found the atmosphere both exciting and a bit frightening.

By the end of their second week, Lizzie had won a significant amount at blackjack, which she lost by the conclusion of their stay. Kathleen had no interest in gambling but thought the other parts of Lizzie's tales sounded like just what she was looking for to expand her horizons.

Harry was not so sure, but after several weeks of badgering, gave in to the ten-day stint. Kathleen was quick to invite Agnes and Nora. Tom, not wanting to be home alone with their now two-year-old, arranged to take his vacation from GE, so the party of travelers went from two to six, all on Harry's tab. Travel arrangements were similar to the ones Lizzie and her gang had made, with the Kern party arriving at the Ambos Mundos in April of 1950. Kathleen and her daughters were absolutely agog, not knowing if their first airline trip was the early highlight or if arriving in a country and city that were so unlike anything they had ever known was. It was so old, so European (though none of them had ever experienced Europe), so charming and exciting.

As Harry checked his group into the hotel, he was offered a selection of three Havana cigars by the hotel's manager.

"You like cigars, Mr. Kern? Havana's are the very best in the world. Try these and see if you prefer one over another. I would be happy to get you a box!"

And, of course, add it to my bill, he thought, taking the keys to the three adjoining rooms. "Thank you, I will let you know."

The family settled into their accommodations and, unlike Lizzie, did not have a pitcher of margaritas sent to their rooms. Kathleen did take a nap, and as she drifted off she wondered how and what it would be like to have Harry once again in bed with her. It was the first time in years, even after acquiring the Shaker Heights house, that Harry would not be in separate quarters. While she napped, Harry took a comfortable chair by the open balcony door and lit one of the cigars he had been given. He also turned his attention to the sleeping arrangements of the next two weeks. Oddly, he was ambivalent about the prospect of sharing Kathleen's bed. Since his dismissal from their bedroom nineteen years earlier, he had grown to enjoy his own room, especially one on another floor. He looked at the furniture in the suite's living room and decided he would commandeer the comfortable-looking couch, change clothes in the large bathroom, and make the couch up again in the mornings. He felt better about this arrangement and began to enjoy the cigar.

That evening the group dined at the El Floridita Bar among pictures of Hemingway and rum drinks. Kathleen had awoken with her excitement unbroken and, with her daughters, was anxious to explore the neighborhood surrounding them. Agnes and Tom had already ventured out that afternoon and were surprised by most everything they saw and experienced. While in the Navy, Tom had visited Havana on at least two occasions he could remember, readily admitting excess drinking had dulled many of his memories. He promised one night, if Nora or Kathleen would keep little Tommy, he would take Agnes for drinks at a place she would never forget because of the entertainment. The floor show consisted of an immensely physically endowed Cuban known as "Superman" having sex with women actors with his fifteen-inch penis!

"He would even invite women in the audience to try their luck."

"Oh my God," Agnes gasped. "Wait until I tell Mother!"

✳✳✳

On several occasions during their stay they visited the Tropicana for a long evening. As the night club did not open until eight, someone had to stay back with Tommy. Dinner and drinking took up most of their evenings. Harry planned to try his luck in the casino but decided to limit his financial exposure to $1,000. Before leaving Cleveland he had purchased a money belt at Higbee's, which he spent an afternoon stuffing funds into. Emergency money, he reasoned, that would be difficult to steal. Meals at the club were extravagant, as were the all-night floor shows. Kathleen and Nora were slightly put off by the nakedness of the female performers, though they thought the feathers used in their costumes were extraordinary.

Tom enjoyed the dancers very much, especially during one visit when one of the women pulled him onto the dance floor, which he good-naturedly accepted. Kathleen teasingly told her daughter she guessed he'd now be hard to keep home. They all returned to the hotel that night at one in the morning—Harry, three hundred dollars richer than when they'd left, Kathleen going immediately to her bed, and Agnes anxious to retrieve her sleeping son from Nora's charge. Tom and Harry decided on brandy and cigars, talking and watching the city's lights from the balcony of the room Harry and Kathleen shared.

Agnes, Nora, and Kathleen began feeling as if they were natives, donning colorful dresses for both daytime shopping and evenings out. Tom enjoyed visiting whatever bars in the Old City he could find open and sampling as many rum drinks as possible, while Harry decided of the three cigars he had been given, he favored the Romeo y Julieta - Churchill by far.

On Tuesday of that week, Harry arranged for a day's charter fishing outing for himself and Tom leaving at nine with a mid-afternoon return, depending how or if the tropical blue marlins were running. The boat's captain was named Hugo, an affable middle-aged Cuban who had been on the water all his life. He promised the Americans a good day, providing sturdy fishing poles, easily winding reels, live Spanish mackerel for bait he rigged himself, and a cooler full of Cuban Cristal beer and fresh Cuban sandwiches. Not really much of a fiction reader, Harry had managed to read Hemingway's *The Old Man and the Sea* published sequentially in *Life Magazine* the previous year. He had enjoyed the short novel, never dreaming at the time he'd be replicating the tale, though he hoped with a better outcome!

Hugo took the boat out thirty miles from its mooring spot before setting up their tackle, the bait rigged to skip and swim in the ocean as the boat trolled slowly. Harry's line was further out from the boat's stern on the port side, while Tom's line was in at starboard. This was a first-time event for both of the Clevelanders. Harry enjoyed surf fishing at Dunkirk during summer visits but thought of this day's adventure as fishing with a capital "F." Hugo offered both fishermen nausea tablets as they left the dock, which Tom refused. The ocean was calm and clear, and he'd never been sea-sick; Harry was pleased with the captain's thoughtfulness.

The morning's trolling proved uneventful, though both men enjoyed the sunshine and Tom the beer. After pausing for lunch, Hugo moved them several miles further out to sea before beginning their afternoon fishing. As he turned the boat for a second troll at the new location, Harry's line took hold of something of great weight, the rod jumping almost out of his hands and his line moving to his left as Hugo cut the boat's motor. Harry let his reel spin, hoping whatever had taken the hook would soon play out. Looking out to where they thought the hook might be, the three men saw a blue marlin leap from the water, the line's tension again pulling to port. Hugo steered the boat in the same direction the fish was moving, and Harry began to wind in his line again as the fish jumped from the water a second time. It took both Harry and Tom to reel the fish close enough to the boat for Hugo to bring the 300-pound beauty to the boat's side with his gaff hook and secure it for the return trip to the dock. Harry remembered Santiago's dilemma in Hemingway's novel when the fisherman attempted to bring his fish to shore while an ocean full of sharks fed off it. Happily, that wasn't the case this afternoon, and the ship and crew made it back to the dock without incident. The marlin was strung up on the dock for all to see. Harry's was the only fish caught that day, and he and Tom had their pictures taken standing on either side of the brute.

Harry had the fish fileted and five nice-sized portions were sent to the La Guarida for their dinner that evening. The remainder of the meat was sold to a vendor at the local fish market. Harry then arranged for the fish to be stuffed and shipped back to Shaker Heights, wondering what Kathleen would say if it were mounted in her living room.

That evening the Kern family feasted on Harry's freshly caught marlin on the huge balcony of La Guarida in the Old City. Agnes had read and informed the party that La Guarida was a favorite among Hollywood celebrities and members of European royal families. The balcony held at least 200 tables, all of them seemingly occupied, so craning one's neck to see someone of note was practically impossible. Throughout dinner, Agnes and Nora would periodically excuse themselves from the table and make bathroom runs to see if anyone of importance might be dining. On their third mission, they were rewarded by finding Marlon Brando dining with Rita Hayworth and an exotic Cuban woman at a table near one of the three bars stationed around the rectangular balcony. Brando's "Streetcar" movie had come out that winter, and while neither of Kathleen's girls had seen the film, he was all they could talk about when they returned to their table.

Dinner concluded, the party walked back to their hotel, Tom walking with Harry, the women following.

Kathleen turned to Agnes and said quietly so no one else would hear, "I've noticed a lot of young women hanging out on doorsteps as we've walked around the city this past week. I suppose they're just taking the air as their apartments are without air-conditioning."

"Oh mother," Agnes said, turning to look at Kathleen, "they're hookers! You are just too cute for words." She giggled.

Kathleen's eyes widened. "Really? All of them?"

"Maybe not all, but I'd imagine most of them."

They entered Hotel Mundos.

"I could use a drink," Kathleen said.

Harry and Tom said they would join her, and the girls took Tommy upstairs. Agnes whispered into Nora's ear, and Kathleen saw her youngest daughter laughing at whatever she'd been told.

✬✬✬

Nora received a constant stream of letters from Sam Price during her time away, which she kept tied together with a ribbon on the bedside table of her room. They had decided to become engaged upon her Cuban return, but were delayed because of Robert's Staunton graduation. The family was to fly to Richmond from Miami, rent a car to Staunton for the ceremony, and take the train back to Cleveland. It seemed to Nora an intolerable delay and she brooded quietly that Sam should have been invited along on the trip. At least her father had made the return a bit shorter by flying them to Richmond.

Robert's graduation was a grand affair in the tradition of the school. He had passed his courses with good grades, was selected to be a member of the Howie Rifles, an elite honor guard and drill team that would perform at the graduation ceremony, and had, in fact, joined the United States Air Force to become a navigator on the B-29 Superfortress. His basic training requirements had been waived because he'd attended Staunton, and as a result of his prior summer's navigational training with the Air Force, he would be assigned directly to a B-29 crew and sent to Kadena Air Force Base in Okinawa, Japan. Harry was stunned by this news, and even Kathleen seemed taken aback by it. Son had served only five years earlier but rarely had seen actual ground fighting. Robert's would be a different experience.

The B-29s, designed and built by Boeing and destined for Korea, were completely redesigned aircraft than the ones flown in the second

World war. They were fully pressurized, allowing the ten-man crew freedom to move about without the bulky pressurized suits worn by crews during the previous incarnation. The planes also had an early computer system designed for a variety of functions, including navigational assists and the plane's protection in flight. The gunnery crew had the advantage of operating all four of the machine gun turrets containing three guns from a single location, rather than having a crew member at each. A flight engineer was added to the crew to ensure all the new systems were working and could be repaired in flight.

For those based in Okinawa, the average tour of duty was fifteen months, with each B-29 crew flying approximately fifty combat missions. Robert would be living on the other side of the world for a year and a half, averaging one mission every eight days. Harry did not like his son's odds, particularly at a high altitude and in the dark, but there was little he could do to stop his going. A week after graduation, Robert returned to Cleveland for two weeks before reporting to Castle Air Force Base in California. Harry wanted to spend as much time with him as possible, perhaps taking him to Dunkirk with Son for a few days.

CHAPTER THIRTY-TWO

A month after the family returned to Cleveland from Virginia, Harry's marlin arrived.

"Oh my God Harry, you didn't tell me you had it stuffed! And you want to put it in my house?"

"It's for that tall wall in my office opposite the fireplace. It won't be seen from anywhere else in the house and will always remind me of Cuba."

"I can think of a lot of other mementos I would much rather have in the house. Won't it begin to smell after a while? I can't believe you didn't mention this to me!"

"Well, I figured you'd throw a fit, and it was a major accomplishment. Took most of an hour to bring it in and was the only marlin caught that day. I felt a lot like Hemingway that afternoon!"

"I can't believe you did this! Just be sure to keep your office door shut." She walked away shaking her head. "I bet it was expensive too."

"Don't worry, I paid for the taxidermy and shipping with my Tropicana winnings. The grandkids will love it!"

Harry had hoped the fish would arrive for Robert to see before leaving for Japan. It would have been the kind of thing he would have found interesting and amusing. He had grown into a very fine young man, Harry thought, and regretted the years he had been away for his schooling. He had lived at Staunton about as long as he had lived with them in Cleveland, and his personality and thoughts were different, molded by other environments.

Robert would have loved the Cuba trip. Its exotic nature would have greatly appealed to his sense of adventure. Perhaps that was partly why he joined the Air Force, to spend time in Japan, even with the threat of losing his life ever-present. He had spent time thinking through his options after graduation, figured he would be drafted into the Army as Son might have been in the last war, and decided to pursue another path. Harry liked that trait and hoped it would serve him well in life. That was what he told the fish anyway as he carried it into his office to install later that week.

✡✡✡

A day after the family's return from Virginia, Sam Price drove from Pittsburgh to find Nora waiting at the door of the Shaker Heights home. It seemed the time away had made his longing for her exceed, or at least equal, the longing she had held for him since they'd parted almost three weeks before. He'd decided to speak to Harry that evening about having Nora for his bride. Harry liked Sam well enough, and certainly his income at Westinghouse was more than sufficient to cover his daughter's needs, but he worried about how Kathleen was going to tolerate having her baby girl living in the Steel City. *She'll just have to adapt,* he thought. She couldn't put her daughter's life on hold.

When Sam did the honorable thing and came to Harry to ask his permission, Harry gave his blessing to the young man. There was no need to huddle with Kathleen to talk the situation over. He fixed himself a bourbon and soda, lit a Churchill, and shut his office door.

✳✳✳

The wedding was to be held in the early fall in the Kern backyard, which was certainly large enough and as yet unincumbered by chickens. Kathleen, while outwardly happy about the match, was despondent about her second daughter living four hours away. However, she and her two daughters threw themselves into the occasion's planning as soon as the engagement was announced. A massive landscaping project was planned using the landscape architect preferred by Shaker Heights residents who promised to spare no expense to make the back landscape as beautiful as the event demanded.

Nora's wedding dress and going-away clothes came from Higbee's, where she was fitted with a wide variety of outfits for the newlyweds' European honeymoon—a gift from Sam's parents. The thought of Nora being in Europe for two months almost made Kathleen take to her bed, and it would have if the wedding was being held anywhere else. As the landscaping progressed, Kathleen ordered outdoor furniture—cream-colored wicker with green-and-white striped cushions.

Agnes managed to keep her jealousy about her sister's good fortune to herself, though she did think of her own honeymoon, shacked up in a motel room in Erie. She did have the first grandson, who Kathleen doted on and would serve as the ring bearer at the ceremony, and she was to be Nora's matron of honor.

La Cuisine would cater the event, with champagne before an extravagant sit-down meal and a full bar. The guest list came to 325, though ultimately only 200 would attend. Kathleen was pleased that fall was generally dry and warm, allowing guests to easily move from the half-acre back property into the home's first floor. That being the case, she turned her attention to the furnishings on the first floor, ordering room-sized matching Oriental rugs for both the living and dining rooms. A large canvas tent for the wedding dinner was to be located near enough to the yard's new water feature so the trickling of water might be heard coming from the mouths of three large, concrete frogs.

All together the event would cost Harry three grand, and suddenly he was grateful Agnes had eloped! His own wedding, he remembered, had taken place in Chester James' living room with a family dinner afterward, and it had seemed just fine. He remembered his father was there and one of his brothers. He hadn't made it to the farm this past summer and felt regret. Pap must be almost eighty and Harry had not visited since he sold the business. *Right after the wedding, I'll go for a long weekend.*

CHAPTER THIRTY-THREE

Unlike Son, who wrote home almost daily during the war, Robert was much more elusive, just as he had been during his Staunton years. Occasional letters would arrive, mostly asking about family and life in Cleveland. He might mention an occasional past mission over North Korea, but in no detail, and mostly wrote about the men he flew with. They were averaging eight missions a month, and he took some pride in writing that his B-29 as yet had sustained no North Korean damage.

His flight crew consisted of young, enlisted men, with the exception of the pilots and the gunner, who were career Air Force. It reminded Robert of being back at Staunton and belonging to a unit of cadets who were together on the parade field as well as when they were not. They were a unit in the air and on the ground, lived in the same barracks, ate and played together—though playing was, for flight crews, limited to their base of operation. His crew's two pilots, because they were both officers, had the benefit of the officer's lounge in which to drink and relax. Their gunnery sergeant and his noncommissioned crewmates would frequent one of several bars and restaurants on base to clear their minds. Flying two nighttime combat missions in a seven-day week meant crews had to maintain a strict personal schedule of when they could unwind with a beer or two and when they could not. Mondays, Tuesdays, Wednesdays, and Sundays were good days to relax in a seven-day rotation, Thursdays, Fridays, and Saturdays were not. In between, crews were on their aircraft looking over equipment, reloading machine guns, checking mechanical systems, and calculating mission routes and targets. As the plane's navigator and radar specialist, Robert played an important role in getting the plane to assigned targets and back to base. He'd spend hours reviewing maps and the fastest routes in and out of danger.

✤✤✤

Son enjoyed showing his father around the construction site of the new Massey dealership. It was certainly much larger than the humble few buildings Harry had put together, and having Buicks available at this time was a good move. The economy was growing, prosperity in Cleveland was evident, and Buicks were sensibly positioned between Chevy and Cadillac models. Harry didn't like second-guessing himself about staying in the business, but the excitement of the new dealership made him wonder what might have been, and he was pleased Son was involved and working for Massey. On Friday he was considering making a trip to Ashtabula to spend time with whatever family was still around. It would be fun to drive his Buick to the farm in the fall and wonderful to see Pap. He knew the house and barn would likely need repainting; perhaps he would help financially with that. He wondered if they were still cooking on Mam's wood-burning stove.

After the construction tour, Harry stopped at their mailbox where the driveway joined Newburn Street. Sorting through the mail, he found a letter from Robert, which he moved to the top of the stack. Then, placing the mail on the front seat, he continued to the house. He could tell Robert's letter had been censored by the military after he mailed it and knew from his experience with mail received from Son this was standard procedure during war time. Agnes's car was parked to the right side of the front door. Entering the house from the garage, he waved the blue envelope at the ladies talking in the kitchen.

"Letter from Robert!"

The women looked up at him.

"How many people did he bomb to death on his last mission?" Agnes asked. "You can't tell me it's just factories and warehouses his bombs are destroying!"

Harry looked at her hopelessly. "Haven't opened it yet to see."

He shook his head at her and slid the envelope open with a kitchen knife. Inside he found a page and a half of Robert's usual greetings to all and a black-and-white photo of his crew lined up beside the B-29 they flew. Robert was easily seen because he was taller than most. Harry passed the photo to Kathleen, and she passed it on to her daughter.

"Cannon fodder," Agnes said, handing the photograph back to Harry. "He looks happy enough, but I can't believe he volunteered to be shot at."

"He'd be there anyway after Staunton. At least he's not an infantry soldier. He's safer at thirty-thousand feet than on the ground."

"Sandwich, Harry?" Kathleen asked.

He looked at both of them and declined the offer. He put the magazines and circulars on the counter, kept what looked like bills and Robert's letter, and retreated to his office.

"He's going to sit with the fish awhile," Kathleen said. "Its smell has finally dissipated, but I do wish he hadn't brought it home."

"It's a man thing, Mom. Tom talks about it after a beer or two. How the thing jumped in the air from the ocean and how Dad worked for an hour or so to bring it closer to the boat. It tasted pretty good as I remember, and you can't see it from the rest of the house."

"That's not entirely true, my dear. The evening of Nora's wedding your father must have left the overhead light on in his office, and as night began to fall, I could see the damn thing through that high window. There it was, staring down at me and everyone else in the yard. I'm sure I saw its glassy eye wink!"

"Oh mother, you're too funny," Agnes said laughing. "That's a good story. Did you tell it to Dad?"

"No, I didn't want him to think I'm getting used to it being here. And I want to keep being mad at him a while longer."

"You two have a very odd relationship, I think. Tom and I argue about small, trifling things, but then we make up, have a drink, and later have sex! I remember when Dad moved to a bedroom on the first floor of the old house and wondered where you two did "the deed," first or second floor. I guess it's still the same now!"

"Your father and I don't do that sort of thing. Stopped when I found out I was pregnant with Robert, after your father raped me one Christmas Eve. I never wanted a fourth child."

"Oh, I remember that Christmas Eve party, when you kissed Mr. what's-his-name in front of God and everybody. He was teaching Son to play that goofy musical instrument."

"Agnes, how do you know about that? It was nothing but a wild exuberance. I'd had too much to drink and, well, Clark was a very good-looking man, and there was mistletoe hanging in the entryway. You were just a child and were upstairs in bed."

"Grandpa Chester mentioned it at another Christmas Eve party. So, were you and Mr. Clarke involved? That might explain a lot of things," she mused, "like why Robert is so different from the rest of us."

"Agnes!" Kathleen said rising from her chair. "Just what do you mean?"

"Well, Robert is taller than the rest of us, his disposition is much quieter, more subdued, his interests aren't like ours. I'm sure if he were around here more there would be other differences we'd see. So maybe your 'wild exuberance' was part of a pattern?"

"Agnes, really, you are reading too many trashy romance novels. Your father's the only man I've ever been with in that way!"

Harry closed his office door, tossed the mail he'd kept on his desk, and thought about Agnes. She really had not changed her attitudes about things in her life or the world. Like her mother, she thought she was better, smarter, and due some extra credit from everyone in her sphere. She had been that way from almost the time she could walk, which came early for her. Also like her mother, Agnes had no time for Robert as an adult or when they were children. She was ten when Robert was born and noticed her mother did not treat him the same way she did Son or Nora. He became the invisible child, keeping to himself.

Nora enjoyed Robert, which was a blessing for him, Harry thought, almost the only company he had. Perhaps that was why Robert did not seem to have an interest in any of those pretty Mary Baldwin girls while at Staunton. He picked up his son's letter and read it through again, then looked at the photograph he'd sent and wondered what it was like to be in that airplane, on a bombing mission 30,000 feet or so in the air at night. It sent a chill through him. Robert had only been in Japan four months, eleven more until he'd be out. Maybe another few weeks after that he'd be back in Cleveland—but to what end? Would he pursue college as Son had? Would he even make it back? Harry pressed the photograph to his chest and shut his eyes for a moment as these thoughts ran through his mind. After a few minutes he left the office, finding Kathleen still in the kitchen and Agnes gone.

"I'm thinking of going up to the farm tomorrow and maybe staying through the weekend to see Pap," he said. "You'll be okay here for a couple days?"

Kathleen looked at him and could see he was anxious about something, even though they spent less time together now than they had at other point in their lives.

"Anything wrong?" she asked. "Did you hear something from Pap?"

"No," he said quietly. "It's just that I haven't seen him in a long while and I promised myself after the wedding I would drive up for a weekend and see how he is. Mary too."

"Ah, sure," Kathleen said and set the small copper watering can she used for the houseplants down on the counter. "I've got plenty to do here. Give them my love. Hope he's replaced that darn old outhouse!"

Harry smiled at that. "I doubt he has. It would be much too civilized for Pap, and as Mary has her own house now, he likely never felt the need." Harry looked at Kathleen, thinking about the girl he had married and all that had happened to them throughout the years.

"I'm meeting Agnes and Lizzie for dinner this evening. Did I mention that? I can call it off if you'd like, since you'll be gone a couple days."

"Oh no, that's fine. I'm heading north early tomorrow morning, so I'll just make something for myself, pay the bills and turn in early. You ladies have fun, and don't let Lizzie lead you astray!" Harry smiled at her, then turned to walk back to his office and the prized fish. "I'll call you if Pap still has a working phone!"

✵✵✵

The following morning Harry was up with the sun, packed a few pieces of clothing, and being as quiet as he could, walked to the garage. It was going to be a beautiful fall day, and he was looking forward to the drive. He enjoyed the Buick he'd been given by Massey and the raw power of its V-8. Turning out of the driveway, Harry headed to the small grocery that serviced many of the families who lived in their subdivision, or village, as it was called by its residents. He pick up food for a couple days and hoped there were not more than maybe two brothers there so he'd have enough to go around. Then it was up the road he'd raced down all those years ago.

He remained astounded at how much the city was growing, passing the newest addition to the Cleveland Clinic on his way. With all those new doctors coming to town, perhaps he should have stayed in the business. He smiled to himself, thinking of all the money he had in the bank and that perhaps he should be investing some of it. Cleveland and the country as a whole were experiencing a strong economy—perhaps there was money to be made in the stock market. He lit one of his Cuban cigars at an intersection, opened his side vent window for the smoke to pass through, and decided to ask Norman who he used to help him invest.

Within two hours Harry turned off Route 2 on the outskirts of Ashtabula and headed toward the 5 Star Hardware Store. He was on mental autopilot and about to make the turn to the farm when he realized Rainey's was no longer on the corner. The building was gone, turned into a Gulf gas station that, while convenient to motorists, was not what he wanted to see. He turned the car around and pulled in. A moment later an attendant came out to pump gas.

"Fill 'er up?" he asked. "This is some beautiful automobile. Don't think I've ever seen one like it before."

"Really?" Harry replied. "I don't remember seeing this gas station before either. Been here long?"

"Well, let me see, I've been working here since it was built and opened, maybe three years. You from Cleveland?"

"Yes I am." Harry put out his hand to the attendant as he got out of the driver's seat. "Harry Kern's my name. There used to be a hardware store in this vicinity somewhere."

"Yes sir, it was right here where we're standing—5 Star Hardware! Got torn down after Mr. Rainey passed. No one in the family wanted to take it over. There was talk of a big hardware chain store moving into the area, so there was a close-out sale and the family sold the building and land."

Harry watched the attendant, whose name was Byron, finish filling the gas tank, wiping it clean with a red rag when he'd finished. He paid and thanked Byron for the information. Harry wished he'd have thought to come four years earlier when he might have seen Mr. Rainey again. *Nothing stays the same,* he thought and grew anxious about returning to the farm.

CHAPTER THIRTY-FOUR

After touring his father around the Massey construction site and show-ing him its architectural plans, Son returned home for lunch. He entered through the back kitchen door as his father had done for so many years and found Rosalee in the kitchen feeding the baby. He smiled at the two of them, kissing his wife and baby boy. They had named him Ogden for Ogden Nash, Rosalee's favorite poet. She had several books of his humor-ous rhymes and had even attended a lecture he'd given during her student days. Son didn't mind. He was Harry Jr. and saw no reason to name ad-ditional males the same. Besides, he liked Ogden's initials—OK—and he was certainly that in all respects.

"Your turn to burp Ogden," Rosalee said and handed Son the baby.

"My pleasure," he replied, putting a clean dish towel over his left shoulder and lifting the baby's head to it. "Come on now, sport, let's give Momma a good belch and then you can take a nap while your mother and I have our lunch."

Son lightly patted the baby's back, walking around the kitchen as Rosalee prepared their lunch. After Ogden took care of all of his baby duties—top to bottom—Son's clean-up duty went well, and Ogden was soon fast asleep in the day crib they kept in the living room.

"Did Harry enjoy his morning with you?" Rosalee asked, smiling at her husband who had just seated her at table.

"Yes he did, I think. The Massey dealership is so far beyond what Dad had downtown it made him both nervous and envious. But I think he's happy to be retired and out of the constant worry over daily sales counts. He mentioned going to the farm this weekend, hasn't seen Pap since selling the dealership."

"I hope he has a good time, then. Kathleen going too?"

"Doubt it, she doesn't like the outhouse in the back yard."

"Can't blame her for that," Rosalee said with a giggle. "Especially at night!"

"When I was a boy spending part of my summers there, I'd just open one of the windows on the second floor and, well, you know. It was better than walking down the steps and going outside."

"Really! Well, that's one of the few biological benefits men have over we of the fairer sex," she said with a smile. "Just remember not to do it here!" They both laughed, then hearing Ogden make noise decided lunch was over.

Harry turned the car onto the secondary road leading to the farm. *It was so very long ago that I headed in the other direction in my racer,* he thought and remembered the trip in an instant. *How young I was.* The road was paved now, so no dust clouds followed from behind as they had when he went off to the race. His Buick had a front windshield, so no goggles were needed either. The goggles he had worn were in a side desk drawer now, along with many other memories from his past. The farm's access road was coming up and he slowed to turn in; another five hundred feet and he approached the farmhouse. The years had not been kind to it, and he knew Pap thought it beyond his station to give it a coat of paint or have a cracked window pane repaired. Anarchists are above that sort of thing, and whichever of his brothers were still living there were kept busy with farm chores. Shutting the motor off, Harry walked to the front door, and as he knocked he called for his father. Pap had been asleep but quickly awoke at the sound of a "stranger's" voice. As he came closer he thought he recognized the man standing there.

"Harry, is that you?"

"Sure is Pap. It's so good to see you. I should have called ahead. I came to see you and whichever of my brothers is here. Want to see Mary too. I've brought some food in the trunk of my car—can I put it in the cold cellar?"

Pap opened the door and hugged his son. "My goodness, it's so good to see you here, Harry. How long has it been, couple of years?"

"Yes, I'm afraid it has, and I hope you'll forgive that. I've been busy with a number of things. Let me get this food in where it's cool and we can talk on the porch."

Pap pulled two wooden rocking chairs from the front stoop to underneath the huge maple trees that had now turned a golden yellow. "How have you and Kathleen been, my boy? Tell me all the news."

Harry sat in one of the rockers, offered his father a cigar, and relayed all that had happened in his life since they had last been together. The story took over an hour to tell, with Pap asking only a few questions along the way. He was sorry to hear Robert was so far away, in a war that, in his opinion, this country had no business being involved in—and in an airplane no less!

"Bobby was always his own best companion," Pap said. "When he was here on the farm, he set his own agenda. He liked fishing the pond, loved Mam, and I'd occasionally find him reading one of the books from the cabinet. Don't think he understood much about them 'cuz they generally put him to sleep! A good boy, though."

"I do wish we hadn't sent him off to a military school when he was so young," Harry said.

"Was it Kathleen's doing?" Pap asked. "I remember her not having much to do with him even as a baby."

Harry looked at his father, not wanting to admit it was Kathleen who wanted Robert out of the house as soon as possible, and that he had allowed it to happen.

"We were both at fault there," he said. "Any of my brothers still living in these parts?" Harry asked, changing the subject.

"Only Virgil," Pap said. "He's not living here anymore, though he does help with the chores in spring and summer. Just growing crops for my own needs now. Virg is living in Ashtabula, got a place downtown over a dry goods store. Works there some. Mary's living in town too. Married a fine fellow who's in real estate, and they have a couple kids who come to visit and see that I'm well. They'll likely come by tomorrow actually."

Harry was glad to hear his sister and her brood would visit before his return to Cleveland.

"Bed's made in her old room if you'd like to sleep there tonight," Pap said. "No point going up to the second floor. Haven't been up there myself in a couple years."

The two men adjourned to the house where Pap lit a fire in its main room while Harry removed the wrappers from two porterhouse steaks he had brought.

"Still using Mam's stove to cook?"

"Yes sir. It still does just fine. Put some wood in like you did as a boy."

Harry did just that, placing one of Mam's large iron skillets on the stove when the fire was good and hot, and peeled two potatoes to cook in the steak drippings. Father and son sat at a table before the fire Pap had made in the main room, ate, and talked about old times. Pap wanted to hear again about the race Harry had won all those years ago.

CHAPTER THIRTY-FIVE

Harry returned to Cleveland that Monday morning. He'd enjoyed his time with Pap, was able to see Mary and Virgil, who had dropped by on Sunday. Virg had found it hard to believe Harry had sold his business, but when Harry explained what his choices in the matter were, he conceded to Harry's conclusion. Saturday morning, Harry had made his way to the grave site of his mother. He was sure she was in heaven, if there was one, and placed some wildflowers in front of her rugged tombstone.

Mary brought a picnic lunch for them when she came, which they ate by the pond while her children played. Always an attractive woman, Mary had grown into a beauty. There was talk of some of their siblings, at least the ones she or Pap knew of, which turned out to be only a few of the nine boys. Harry could tell it grieved Pap that so many of the boys had disappeared, leaving little knowledge of where or how they were. It bothered Harry too, even though he knew he'd been the first to leave.

✲✲✲

"Harry, do you think you'll be back at the house mid-day?" Kathleen asked when he'd called from Pap's before returning. "I'm expecting a delivery that requires someone to be here and I'm attending a casual luncheon in Bratenahl for Meg Hamilton at Lizzie's home. You remember Meg, or Margret as she's come to be known—she was with us at the first picnic we went on, right after your race. She played the Wicked Witch in that movie with Judy Garland about Oz!"

"Yes, I suppose so. It must be sizable if someone has to be there to let the delivery people in."

"It's not all that large, but it can't be left outside on the front stoop. It's a baby grand piano and it's to go in that back corner of the living room. I've had my eye on it for quite some time and it finally went on sale. I do play the piano, and it will be wonderful to have during holiday gatherings or at parties, and it will look just so fine in the room!"

"What did it cost, with the discount and all? I can't believe you bought a piano without our talking it over."

"It was only four hundred with the discount, and they threw in the matching bench, which also stores sheet music. It was quite a good deal, don't you think?"

"That's about what the trip to Cuba cost! I can't believe you've been planning this purchase for some time and never mentioned it to me before the damn thing comes rolling through the front door! Really Kathleen, you've got to slow all this spending down. Our bank account has to last us the rest of our lives, and I hope that's at least another forty years!"

"Well, it will. I've just about got this place where it needs to be."

"I'm glad to hear that because there is hardly a place in the living room, dining room, or hallways where there's not a piece of furniture taking up space, then there are the mirrors and paintings. I sometimes think I'm in a museum. Perhaps we should have a couple suits of armor standing around to complete the setting."

"Now, now, don't get theatrical Harry, it's just a piano...and a console TV!"

✷✷✷

Harry arrived at the Shaker house before one. Kathleen wasn't home. The weather was cooler than it had been at the farm; lake effect, he reasoned and started a fire in the immense living room. He also turned up the furnace and soon heard the pinging of the radiators. Fixing himself a bourbon and water, he took a seat in a new wingback chair Kathleen had purchased along with numerous other new pieces since he'd sold the business. *Keeping up with the Hannahs is going to bankrupt me,* he thought. At that, a delivery truck stopped at their front door.

✷✷✷

Kathleen returned before five that afternoon and asked about his weekend at the farm. Harry found he was pleased to see her and might have actually missed her. Before sitting by the fire in another new lounge chair, she made herself a gin and tonic and admired her new piano in the room's corner. Harry relayed all he had seen and done over the last couple days. She was saddened to learn Rainey's Hardware was gone because she had enjoyed meeting Rainey once upon a time. She was further saddened to hear the farm looked to have seen better days and Pap seemed as if he were beginning to fail. The closest doctor was still in Ashtabula, and with Pap's telephone out much of the time.... Harry assured her he had given Pap money to cover his telephone bill for the remainder of the year, but with his party line there could still be an issue getting medical attention to him. Harry didn't tell her he had considered bringing Pap to Cleveland to live in one of their many guest bedrooms, but thought if whatever happened to Pap didn't kill him immediately, it just might just come to that. First the fish, and now possibly Pap—that would be his strike two!

✷✷✷

Norman Minor was only too happy to meet with Harry and discuss his investment strategies. He arranged for a light lunch for three to be delivered to his downtown office where he, his financial advisor, and Harry met two days after the piano's arrival. Irving Copland was a broker at Merrill Lynch; Harry remembered once selling an automobile to him after Norman reintroduced them.

"Love that car, Harry. Still have it, as a matter of fact. My wife and teenage daughter drive it around."

"It was a Dodge Custom Coupe," Harry remembered. "They were great cars when they came online in '42. I'm pleased to know it's still giving you good service."

"I was saddened to hear you sold your dealership in the Flats, but Norman filled me in on the reasons. Without knowing specific numbers, I'm assuming you did well financially with your decision."

"I did, yes," Harry said, "but my dear wife Kathleen seems bound and determined to spend what was left after the government took its cut. Which is why I asked Norman about investing, to hopefully begin to restock the bank account."

The two men smiled at Harry, Norman nodding his head in agreement. "For policeman's daughters, those James girls do enjoy having things," he said. "It comes from hanging around those Hannah folks I'm guessing. Mary just returned from a week at their Georgia plantation. You can just imagine what I thought of her being there! She took a steamer trunk of new clothing with her and now wants to buy a horse. We live in the city!"

"Well, our current economy is strong and growing," Copland began. "I'm sure you both see the growth all around us here in Cleveland. The stock market is steadily moving upward, new businesses are being born every day. It seems to us at Merrill this is a good time to be in the market. When Norman first came to me to discuss investing, we spent a good deal of time thinking through a financial strategy to meet Norman's needs and comfort level. That strategy is working, I think Norman would agree. I'd be pleased to work with you Harry if you have an interest.

Perhaps we can at least keep up with your wife's appetites!" The three chuckled and Harry made an appointment to meet Irving at his office the following week. Norman walked his brother-in-law through his office to the elevator.

"So what are you going to do with a horse, Norm?" Harry teased.

✺✺✺

After several meetings with Irving Copland, Harry felt his first foray into investing was solid enough to venture $5,000 into a varied growth-oriented portfolio. The Merrill Lynch office had real-time stock readouts running along the top of its reception wall—a sales gimmick to be sure, but an easy way to keep track of the market's movement. Harry made careful note of his stock's values, dropping by the Merrill office daily to see if they increased. After a year of this activity, Copland made a small desk and chair available, where Harry read the financial news reported in *The Plain Dealer*. The investments he and Copland made were producing income for him and coming close to keeping up with Kathleen's extravagance. That initially was all Harry had intended for them to do. But in his third year of investing, Harry began to think of the market as a legalized form of the gambling he had enjoyed in Cuba and began making purchases on his own.

Harry found Kathleen at the kitchen table after he returned home from one of his usual late lunches downtown. "And how is Mrs. Kern this afternoon?"

"Oh, just tip-top, but I can't get this checking account ledger balanced with the statement that came in the mail."

"Glad to see you're giving it a try—very commendable."

Harry had opened a separate checking account for her after the dealership sale with a balance of $2,000. He knew she needed funds for furnishing the new house, and it relieved him from writing checks.

"Can I help you with it?"

"You can just do the damned thing," she said in her frustration and threw the checkbook at him. "I need a drink. Is it too early in the afternoon according to your schedule?"

"Well it's not quite three. Cows aren't in from the pasture yet."

"Ah yes! I nearly forgot you're a country boy," she said, walking toward the living room liquor cabinet. "Everything in its time and in its place," she said loudly as she poured herself a vodka on ice.

"I'll be in my office, working on your checkbook."

"Go to hell, Harry! Hey, I like the way that sounded."

Harry shut his office door, still hearing Kathleen carry on. It was not the first drink she'd had that afternoon, he reasoned. Probably had a beer or two as an appetizer. He smiled up at the fish before attempting to balance her account. It was a mess, but after thirty minutes he found she had spent almost half her balance at Higbee's on one thing or another. He brought down the balance, checked it with her bank statement, and re-entered the kitchen to give her book back.

"Here you are, all checked and reconciled with your bank statement."

"I suppose you've got some smart remarks to make about the things I've used it for." The vodka had brought a redness to her face.

"No, nothing like that. You needed to furnish our home here and have clothing comparable to things Lizzie and our neighbors wear. I understand men can get by with a suit or two but women require a broader inventory. Just remember, we're still young with a lot of years ahead and don't want to end up living in the poorhouse."

"Go to hell, Harry," she said again and left the room.

CHAPTER THIRTY-SIX

By May of 1953, the war in Korea seemed to be winding down, and Robert's enlistment was coming to an end. Miraculously, his was one of the few crews that had not sustained damage from enemy fire during their deployment. He briefly considered signing up for another tour, but knew peace was being discussed by both sides and decided he'd had enough military living, what with Staunton and the time he had just served. He was honorably discharged and flown back to Virginia with other discharged airmen. Several days later, he took the overnight train to Cleveland where Harry met him at the station. Robert was not quite prepared for a return to full civilian life. He had been thirteen when enrolled at Staunton. Now twenty-two and moving into his parent's house, he felt his life was moving backwards.

"You're going to need some civilian clothes, Bob," Harry said as they walked through Union Terminal. "We'll see to that first thing tomorrow. Sure wonderful to have you here with the family. Your mother has planned a small dinner this evening to welcome you home. It will just be Agnes, Tom, Son, Rosalee, and Nora and Sam, who are driving down from Pittsburgh. I'd asked her to give you a few days to adjust but, well, you know your mother!"

Robert thought to himself as they arrived at Harry's car, *No, I really don't know my mother all that well.*

"Look at you," Kathleen exclaimed as Robert and Harry came through their front door. "You're all grown, and an Air Force pilot!" She gave him a hug. "I think you've gotten taller since we saw you last—and very handsome!"

Robert hugged his mother and smiled down at her. "I was a navigator, gave the pilot directions."

"Oh yes, how silly of me. I knew you got your plane where it needed to be for a mission and then back safely to base. That's much better than just flying a big old airplane."

"Bomber," Robert clarified.

"Yes, of course! Well your room is all made up on the third floor. I'm sure you'll want a shower before dinner, and maybe a beer or something like that to help you unwind. Your father will help you upstairs with your things and get settled while I attend to getting your homecoming dinner ready."

✵✵✵

In the fall of 1953, Robert was admitted as a student to John Carroll University in Cleveland looking to major in English with an emphasis in business writing. His wartime experience had added to his introspective nature, and he found pleasure in writing accounts of his time in Japan. Often these memories became short stories he occasionally asked his university advisor to read. He enjoyed this college experience, though it was a new kind of socialization. He was older than the other first-year students and certainly had more life experience than the average eighteen-year-old freshman. He could not help feeling like an outsider and largely kept to himself.

Harry had purchased a car for Robert—a Buick Special Son found, which had been a demonstrator at the Pittsburgh dealership. While technically still a new car, it was sold to Harry as a used vehicle. It was green with a cream-colored hard top and made Robert happy just looking at it or washing and waxing it in his parents' driveway.

His third-floor room was small but adequate and included its own bath. He had unpacked his belongings from Staunton and the few things from his military service, purchased a portable typewriter, and began to adjust to his new life. When on campus and not in class, he spent time in the student union lounge reading, drinking coffee, and watching the world around him. Robert was shy around women and attributed it to the fact his mother never had much to do with him. Here he was, seemingly surrounded by young women he could tell found him attractive. He rarely began a conversation, but would talk if spoken to and participated in class discussions, not being shy about voicing his opinion of an assigned author or passage. His grades were good, allowing his easy matriculation through his college years.

At the beginning of his senior year his faculty advisor changed due to retirement, and he found himself assigned to a female PhD in the English department who he had taken a class or two with. He had enjoyed her lectures in comparative literature, finding them geared often to female characters even if they were not necessarily principal characters. While there were two or three other female instructors in the department, Dr. Hughes was certainly the youngest, perhaps only in her late twenties or early thirties, and attractive. He would never have thought of her in this way had he not felt a kinship from being one of her students. Somehow she seemed approachable, someone he would enjoy talking with.

At Robert's first consultation, they discussed his course selections for the year, making sure he would have enough credits to graduate the following spring. He found it difficult to keep from thinking of her as something other than his advisor. She was almost as tall as he was, with long auburn hair, bright blue eyes, and the fair complexion of a red-head. She was focused in their meetings, very business-like without being dictatorial, and seemed to enjoy their conversations about his time at John Carroll and his future ambitions. He would be her student in two creative writing classes that year, and she suggested he make occasional appointments with her. She was interested in the fact that he was an Air Force veteran.

CHAPTER THIRTY-SEVEN

Harry continued investing in the stock market on his own. Most every morning he would motor to the Merrill Lynch office to read the paper, watch the performance of his investments, listen to Copland's strategies, and lunch at the NY Spaghetti House. Mostly he enjoyed these mornings because it gave him something to do and got him out of the house. Kathleen had become—well, she had changed from the young woman he married to someone harsher, more opinionated, and certainly less kind to him. She was more involved with Lizzie Hannah and the women in her circle than ever, planning events that would take her out of their home for dinner and leaving Harry to his own culinary and evening's devices. She would generally see him at breakfast before he would leave for Merrill and perhaps have a kind word, but they were living separate lives. This arrangement only changed for holiday gatherings of the family, when she enjoyed being hostess, playing her baby grand or plotting with Agnes on any number of future plans. He was not about to rock the boat over this lifestyle, but he did miss the Kathleen he'd met the day the race ended.

In his investing thus far he had made a bit more money than he had lost, but not enough to feel he was building for the future. He had holdings in each of the three major automobile corporations and General Electric, all of which were making him money, while some of the less solid companies he thought might greatly increase in value did not. He wished he had listened to Irving when he tried to interest Harry in something called "Big Blue" in 1951. *What good would these contraptions be,* he had thought, and opted not to invest in the IBM 701 mainframe computer.

✳✳✳

Two weeks after his graduation from John Carroll, Robert made an appointment with Dr. Hughes. He had started looking for work as soon as he walked down the aisle with his diploma and now sought her advice on preparing a resume. For the post-graduation meeting, Robert wore a suit and tie because he had attended a Career Day event. Used to seeing him in less formal attire, Dr. Hughes was briefly taken aback as he entered her small, light-filled office.

"Well, you clean up nice." She rose from her desk and shook his hand. "So how was Career Day?"

"It was large! Cleveland apparently has a booming business sector. I met some very nice people, have a small stack of business cards in my pocket, and intend to lose a lot of shoe leather on downtown sidewalks."

"Eager and determined—that's the way you need to be. Your military service and honorable discharge should help quite a bit since many corporate people served in the last world war."

They then spent an hour working on his resume. She had no other student appointments the remainder of the afternoon and had decided to leave for the day after meeting with Robert.

"May I buy you an ice cream?" Robert asked. "Or maybe a beer would be more appropriate."

She blushed at the invitation, then quickly decided they were both adults after all, and he was no longer one of her students. A beer was just what this afternoon needed, she agreed.

CHAPTER THIRTY-EIGHT

The Cleveland Massey dealership had been open six years and Son was now its general manager. Automobile sales came easy to him, and much ado had been made about a second-generation Kern being back in the Cleveland car business. During the coming summer he would again be spending two weeks at GM Tech, this time in management, but he fully intended to have a crack at the assembly line again. He wanted to know everything about new technologies the manufacturer was using and how they worked.

The dealership building itself was of a new design—lots of floor-to-ceiling glass and an exterior of twenty-four inch white ceramic tiles applied over concrete block. On sunny days the building radiated modern style, and in the evenings when the business day was finished, the inside lighting made the cars stand out when seen from the street. *Life for the Kern family just couldn't be any better,* he thought, driving home after work on a Friday afternoon. Harry was in good health; Kathleen seemed well and was enjoying spending money at every turn; Agnes and Tom—well, who knew about those two; Nora and Sam lived in Pittsburgh much to their mother's chagrin; Robert had been hired as a technical writer at Republic Steel.

Son and Rosalee loved living in the house he and his sisters grew up in, and Rosalee was pregnant again as Ogden turned seven. The dealership had had record new car sales since its opening. In 1957, Buick had sixteen body styles for customers to choose from, and Massey had at least one of each on the lot or in the showroom. It was rumored as the decade came to a close the Buick body style was going to change radically, and Son wondered how the public would react. The drawings he had seen in Detroit were exciting, with the models going from a boxy style to one with rear fins like a spaceship, or at least the Hollywood movie version. *Maybe corporate could get the actors from Buck Rogers or Captain Video to make appearances when the new model comes out! I need to make that suggestion to Mr. Massey.*

Rosalee was picking roses from the plants he and his father had once planted in the backyard as he pulled into the driveway. Pregnancy suited her—she just glowed.

✪✪✪

The telephone was ringing as Harry entered the house from the garage. He wondered where Kathleen had gotten to since she didn't pick up the call as she generally did on the second or third ring. He ducked into his office to pick up the receiver.

"Harry Kern here."

"Oh Harry, it's Mary. She paused. "Pap has died. Virgil found him in his bed and called me to come as soon as I could. We guess he just passed in his sleep and it was very peaceful."

A thousand thoughts and images passed through Harry's mind within a moment of Mary's news. He wondered how many of his brothers could be contacted, and if some of them were even alive.

"I can be there in a few hours," he said. "Is there anything I can bring? Anything you and Virg need from here?"

"No, I don't think so, thanks. I'll be meeting with our new undertaker shortly. He bought old Mr. Perkins' business a year or so back. I don't guess we'll arrange for any sort of viewing, I don't think Pap had much of a circle of friends. He wanted to be placed beside Mam. I think he began to think about some sort of afterlife in his later years. Funny to think about—Pap with a soul."

"Mary, I'm so glad you're there. I'll pull some clothes together and head north. Be at the farm in a couple hours and will see you or wait for your arrival there. Virgil still there?"

"Just left. Said to let him know when you arrived. Said you'd know what to look for among Pap's papers. Thanks for coming," she said and hung up.

Harry replaced the receiver as the full impact of Pap's death seeped into his consciousness. The thought of his father's passing had never really been a consideration for him before. He took a notepad from his desk drawer and scribbled a note for Kathleen saying he'd call her that evening with more information. After packing a small bag of clothing he left for the farm perhaps, he thought, for the last time.

Of the nine brothers, Mary only knew the whereabouts of Virgil and Harry for sure. Graham and Homer were last known to be living in Chicago, and she remembered hearing one of their number had gone to live in California, but could not remember now which one. After Harry arrived they headed for Pap's room, the inner sanctum where he had kept his books and records. Surprisingly, Harry found his father did have a will, apparently written after Mam's death based on its date. It named Harry as his executor, directing him to sell the farm and livestock, and with the proceeds, settle any outstanding debts. The remaining funds were to be distributed equally among those of his children who were alive and could be found within twelve months. As of the document's writing, there was no outstanding debt on the property or its contents, and he wished all his progeny a long life. *Just like Pap,* Harry thought, and wondered if he paid federal or state taxes. He could find no evidence of payment in a quick review of his desk drawers.

"I'll want to have Norman Minor look all this over," he said to Mary. "You remember, he's husband to Kathleen's sister, Mary, a big-time lawyer in Cleveland. Among other things, I'm not sure how you sell property with people buried on it. I'm assuming that's still the plan?"

She nodded her head. "We were thinking the day after tomorrow, it's not supposed to rain." She smiled at her brother. "It's been a long day Harry. If you don't mind, I think I'll call it quits and go home. I think things are reasonably clean in my old bedroom, and there's likely some food in the icebox, but don't eat anything that looks old or smells."

They both laughed and Mary left, saying she'd return the next afternoon. Harry sat alone in the house he knew so well and began a further examination of his father's papers. He found a bank deposit book showing a small positive cash balance, a dark-green metal lockbox containing fifty dollars, and a recent land appraisal completed by a real estate firm in the next county. Harry wondered about the appraisal, as he wouldn't have thought Pap would go to the trouble to obtain one, and was surprised by the cash value the company had come up with. The stresses of the day caught up with him suddenly. He turned off the desk lamp and wandered into the kitchen, though he was not hungry in the least. He found eggs, a slice or two of ham, and three bottles of Red Cap beer in the icebox. He grabbed a bottle and closed the door. He hadn't called Kathleen since he arrived, and she hadn't called either. He'd try first thing in the morning.

Perhaps it was the events of the day, being in this house with its memories in every dark corner, or merely the time of night, but Harry could not help but think about the lives people lead and their effects on those around them. Pap was always something of a mystery, at least that was how he'd felt growing up, and he really didn't know how his siblings felt. They lived here longer than he had, so perhaps Pap's life and thoughts came into focus for them finally. Maybe that's why all his brothers but one left—some for points now unknown—like the milkweed seeds that take flight in whatever directions the wind blows them. He regretted not knowing where so many of his brothers had landed, how they were, and what they remembered of life in this place when they chanced to recall any of it. Finishing his beer, he walked back through the house, turning off lights and locking both the front and back doors. He collapsed into Mary's bed, threw one of Mam's comforters over himself, took a deep breath, and fell asleep, dreaming nothing of the day he'd just lived.

Harry awoke to the sound of loud knocking at the front door and his name being called. He pulled on his pants and went through the main room to find Virgil standing outside.

"We never lock doors around here," he said. "Just you city folk do stuff like that. Got coffee going yet? Even got the stove going?"

He was being a pissant Harry thought, trying to show off to his older brother. "No, waiting for you to come show me how it's done. Only takes a twist of a dial in the city. I'll finish dressing."

Harry left his brother standing inside the door holding a loaf of white bread under his arm. He rejoined Virgil in the kitchen some ten minutes later after a visit to the outhouse. The morning was full of sunshine, but the air was cool. He wondered when the mortician's crew would stop by to dig next to Mam. Virgil did indeed have the coffee pot going and was toasting several slices of the bread he brought in one of Mam's iron skillets.

"Have to drink the coffee black, or maybe with sugar. The milk's soured and the cow seems to have run dry lately. She's pretty old now, you know."

Harry enjoyed listening to Virgil talk. Everything was so simple and uncomplicated for him.

"You have a girl, Virgil? You must be what, thirty-three by now. Must be some little Miss Sunshine around."

"Ha! No time for that. Too busy with chores and work here, then spring and fall I help out at the Butler farm down the road. They have a big spread. Anyway, no girl in her right mind would want anything to do with me. Destined to be a bachelor farmer."

He poured an egg into a hole he'd made in each of the four pieces of bread and tempered the fire in the stove. "Make any sense of Pap's papers? I suppose there will be a notice of his passing in the afternoon paper."

"Pap ever mention to you anything about having the farm's value appraised? I found some documents in his desk showing he had it done eight months or so ago."

"Don't remember his saying anything, and don't remember seeing any strangers wandering around the farm. Course I'd have been busy getting the Butler farm ready for winter then."

"I've got more things to go through in his room this morning. Mary said she'll be over in the afternoon. Do you keep in touch with any of our brothers? I need to contact as many of them as I can find."

"Heard Elliot is living in California, Los Angeles I think. Melvin's maybe still in Chicago, but that leaves four more out there somewhere if they're still alive."

"Pap's will was specific about the time I should allow for finding them. I suppose I'll have advertisements placed in major regional newspapers looking for each of the brothers we can't account for and see what kind of response that produces. Heck, maybe there are even some in Ohio somewhere. It'll give me something to do besides playing the market back in Cleveland."

Harry cleaned up the breakfast dishes while Virgil went to the barn to look after the animals. He remembered his mother standing where he was, doing the same simple chore. *How did she find any time for herself,* he thought, then remembered he wanted to call Kathleen. Finishing up, he went to the telephone on the wall between the kitchen and the living room. It was a crank style with a party line he hoped was currently not being used. He turned the crank to get an operator and sent a long-distance call through. Kathleen picked up on the fourth ring.

"Hey there, how are you?"

"Just fine, thank you. How's things there? I'm sorry to hear about Pap. Always a sweet old fellow."

"Well, sweet is not the adjective I would use, but I'm glad he came off that way to you. Funeral is tomorrow, then I'll need another day or two to make sure I'm not missing anything in his financial affairs and to try to contact any of my brothers who might still be living. I hope to be home by the weekend."

"Take as much time as you need. I'm here and just fine. Lots to do. Agnes and I are thinking of joining a new mystery club in town, and of course there is always Lizzie to catch up with. Then there is spending more of your money...."

"Well, try not to spend it all before I get back," Harry said and hung up.

CHAPTER THIRTY-NINE

Agnes Keck felt boxed in by her life. The house she and Tom purchased ten years earlier now seemed too small for her needs—or at least her desires. The son she and Tom were raising was too much like her. A conniver, he always found ways to get what he wanted or at least to come out ahead. Tom enjoyed his work at GE, often working a double shift if asked, leaving her stuck in their home awaiting both the men in her life to return from school or the plant. Her sister had found living in Pittsburgh agreed with her, as did married life. Sam was an executive at Westinghouse, where his father served on the company's board, and she fell right in with the country club set. Nora had a much larger home than Agnes's squalid little bungalow and had quickly gotten herself pregnant—*all nice and tidy,* Agnes thought. Then there was her mother, the newly rich matriarch. She wondered just how much of Harry's fortune would be left for her to inherit after they were both gone. Her parents were still relatively young. Would it all get spent during their lifetimes? She took another bottle of beer from the refrigerator. It was her third since breakfast but helped her cope with the miserable life she felt she was leading. *Just another beautiful day in paradise.* She finished the beer and slipped the empty bottle into its cardboard carton. She would need to refrigerate another before Tom's arrival and eat a little something so she wouldn't appear as tipsy as she felt.

✵ ✵ ✵

Pap's three children in attendance had the undertaker dress him in the one suit he owned and place him in a wooden coffin. Three grave diggers arrived and carried out their grim trade two feet from where Mam rested, and the next morning, a beautifully sunlit October day, Pap was laid to rest beside her. Mary's husband and their three children came, as did the mortician and the preacher from the local Methodist church, who was given twenty bucks by Harry to say some brief words about a man he had only seen a few times. After each of the children shoveled a spade of dirt into the grave the diggers did the rest.

"Pap would have admired this handsome day," Virgil said to no one in particular. "He loved the fall. Hated the winter though."

"I'm sure he did," Mary said. "I felt him here. Kind of spooky but I did."

The seven mourners walked back to the house. Mary had brought a baked ham for their lunch, after which Harry outlined his plan for trying to find their siblings through advertisements in regional newspapers in the Midwest and on the West Coast. He also was going to contact the real estate company that had appraised the farm to find out why Pap had engaged them, then he would head back to Cleveland. Virgil was to move into the house to protect against vandals, giving up his room in town.

A day and a half later Harry drove back home and found Kathleen, Agnes, and the very pregnant Nora in residence.

"You look like you're going to bust," he said to his youngest daughter in jest.

"I know! The doctor thinks it's twins but it's too early to really tell. You look tired Daddy. I'm sure Pap's passing has been hard."

"Yes," Kathleen agreed. "I'm having the family together for a pot-luck dinner this evening. I thought it might make you feel like you're home and among your own. I hope you don't mind."

"That will be nice. Thank you. It has been a long few days up there. It was easier with Mam, for some reason. She had all those children, all that cooking and laundry. I was amazed she lived as long as she did. But Pap! He just seemed eternal to me, and now he's gone."

"Go have a shower and maybe a short nap before dinner and the three of us ladies will ready things."

Harry thought that a good idea as the bathing facilities on the farm were limited at best. He attempted to hug Kathleen, who squirmed out of the embrace.

"You stink! To your bathroom before you bring flies into the house!"

She pushed him away from her with such force that he lost his balance and fell onto the thick Oriental rug.

Agnes helped her father to his feet remarking, "You are kind of ripe!"

✬✬✬

The Kern family gathering was low-key and informal as promised. Robert and Son reminisced about their summers on the farm and being around their extended family. Son even told the story about his horse ride to the barn that one summer and was amazed it had not reached his parents' ears before. There were questions about what would happen to the property, if Pap left a will, and if all the brothers could be found, which Harry discussed in turn, indicating Pap had left a timetable for when all his wishes should be concluded.

"Who would know," Agnes asked, "if his loose ends took more than a year from his death to resolve themselves? Who would know or even care? Pap's gone."

Harry agreed but said he hoped to be able to honor his father's wishes if at all possible. "Finding my brothers will be the most difficult part—if it's even possible!" He yawned. "Family, I've had a long couple of days and I'm very tired. Thank you all for your company this evening and for the wonderful meal you put together—to say nothing of the lemon meringue pie Rosalee brought—but I'm going to call this day over and bid you all a good night."

Kathleen's daughters and daughter-in-law cleaned up the kitchen while Son and Robert continued to reminisce about their childhood memories at the farm. Kathleen sat quietly with them, holding Ogden and watching Rosalee interact with Agnes and Nora. Finishing their work, the three women rejoined the others. Rosalee was the only one whose spouse was actually in attendance.

"Tom working tonight?" she asked Agnes.

"I suppose so. He often gets a second shift call, and the money is good. Didn't get a cushy job like Son here with the Massey organization! Need any hard workers over at that fancy dealership, Son? Share the wealth with the family?"

"Tom know how to rebuild a Buick transmission?" he said smiling. "Our mechanics are trained at the factory in Detroit and know every nut and bolt that goes into one of our cars. Besides, I think he makes more money at GE than he'd get working at Massey."

"Oh, I was thinking about something in sales, start him off as say assistant sales manager. He wouldn't get all dirty talking people into buying a new car. What do ya think?"

Son smiled at her again. "I'll take it under advisement. In the meantime, I think it's about time I take my sweetheart here and my little boy on home."

Robert rose and said he'd walk out with them. Good nights were said, and the three women adjourned to the living room. Agnes wandered to the bar, fixing herself a vodka on the rocks and swallowing half of it before turning around to where her mother and sister were sitting.

"Well, that was a fine little family gathering," she said. "Seems as if the male Kern members have the world by the ass and don't give a shit about the lives of us females and our families! You'd think Son could spread his largess around just a bit. Think I like seeing Tom come home from work—when he actually does—dirty from a day's labor at the plant? And then there's Robert—graduates college and right away gets a white-collar job writing about steel. He's smart and crafty too. He'll see where this job takes him and turn it into something better." She looked at her sister. "You've got it made too, Sis, up there in Steeler Town. Husband with family connections to a growing company, big home, country club set, all the goodies." She finished her drink. "I'm not holding it against you, you played it smart hooking old Sam. But you all got me looking up to your accomplishments when I should be on top! Hell, even that little Rosalee and her lemon pie has got it over me, at least in Harry's mind. Damn it all to hell!"

CHAPTER FORTY

The Who Done It Club, as it came to be known, began as a females-only social, a book-club-like gathering that included monthly luncheons at one of the ladies' homes followed by a presentation by one or two of the group on their version of how to commit a perfect murder without being caught. Occasionally there would be guest speakers invited. The famous G-man Elliot Ness was one such guest after moving his family to Bratenahl. He assured his audience crime really does not pay, as had Norman Minor when the group's meeting was held at his home. Kathleen and Agnes found those meetings particularly intriguing, allowing their imaginations to run with clever scenarios for committing a murder, then deconstructing their theories to see if they actually held up. Agnes was particularly skilled at creating situations where the murderer would simply fade into obscurity.

After a member's presentation, the group would discuss and work through it to see if the crime could indeed not be detected or if it had flaws. Then they would have lunch and decide who would give the next month's murder scenario. To a disquieting degree, the group's presentations seemed to focus on the demise of husbands. Happily none of the group's spouses had gone to their final reward, but the number of mariticides was duly noted.

It was also noted by Kathleen that Agnes, more often than not, would arrive a cocktail or two ahead of everyone else, even though she was savvy enough to have imbibed on odorless vodka. It wasn't until she began noticing her daughter's overall personality changing in a manner perhaps only a mother would that she grew concerned. Agnes's recent tirade about Son giving Tom a sales position at the dealership would not have been so flagrantly expressed five years earlier, though she likely would have thought it then. Kathleen was sure Tom was a hard man to live with, and they probably often had arguments ending in bruises to both their bodies. She was sure her daughter's participation in the club was more focused on results than those of the others, and her increased consumption of liquor was meant to help her overlook the inequalities she felt but made her more easily express them. Agnes didn't realize how few marriages were totally enjoyable, even with money, but Kathleen was sure she would never convince her. Her own, Kathleen knew, had gone off-track when she learned Robert was coming into the world and she couldn't forgive what Harry had done to her. Now it was his constant harping about her spending habits. *What use is it to have money if it's not going to be spent and enjoyed? Oh, it was okay for Harry. He bought that fucking fish and hung it up in my beautiful home!*

✵✵✵

Classified advertisements were published in the *Chicago Tribune*, *The Kansas City Star*, and the *Los Angeles Times* in an effort to find Pap's other sons. Three were located: two in the Chicago area and one in California. There were four other responses, but none were Harry's brothers, probably just men looking to make a quick buck from responding. The three legit brothers were pleased to hear from Harry, sorry to hear of their father's passing, wanted nothing to do with the sale of the farm, and were happy to allow Virgil to live in the house if he chose to do so. Harry's inquiries as to if they knew where other brothers were living or if any had passed proved fruitless. The others had simply disappeared.

His investigation into whether or not Pap paid property taxes uncovered he had up until two years earlier, when he apparently just ignored the notices. Harry covered these and the associated penalties, making Virgil promise to pay future assessments if he planned to live on the property. Mary was given a few items from the house that had been her mother's; Harry wanted nothing, leaving Virgil a mostly intact residence to occupy, which he did for the next ten years. As for the farm's property evaluation, Harry found a small black leather notebook his father kept in a drawer of his desk outlining Pap's supposed plan to sell the farm to Antioch College. It seemed a philosophy professor and a band of his students were interested in recreating a Brook Farm-like utopia a la George Ripley's experiment in communal living. Also folded neatly in the notebook was the article from the *Yellow Springs News* where he had read of the effort and got the idea. He apparently had not pursued his plan to make this connection to his hero.

Rosalee and Son had their second child in 1957, a daughter they named after each grandmother—Mary Kathleen. The dealership continued to do exceedingly well. Son was made vice-president of Massey Corporation when Don Massey retired to the east coast of Florida and his son took over as president.

Robert Kern and Allison Hughes became engaged almost a year after their first non-academic date, and married in June of 1959. She continued to teach at John Carroll, while he took a position at Burson-Marsteller Public Relations as an Account Executive in the firm's Cleveland office. Robert came to enjoy being the "man in the grey flannel suit," and the couple moved to an expensive apartment in a new, highly touted building downtown with floor-to-ceiling windows overlooking Lake Erie. At a university function with Robert, Allison was casually asked by a female colleague what birth control she intended to use. It seemed to Allison a personal question, but responded they would not be using any of the recently approved pills being offered by pharmaceutical firms, having complete confidence in the rhythm method; she was pregnant within two months. Allison continued teaching up until a week before her water broke.

Agnes became a functioning alcoholic, with Tom and their son bearing the brunt of her disease. At the year's end they separated, with Tom taking full responsibility for the boy, who was nearly finished with elementary school, by adjusting his work schedule at GE. Though she occasionally attended AA meetings, Agnes found the pleasure of a bottle of vodka difficult to ignore and spent many of her evenings passed out on her living room couch. Hampered by the fact that Tom was giving her just a third of his weekly earnings, she turned to Kathleen for financial assistance, which she received without Harry's knowledge and without Kathleen cutting back on her own spending. As the year came to a close, Harry decided to temper his attempts to accrue wealth in the stock market, having lost more than he'd gained in 1958. Without telling Kathleen, he listed the Shaker Heights house with a private realtor and began looking for a residence he hoped would appeal to his wife in an area where property taxes were lower and would be less expensive to maintain. By spring his realtor had found a prospective buyer willing to pay what Harry wanted for their current home. Coincidently, he had located a property in Walton Hills situated on two acres of wooded land. It was almost the same size as the Shaker house and a good price, making him a profit on the transactions. The trick now was approaching all this with Kathleen without accruing additional marital penalties. He decided to repeat his former success in announcement-making by inviting the family for dinner.

Harry told the family at Sergio's he'd been made an offer for the house that was just too good to pass on, which was sort of the case, he reasoned. Their new place was in an area of the city where property values would increase over time. Kathleen did not object to the move, perhaps because some part of her realized her spending habits were getting out of hand, and the money she was giving weekly to Agnes was not helping. She hoped this assistance would be short-lived, as Agnes had indicated her relationship with Tom was improving and they were spending more time together. *Horny bastard,* Kathleen thought. Agnes knew exactly how to play him and was embarrassed she could think of her daughter in those terms. But wasn't that the way of the world? Certainly it was in some circles. After dinner broke up, Kathleen and Harry drove home. She was feeling confident in him now. He had solved a concern of hers without realizing it. *Perhaps I won't kill him off after all,* she thought, and smiled as he handed her a night cap.

✪✪✪

By June of 1960 the move to Walton Hills was complete. Kathleen bid farewell to her assorted friends and left her prized home in Shaker Heights for the new location, which she came to like even though it was further from downtown, Agnes, Son, and her Bratenahl cronies. The fish, at her insistence, stayed at the Shaker house.

Kathleen had begun to warm a bit to Robert after his marriage and his seeming success in public relations. He took her to lunch at the Cleveland Press Club, where she was introduced to television personalities from local news stations. Robert seemed to know all of them; she listened to the small talk and jokes they made, which increased his stock in her eyes. She found Allison to be pleasant enough, but too intellectual for her comfort, and with decidedly alternative ideas about child-rearing. Their baby was a sickly little thing and a worry to her parents. Kathleen thought the only good thing about their apartment was its proximity to a Cleveland Clinic emergency location.

"I've decided not to become too close to that child," Kathleen said to Harry one afternoon, "as I would find it just too sad when it dies."

"How can you say such a thing?" Harry responded. "She's not an 'it,' she's your granddaughter and needs our love. And Robert and Allison need our support, not abandonment!"

"Oh, Harry," she said, turning away from him, "you always take Robert's part in things. He's much more your son than mine, so that little girl is much more yours than mine too."

CHAPTER FORTY-ONE

1964

"I am sorry to tell you, Mr. and Mrs. Kern, your daughter has a hole in the left ventricle of her heart, which is causing a loss of blood."

The physician continued matter-of-factly describing something that struck Robert and Allison as horrific.

"Her body is currently assimilating the leakage, but as she grows it will be more difficult for her body to do so."

Allison moaned and began to cry. Robert was stoic but worried. Their only child, Veronica, had recently turned four, and they both had noticed signs of something affecting her negatively over and above the normal illnesses she had suffered through since birth.

"Here at the clinic, we have been experimentally treating adult patients with a new procedure that keeps their hearts beating while surgeons close a tear, and we have had increasing success with it. But we've never tried the procedure on a child, and it is reasonably expensive. I've read articles out of Stanford University stating this type of procedure is part of a new study being conducted at their Children's Health Center.

They are, I believe, waiving the cost as an incentive for children of California residents."

Robert looked at the physician quizzically. "As an incentive for what?"

"Well, for finding young patients to treat and improve their technique."

"And you can't treat her here?"

"No, we're not working on children. She would be a total experiment, even if the physician review board decided to take the case. California is far away, I realize, but at least Stanford has had success in children with this type of surgery. I can put you in contact with the surgical team there if you'd like. She doesn't need the procedure tomorrow, so there is some time, but should you decide to take her there you would need to establish residency."

Allison and Robert looked at one another and walked the short distance to the room where Ronnie had been taken after her X-rays.

"Hey there little girl," Robert said, smiling down at her. "How are you feeling after all that? As soon as you're ready and the doctors say we can go home, we'll get some ice cream at Pierre's. How's that sound? Just the three of us."

Veronica smiled up at her parents, though she still was a bit traumatized from the X-ray procedure. Later that evening, after she was tucked into bed, Robert and Allison began making plans for a move to the coast.

"Happily, if there is something in all this to be happy about, we have some time to plan," Robert said.

"Yes. I'll begin looking for teaching positions in the area. There are quite a few institutions, even community colleges, to get us by until, well, until we can come back."

"I know Burson Marsteller has an office in Los Angeles, but I'll check to see if there is anything closer to Stanford. The company is growing like a weed, so I'm sure I can get something. I'll check on residency requirements as well."

It took six months, due largely to Allison's teaching schedule, for the Robert Kern family to ready themselves for life in California. There was no office for Burson Marsteller in Stanford, but there was one in San Francisco, forty-one miles away. Robert easily transferred and made about twice as much due to the living costs being much higher. The city of Stanford was comprised of the university and the university hospitals, with most of the closer residential area taken by student housing. Working by phone with a realtor, they were able to find a furnished rental home in Palo Alto County and stored their Cleveland apartment belongings in a long-term facility.

Residency status required living in the state for one year, which meant Ronnie would be at least six when her surgery could be added to the hospital's schedule, and no one knew how long it would take after that. In the meantime, Allison would look for a teaching post close to where Ronnie would be attending school. It was a lot to hope for, but she and Robert were both being positive about her finding something and the success of their daughter's surgery. Son put both Robert's and Allison's cars in his used lot, selling them prior to their move, and put the money down on a newer vehicle for the family's drive west. They planned to make the trip over five days as a bit of vacation they could enjoy along the way. However, the reason for the trip was never far from either of their minds, tempering any enjoyment they might otherwise have taken in it.

"I think we should travel more, Harry!" Kathleen said one afternoon a month or so after Robert and Allison moved to California. "I'd like to see Paris and the artwork in all those big museums. It might stimulate me enough to get back to my own painting. People said I once had promise, particularly in watercolor, though I think it is a difficult medium, very hard to correct if you make an error. And then there's the food over there!

It could be just the two of us, maybe for a month of sightseeing. We've surely got the money after selling the house!"

Harry sat still, listening and wondering where this all was coming from. It wasn't like Kathleen to suggest things out of the blue. This revelation had its roots somewhere—probably somewhere like Bratenahl.

"Neither of us speak French," he said quietly, taking his cigar from his mouth. "We'd be seen as American tourists ripe for the picking."

"Oh Harry! Everyone over there speaks English, at least that's what I hear and read in travel magazines. I can line up our complete itinerary and arrange for side trips with French guides. It would be something to always remember and might even spark an interest in you to explore other new locations. In a way it might remind you of the big race you won and coming to the sinful city of Cleveland all those years ago."

Harry smiled, which was all the encouragement she needed to make several appointments with the same travel agent she'd used for their Cuban trip. Harry was sure the cost of getting to Paris and back—along with hotels, restaurants, sightseeing trips, gratuities, and souvenirs—would be the least of the expenses. He worried about the furniture, carpeting, and artwork Kathleen would decide she absolutely needed to have to make the trip a success in her mind. He could easily see a home addition in the future and was again thankful for moving away from Shaker Heights.

✲✲✲

Paris fit Kathleen, Agnes, and Nora like handmade calf-skinned gloves. Originally conceived as a trip for Harry and Kathleen, it quickly enlarged to include the girls as news of its planning became known. The costs involved with adding Agnes were born by Harry, while at least those incurred by Nora were largely covered by Sam, who had already planned to be in Paris for a corporate trade show. For Kathleen, being surrounded by the sheer extravagance of the city's interiors—hotel lobbies, restaurants, museums—to say nothing of the historic structures themselves, set her off in a renewed decorating direction. In particular, it increased her fondness for additional white marble sculptures of semi-nude females perched on gilded metal stands.

Upon their return, the furniture Kathleen had purchased for the Shaker home was sold to a used furniture dealer in a better part of the city and was replaced with everything reminding her of France. The piano stayed, as did an electric organ she'd purchased for the living room, relegating the piano to a less formal gathering room off the garage. All told, the trip and new furniture cost Harry $2,500, and at sixty-six, he hoped it would be his last excursion abroad.

Agnes learned to like anise during the Paris trip. Its forty-percent alcohol content allowed her not to have to drink as much to achieve the buzz she required. She was also partial to the small dark cafés near their hotel she frequented once Nora, Sam, Harry, and Kathleen had retired for the evening. She was never alone for long, picking up men who easily lured her to their apartments, then returning to the family's hotel before dawn through a service door left unlocked. She found she enjoyed the French men she met and was never with the same one twice, not wanting any serious attachments. They were always polite, caring for her comfort, never in too much of a hurry to consummate their lovemaking, and never rough with her as Tom sometimes was. Some would walk her back to her hotel in the early morning hours, sometimes she would walk back alone to smell the fresh air and experience the waking city on her own. She never was afraid for her safety, likely due to the accentuated confidence the anise instilled. Her parents and Nora never knew about her liaisons.

Some of her acquaintances used marijuana, which Agnes found very freeing. She enjoyed the mindset the drug allowed, the freedom from convention and societal rules. At first it was easy for her to keep the anise and marijuana compartmentalized, but toward the end of the trip she found it harder to keep these pleasures at bay. She was able to pack several bottles of anise among her belongings, and even a bit of marijuana to get her back to Ohio, but the trick would be how and where she would get it once stateside. One other thing would go back with her—a burning sensation between her thighs, especially when urinating.

CHAPTER FORTY-TWO

When Ronnie's surgery was scheduled she had just turned seven. Her condition had worsened slightly since the move but was monitored weekly by hospital staff. While they had made the move to California expressly for their daughter's condition, the realization of the surgery actually taking place weighed heavily on her parents. And as the date grew nearer, both Robert and Allison's anxieties intensified. Allison's mother offered to be with her daughter and son-in-law for the surgery, an offer that was accepted. Robert had written to Harry and Kathleen about the procedure, resulting in the receipt of "Oceans of Love" cards from Kathleen.

Ronnie had adapted well to California, attending a private school not far from their rental home that catered to children with special medical needs. She quickly made friends with other students there, participating in most activities except active sporting events. For the surgery, Ronnie would miss six weeks of school if all went well, longer if there were complications, and no one wished to think or talk about any bleaker outcome. Allison arranged a cookie and ice cream party on Ronnie's last day at school prior to her surgery, and Robert took the day off to help and try to enjoy this bittersweet moment. It was one of the few times he had been able to share an event with his daughter during a school day, and it was clear she enjoyed having him there. At the end of the afternoon the Kern family left the school together.

Robert decided to document what occurred during Ronnie's hospital stay, perhaps write an article or two for other parents or just for his own memory. He had taken the next week off so he could be there for Ronnie and Allison. He had faced many trials in life and had learned to endure, but this one—even though it had been planned for and carried out to the letter—was nearly more than one could bear.

While surgery was scheduled for Wednesday, Ronnie was admitted the Monday before. There were a number of tests, X-rays, and parental consultations required. Robert and Allison decided to take turns staying nights in Ronnie's hospital room, sleeping as well as possible in an over-sized leather chair that reclined nearly flat, allowing the other to drive to their home for a shower and as normal a sleep as could be mustered.

The wait for Wednesday morning seemed endless, then when it finally came everything seemed to happen in a rush. Surgery was scheduled for seven, the second on the morning's schedule. Three teams of pediatric heart surgeons would work the day's patient load, each performing two procedures, with the first beginning at five-thirty. Robert spent Tuesday night with his daughter, sleeping very little with the constant interruptions of nurses checking on Ronnie throughout the night. He was up at six, splashing water on his face when the first day nurse arrived. Forty-five minutes later Allison arrived. With one parent on each side of her hospital bed, Ronnie looked as happy as she could under the circumstances.

The nurse who administered an IV in Ronnie's right arm was exceedingly skillful and caused her no pain. A bottle of clear fluid dripping from the line contained vitamins and a small bit of sleeping solution to calm her prior to the surgery. Before Allison arrived, Ronnie's surgeon had come by to greet his patient. Robert thought he looked so different in his green scrubs from when they had been in his office. He brought Ronnie a small stuffed bear also wearing scrubs, and she smiled and even managed a laugh when he told her he'd be seeing her again soon, but the bear would need to wait in her room for her return.

A few minutes before seven a group of nurses entered and whisked Ronnie and her bed out of the room. Robert hugged his wife, who was crying, and her mother. While none of the three were hungry, they headed to the cafeteria for coffee and to wait a bit before going to the family lounge. After three hours Ronnie's surgeon came to tell them everything went well, the hole had been closed successfully, and the patient was asleep in recovery and would be back in her room in an another hour or so. Alison began to cry again and thanked the doctor for taking good care of her baby. She generally was very stoic about her feelings and rarely expressed them in public. Robert hugged her again, which she happily accepted.

The three of them left the lounge, and Robert left the two women in Ronnie's room while he went home to shower and get a change of clothes. Upon his return, Ronnie was sleeping with the scrub-wearing bear under her arm, and the two women were silently keeping her company. A second IV bag had been added, containing who knew what. He had made copious notes about the procedure and wished to add this new item to them. Suddenly Ronnie awakened and was crying, as if waking from a bad dream. Allison was immediately by her side holding her hand.

"It's all over, my angel. You don't need to cry. Are you in pain anywhere? Daddy and Nana are both here too. Here's your big, strong daddy, sweetheart. We're all together."

Robert bent over his daughter and squeezed the small bear her doctor had given her earlier. "Look, here's the bear doctor. He's been waiting all this time to see you and make sure you're okay."

Groggily Ronnie reached for the bear and kissed its forehead. "Hello there, doctor," she said. "How are you feeling today?" She smiled, gave the toy a hug, and fell asleep again.

Allison noticed the tears in Robert's eyes and the relief in his posture as he stood back up. She smiled at him as their eyes met over their daughter's sleeping body, and for the first time in many days they both began to relax.

CHAPTER FORTY-THREE

1967

Nine months after her surgery, Robert, Allison, and Ronnie were permitted by the Stanford surgeons to return to Cleveland if they chose to do so. The three had come to enjoy living in California, though for Allison it seemed increasingly burdensome to be so far from her family and friends. Robert was perfectly happy to work in San Francisco, having spent the largest part of his life away from family. He made friends easily and the work was going well. Clients on the West Coast seemed much easier to work with and accepting of new ideas that would have never gotten off the ground in the Midwest. Ronnie had made friends and seemed happy at her school, but Robert thought about their Cleveland possessions in storage as he paid the monthly bills and eventually began to find their rental house confining.

The medical staff had stipulated Ronnie would need yearly weeklong check-ups for at least three years, so if they did return to Ohio there would be annual flights west; then there were the Cleveland winters—the cold, snow, and ice about four months each year. All that considered though, the family decided to return to Ohio prior to the beginning of the next school year for both Allison and Ronnie. They found a home to purchase in Shaker Heights and moved their stored belongings into it. Ronnie was enrolled at the Laurel School and Allison returned to John Carroll University as a full professor.

Robert took two weeks off from Marsteller to get his wife and daughter settled before returning to San Francisco. He needed to finish a large and involved project—rebranding the McKesson & Robbins Company still reeling from the scandal brought about by the firm's then-CEO, Phillip Musica. Two months later he was able to return, just in time for Halloween, rejoining the Marsteller Cleveland office as a senior account executive with company stock options and a substantial year-end bonus. He was pleased his "girls" were happy in their surroundings and schools. Laurel, a school that prided itself on both the physical and mental development of its students, was willing to adjust Ronnie's physical activity based on the instructions from her California medical team. Yoga became her salvation from academic rigor. The following June the family flew back to Stanford for eight-year-old Ronnie's heart evaluation, and with a radiant Allison carrying an unborn family addition.

In October, a second daughter was brought into the world. She was named Autumn in honor of the season and her strands of red hair. It was 1968, and the world was in a state of flux. The 60s saw a young American president—who had faced the reality of Russian missiles poised in Cuba within minutes of possible US targets—assassinated, along with Martin Luther King Jr. and the president's brother, Robert; racial unrest grew in the South after James Meredith was enrolled in the all-white University of Mississippi, escorted on campus by US marshals; NASA had begun its first Apollo activity, looking to land Americans on the moon; the James

Bond film, *Thunderball,* was turning Sean Connery into a megastar, and the Beatles' *White Album* and *The Graduate* were released.

Robert found the rapidly changing societal remodels exciting, fantasizing about trading in his gray flannels for bell bottoms and boots. However, a change of that magnitude was not going to occur at the Burson Marsteller Cleveland office, and the money was too good to leave. Allison, as part of a university environment, found the changing ethos much easier to accommodate, and the relaxed attitude toward women's dress increased Robert's interest in attending the occasional English department's social gatherings.

Between classes at Laurel and her enthusiasm for her baby sister, Ronnie was completely happy living in Ohio. She made a new friend at school—Alice, who also was not a boarding student. A very active girl, Alice excelled in field hockey, which was much too strenuous for Ronnie, but she enjoyed attending the games and cheering for the school's team. At home, Ronnie was keen to help her mother with Autumn, including occasional bottle feedings when Allison could not breast feed and other less desirable duties. She wondered how such a small being could produce so much poop!

Ronnie, like her father, was aware of changes in her immediate environment. An RCA color television had recently been purchased—one of the first in their neighborhood—causing friends to drop by weekend evenings, which she enjoyed. She often fell asleep next to her father on the leather living room couch. Seeming never to make it to the eleven o'clock news, Robert would carry her to her room while Allison dealt with Autumn. Allison's mother was an enormous help during the first years of Autumn's life, providing weekly nanny duties through the winter months. Robert was aware of all she was doing for them, as opposed to Kathleen, who rarely came to visit or help out.

Harry came frequently, bringing Ronnie candy or picking her up from school on days Allison was delayed at John Carroll. He frequently babysat on a weekend night so Robert and Allison could have a bit of time alone and dinner out. He particularly enjoyed Friday nights when he could watch *NBC Friday Night Fights* on the color television and de-cided to add a set to the Walton Hills house if it could be budgeted among the latest of Kathleen's desires. Harry often thought Ronnie's skin too pale, though it was winter in Northeast Ohio, a time when sunlight was at a premium. Still, with her heart condition he was wary and mentioned her color to Robert when he could get him alone, not wanting to unduly worry Allison.

"She's one of the most monitored children in Cleveland," Robert assured him. "The nurse at Laurel looks her over every morning, and she's seen by her pediatrician twice a month, to say nothing of our annual trips to the West Coast. I'm glad you are keeping tabs on her, but I really think the Cleveland winters are to blame."

That spring Ronnie's color improved, and by the time of their Stanford return, Ronnie's skin was lightly tanned. However, her medical team did find another leak—much smaller than the one they had repaired—in a different location they wished to monitor during a second week's stay. Arrangements were made, with Robert again traveling to the San Francisco office to make calls to his Cleveland staff and clients, but only staying for an occasional afternoon. Allison, Ronnie, and Autumn were transported to the hospital for testing if Robert was away, and they enjoyed the amenities of the Hotel Citrine in Palo Alto during their stay.

The consensus of Ronnie's medical team was the second hole was too small for additional surgery at this time. If Ronnie began to feel exceedingly tired, was unable to function at her school, or started sleeping longer than normal, additional surgery would become necessary. This could be accomplished at Stanford, or quite possibly at the Cleveland Clinic, where significant advances in adolescent heart surgery had been made since several former residents from the Stanford program had relocated to Cleveland.

CHAPTER FORTY-FOUR

The Who Done It Club had grown significantly and elected Kathleen as its leader for the coming year, a post she took very seriously. Their number had outgrown home-hosted sessions, so gatherings were now held at the Cleveland Public Library on Superior Avenue, with lunch following at a local restaurant for those interested. Kathleen's search to devise the perfect unsolvable murder led to many hours of research, studying crimes reported in back issues of *The Plain Dealer* as well as dinners with Mary and Norman.

She was only mildly conflicted knowing the scenario she was concocting centered around Harry's fictional demise; she named her intended victim Glenn. Glenn was a resident of Manhattan, in and of itself reason to die, she thought, living childless with his wife in a high-rise building on the upper West Side. Like her brother-in-law, Glenn was an attorney in a prestigious firm located in the city's financial district, his practice limited to four clients. One was a Texas oil multi-millionaire who had fathered three children with two women, neither of whom he ever married. He kept each family in different Dallas suburbs where the children wanted for nothing and called him "Daddy."

Glenn's second client was a female movie star of prominence living in Hollywood, whose films were very popular in the 50s and 60s. Unlike the Texan, she'd had several marriages to actors, directors, and others in the film industry whom she divorced regularly. Glenn was charged with making sure this client remained free of financial encumbrances. The third and fourth clients were Manhattanites. One was an eighty-nine-year-old third-tier member of the Rothchild family with a new wife the age of several of his now-adult children, whose considerable assets Glenn was managing through non-taxable interest-bearing instruments. The fourth client was the Spanish artist Salvador Dali, who Glenn enjoyed but thought was living longer than his fame as a Surrealist could accommodate. Salvador wished to build a museum in Florida for himself and hired Glenn to see to the particulars.

In Kathleen's fiction, Glenn's wife decided she would be happier living without the husband she never saw or spent time with, but didn't want the hassle and uncertainty of a divorce. Glenn's income was significant, and he had invested wisely. His net worth would become his widow's per his last will and testament, just like Harry's!

✡✡✡

Veronica Kern lived four more months after the family's return from their two weeks in Stanford. Unlike the scenario outlined by her medical team the prior summer, her death was not a gradual decline. Instead, the small hole in the superior vena cava simply burst one afternoon as she walked from her last class at Laurel to the athletic building where she took yoga. She never felt a thing, the emergency room physicians told her parents later. One moment she was alive, the next she was not. There was nothing that could have been done for her even at a hospital.

Robert was thankful it was quick for his daughter, and he hoped as painless as he and Allison had been told. Seeing their first born lying on a cold metal slab awaiting a final disposition was brutal nonetheless. There was no way a parent could endure such a thing, no matter how many times it might have been considered. Children just should not die before their parents, or grandparents for that matter. A kind and gracious God would not allow this to happen.

As he had been taught at Stanton, Robert held his pain inside. Allison became hysterical, throwing herself over her daughter's body. He knew Allison needed to expend her grief and wanted to comfort her, though he didn't quite know how. A hospital orderly came to inquire where the body should be sent. Robert did not have an answer, thinking it ghoulish to plan for such a thing before the fact. The Stanford doctors had failed him and his daughter. It wasn't supposed to end this way.

"I don't know," he heard himself tell the orderly. "Where's the best place? I don't expect my wife and I will want a public visitation. We don't even have burial plots."

"I understand this is all so very sudden, and I expect you and your wife are experiencing considerable shock. If you'd permit me to ask the recommendation of the Laurel School headmistress? She's here, she came straight away."

"Thank you. I should speak to her. Please go ahead and tell Mrs. Simpson Allison and I will meet with her in just a few minutes. I'm sure we'll be pleased with her recommendation."

Allison's parents had purchased six plots at the Erie Street Cemetery—the oldest in the city—fifteen years earlier, intending them for themselves, their two daughters and their husbands if they married. Robert gave his up, announcing he wished to be cremated when the time came, or he could lodge with Allison or Ronnie for that matter. A small group assembled at the gravesite a few days later. Kathleen did not attend, saying it was too sad for her, but Harry went, along with Son, Rosalee, Ogden, Mary Kathleen, Allison's parents, and her sister. Prayers were offered for Ronnie's soul, for Allison and Robert's suffering to be lightened by their memories of their beloved first child, and for the family in attendance. Allison was seated facing the casket, within arm's reach, and as its small white form began to lower into the ground, she screamed her daughter's name and leaned forward as if to follow it into the darkness.

Fearful she would do just that, Robert grabbed her by the waist, pulling her back.

Ronnie's passing left her parents struggling with their lives, their careers, and finally their marriage. Their divorce nineteen months later, in September 1971, was reasonably painless. Allison got the house; Robert was assigned a modest child support payment for Autumn. Allison kept her position at John Carroll, where she remained until she retired, and never remarried. Robert left his job at Burson Marsteller in 1972 and moved to Florida, taking a job at the local newspaper, the *Palatka Daily News*.

CHAPTER FORTY-FIVE

That Kathleen did not attend the funeral was not lost on Robert, the Hughes family, or Allison. The Kecks did not attend either, nor did Nora and Sam Price. It was also not lost on Rosalee or Son, though he made excuses for his mother, alluding to her sensitive nature. Most of all, it was a cross to bear for Harry, one of the many related to Kathleen since the dealership was sold.

Arriving home after the service he found the house quiet and dark. A light snow was beginning to fall. He fixed himself a bourbon and branch in a tall glass with cherries and crushed ice and sat in the living room. Most recently Kathleen had decided she was artistically gifted and spent her time and energy painting. She turned one of the three second-floor bedrooms into a studio, purchasing a sturdy wooden easel, tubes of every color of oil paint offered, numerous brushes, and several palette knives. Boxes of pre-stretched canvases in a variety of sizes had been delivered as well, and she set about producing paintings based on photographs cut from magazines. Harry assumed she was now in her studio following her "muse," as she often referred to her artistic gift. He could smell roast beef cooking in the kitchen and guessed they would be dining at home on what had become quite a dismal evening. The bourbon was easing the pain he felt for Robert and Allison over their failed attempts to keep their daughter alive. He was considering their futures when Kathleen swept into the room smelling of oil paint and turpentine.

"Did I miss much?" she asked. "Is the poor little thing securely resting?"

"If you're referring to Ronnie, yes she is at peace. If you are referring to Allison, I'm not sure she will ever be completely at rest."

"And Robert? How is he taking all this?"

"Stoically I would say. Something he learned at a young age living with the two of us, and something that Stanton, I'm sure, impressed upon him. They are both grieving in their own way. I'm glad little Autumn will give them some comfort."

"Autumn. What a dumb name. What were they thinking? It must have come to them while in California where all those hippies live."

"I wish you'd have come to the funeral, Kathleen. It would have meant a lot to Robert, and to me. Son and Rosalee and their children were there, but no one else from our family. I found that sad and disappointing."

"Oh, I'm sure Rosalee, who can do no wrong in your book, looked appropriately grieved and wore black head to toe. How in the world Son got mixed up with that woman is a mystery to me. He must have been shell-shocked, just back from the war with a mouthful of bad teeth compliments of the Army."

"Kathleen, I am not going to listen to your self-serving whining on this or any other matter this evening. I'm having another drink and am happy to fix you something before dinner."

"Nothing for me. I'm working upstairs and need to keep my senses sharp. There is a pot roast that should be just about finished in the kitchen. I'm taking a plate up to my studio and will see you in the morning."

Harry watched her leave and headed for the kitchen, thinking of the woman she used to be when they were young, before she decided Son needed music lessons. Would she have left him for Clarke if she hadn't been pregnant with Robert? Probably not. Clarke knew better than to divorce Cynthia—poor musicians are a dime a dozen. Was having a fourth child really such a burden? Sending him away at such a young age—Harry should have never let that happen.

The following afternoon Kathleen mentioned she and a few artist friends were thinking of taking ten days or so in Italy to view the masterpieces of Florence as well as to paint and sketch. Did he want to go along?

As far as Harry could tell, the time Kathleen spent in Italy did not help her artistic efforts, but it did cost more money than had been allotted. It was yet another occasion when Kathleen seemed to think spending would have no real consequence on the amount deposited from the sale of Kern Motors, regardless of what Harry told her. He considered moving again to a smaller house in another part of Cleveland where they could spend their remaining years. At sixty-five he applied for Social Security benefits and hoped to augment it with some sort of part-time job. He found, however, that scenario was not possible until he turned seventy, and for the ensuing five years sought to limit their spending as much as Kathleen's extravagances would allow.

At the age of seventy-one Harry went back to work part-time at White Motors, cutting engine gaskets in cork and rubber. It was something he'd learned when working there all those years ago. He would even hold weekly instruction on the process for the younger White employees. He fell in easily with the other men in his department, enjoying the comradery, his union membership, and a cigar after finishing his brown-bag lunch. Most of all though, he enjoyed time away from Kathleen and a paycheck every week. It wasn't a great deal of money, but it did help with the monthly bills, as did the regular checks he received from the government and Son. Harry was no longer buying his cars from the new car lot, so when the time for a vehicle change came, Son would be on the lookout for a good buy. Harry preferred station wagons, feeling they were heavier than the sedans Buick was putting out. Leaving the car for Kathleen's use during the day, he would ride the bus to work and back each week.

In 1971, Harry and Kathleen moved to a smaller home in Lyndhurst, developed a decade earlier. Kathleen refused to sell any of her furnishings, so everything was squeezed into the smaller confines. The three-bedroom home found Harry living on the same floor as Kathleen, with the third bedroom again becoming her studio, used less now than before. The Walton Hills property sold for more than Harry paid for it, covering the cost of their new location and providing a cushion in the checking account. Turning seventy-five, Harry decided to leave his job at White after injuring his right hand and almost losing a finger cutting a camshaft gasket for a truck. The company gave their oldest employee a well-deserved send-off with a full lunch catered by The Harbor Inn. He was touched by the attention, the luncheon, and the box of Churchill Cuban cigars somehow smuggled into Cleveland by an anonymous donor. Although invited by the company's foreman, Kathleen did not attend.

✧✧✧

Robert became editor of the *Daily News* two years after joining the paper. It was more of a default promotion as the former editor and owner sold the publication to the *Sun-Sentinel* in Deerfield Beach—one of many regional newspapers owned by Tribune Publishing—and retired. It was a position Robert never really wanted or expected. He enjoyed writing local articles for the *News* because the pace was nothing like what he'd been used to at Marsteller. However, the promotion paid better than the salary he'd been hired at, and there were no other internal candidates for the job. He stayed in the position just long enough to put money aside for a used Diamondback airboat. He liked evening cruising on the St. John's River and hunting gators on Saturday afternoons with a couple six-packs in a cooler and a Smith & Wesson 44 Magnum pistol from his Air Force days secured in a chest holster.

One February Saturday evening, an electrical storm began brewing, and he was further from his dock than he wanted to be. The desire to get back before the storm broke caused him to travel faster on the water than was safe, which he knew, but the boat had no shelter from the elements. Rounding a narrow turn in the river he suddenly came upon a half-submerged tree downed by lightning. The crash sent the airboat eight feet into the air, turning it to the left as it again hit the water, throwing Robert overboard and dragging him by a tow rope tangled around his left leg. His drowning was one for the gators.

Kathleen had turned in early that night, and Harry was dozing in a high-backed French reproduction upholstered chair when he heard the telephone ringing in the kitchen. He rose and made his way to the noise, his legs a bit shaky.

"Hello?"

"Hello. This is Sheriff Hugo Gage. I'm calling from Palatka, Florida. Do you know a Robert Kern, sir?"

Harry was now wide awake. "I have a son by that name, and last I knew he was living in Palatka. Is he all right?"

"Mr. Kern, I am very sorry to inform you that your son died this evening in an airboat accident on the St. Johns River. We believe he was trying to get out of an electrical storm and hit a tree felled by the wind. He was thrown overboard and dragged by the boat before it came to shore. I'm so sorry to report this to you. There will be an autopsy here tomorrow to confirm the cause of death. Do you know if your son had made any advance directives concerning funeral arrangements?"

Harry was trying to take in what the sheriff was telling him. It didn't seem possible. "Ah...no. I don't know if he ever had plans along those lines. I'm sorry."

"Certainly, I understand. A couple of my deputies will go by his apartment in the morning to see if there are any helpful documents there.

I will let you know if we find anything just as soon as possible. And I am so sorry for your loss. Goodnight."

The phone went dead, just like Robert. Harry heard a shriek from the second floor; Kathleen had been listening to the conversation on the phone in her bedroom. He went upstairs. Looking in from the hallway, he found Kathleen curled up in her bed, arms wrapped around herself, weeping uncontrollably. Harry entered her room, a shrine to eighteenth century French furnishings, and sat gingerly on a corner of her bed. He watched the ensuing drama, wishing it were genuine.

"Kathleen." He put his hand lightly on her satin-covered arm. "You heard the conversation?"

She stopped crying and nodded her head.

"Robert always went his own way, even before he had to. I remember Pap telling me once about a confrontation he had with a bull one summer on the farm. He wasn't as lucky this time."

Kathleen again went into hysterics.

"Now, now," Harry soothed. "He's with Ronnie now, and she's happy to see him. And with Pap and Mam too."

That got Kathleen's attention. "Do you really believe what you're saying?" She sat up. "Honestly Harry, sometimes you say the stupidest things. Those four people are dead, cold and gone. Nonexistent!"

"You don't believe in a life beyond this one?" he asked her. "That is so very sad, you've got nothing to look forward to."

Kathleen jumped up from the bed, "You old fool! I bet you believe in Santa and the Easter Bunny too. You're nearing eighty, for heaven's sake!"

"My age is all the more reason to hope for an afterlife," he said.

"I suppose you think that fish you brought home is somewhere up there too, in a big, blue ocean of love!"

Harry didn't respond. Still sitting on a corner of her bed, he looked down at the white Oriental rug on the floor, then at the white gilded headboard.

"You could have loved him more as a child," he said finally. "We should have never sent him to Staunton at such a young age. It must have felt like being banished from home without understanding why."

"Don't you dare blame me for his death down there tonight. If anything, Robert's death is your fault—he should have never been conceived and never been born. That was all your doing!"

Harry spent that night on the living room couch, which being more decorative than useful, added to his grim mood. Even in death, Robert was not wanted by Kathleen, despite her bedroom theatrics. She now had her little family of three restored. He was sure Son would mourn his brother's passing, Nora would find it a dreadful loss, and Agnes would not think of it at all.

The following afternoon Sheriff Gage called back to say his deputies did find paperwork Robert had signed and had notarized to have his cremated remains buried at the Florida National Cemetery in Bushnell. All expenses incurred in getting his ashes there and buried would be covered by the federal government. He also had a will leaving all his possessions and checking and saving accounts to his former wife, Allison Hughes Kern, living in Cleveland.

CHAPTER FORTY-SIX

Robert's death was a sore that just wouldn't heal for Harry. Allison and Autumn drove to the military cemetery for his interment, received a neatly folded American flag, which they gave to Harry upon their return, then drove to Robert's apartment, where they spent the better part of the week seeing to the distribution of things left behind. His car, found at the slip he rented for the airboat, was sent to Son to sell. There was not much of the airboat left to deal with, but the wreckage was finally sold to a dealer for parts. The apartment's furniture was rented, as was the apartment for the next two months. The rent was kept by the management even though Robert had died, but his deposit was returned. He had a bit over $5,000 in a checking account, and Allison found several personal items in the apartment, including pictures from their wedding and some of Ronnie taken in California. Autumn was old enough to remember some things about the sister she lost, but the photographs Robert had saved were helpful for her. Allison could not help but feel anguish at seeing these reminders of the lives they once led. Returning to Cleveland, she met with Harry to show him pictures of the Florida cemetery and relate as much as she thought would interest him about Robert's life in Palatka. He had died doing something he enjoyed, though he had picked the wrong night to do it.

Harry had the flag framed and hung in his room.

"I'm glad you didn't put that somewhere it can be seen by visitors. Unless you're having visitors upstairs," Kathleen said, looking in from the doorway. He glared at her and walked past without speaking. "I suppose you're going to make him a martyr around here, make him your favorite above everyone else."

"That would be easy to do. Agnes doesn't count for much, and we never see Nora. Son's busy with his Cleveland and Pittsburgh dealerships. He's traveling all the time. That just leaves you and me Kathleen, and while I was in a rage that Christmas Eve after seeing you kiss Clark Clarke, who you may or may not have had intimate relations with, I decided to claim my wife back. The result was a second son that for some crazy reason you could not stand because he caused the family's number to increase by one!"

Harry stormed down the hall with Kathleen following closely behind, screaming at him with every step. Harry ducked quickly into the bathroom to get away from her, but her toy poodle Topaz somehow got underfoot as he entered, and Harry lost his balance. Seeing her chance, Kathleen pushed him hard from behind. Stumbling, he hit his head on the corner of the marble countertop and fell to the floor between the vanity and the commode, blood leaking from his left ear. Kathleen decided to leave him there until he regained consciousness and an hour later called Agnes. After waiting a second hour before deciding to seek medical help, they realized Harry was dead and called the police. His death was ruled an accident by the coroner and was subsequently reported in a lengthily obituary article in *The Plain Dealer*.

Kathleen turned to Son to sort out Harry's financial affairs and advise her on to how to proceed without him. Son found the one million dollars his father had received from the sale of his business largely depleted. He told his mother her home and its furnishings were nearly all she had left financially and that she should spend as little as possible. She had long since given up driving, so many activities outside the house had to be given over to others. Agnes was most available, though Nora would come from Pittsburgh for an occasional week's stay to help. It soon got to the point where an alternate lifestyle was needed for the widow of Harry Kern.

CHAPTER FORTY-SEVEN

The Brookhaven Retirement Community opened for occupancy a year and a half later. After visiting as a prospective resident, Kathleen Kern decided it was where she was going to live and told Son to make it happen as quickly as it could be arranged. She selected a larger room with wide windows, a private bath, and a meal plan that allowed her to take most of her dinners in her room. The questions Son now faced was how long her financial resources would last and if she would go to her just reward before they ran out.

Most of the furniture from her bedroom at the house was moved to her new quarters: the white and powder-blue Oriental carpet, the white French-style twin bed, the gold and white dresser with a matching end table and tufted chair. Every flat surface held marble figurines she had brought back from France, and six of her paintings in gilded frames adorned the room's walls. The community's management was so taken with how the room turned out that Kathleen was photographed lounging on her bed surrounded by the room's opulence for a magazine advertisement.

Meanwhile the financial clock was ticking, forcing Son to begin the process of turning his mother's remaining assets into cash. The Lyndhurst house had not been thoroughly cleaned in some time and became a priority he and Rosalee took on rather than hiring a commercial cleaner before putting it on the market. A week later the house and contents were in a reasonable selling state, and Son arranged for a sale of furnishings and other possessions to be held the next weekend. Hearing of this, Agnes and Nora went through the house twice, taking things they wanted. Son tried reasoning with them, explaining many of the things they took were of a higher value and they should remember the goal of the sale was to provide funds for their mother's care. The logic of his argument was lost on Agnes, who sold all her items to a pawnbroker, using the cash to buy drugs. Items not sold were carted off by Goodwill. The house was turned over to a realtor who found a buyer willing to pay the asking price. Son opened a checking account for the proceeds and, to keep them from being used inappropriately, was the only authorized signatory. Kathleen lived in her regal splendor for two years before dying of heart failure one evening after she'd finished her dinner and a bourbon nightcap. Agnes laid claim to everything in Kathleen's Brookhaven room.

With their mother and father both gone, there was little reason for the Kern children to spend time together. Nora and her family were in Pittsburgh; Agnes was increasingly involved in get-rich-quick schemes that, when described to Son, sounded more than a tad illegal. Son was thinking of taking an early retirement and moving to Naples, Florida. He knew Rosalee was anxious to escape Cleveland winters and be in a warm climate. He thought about Harry and his brothers going their own ways once upon a time and wondered if this was what happened to most families. Ogden was on his own living in Atlanta, and his sister would be away at college in another year. Would they also just drift away for jobs or wives or husbands? The thought troubled Son, but it did seem to be the one constant in the Kern way of life. *Perhaps we should make Florida a winter home for now and see where our kids end up before making any major moves*, he thought for a moment. *Nah, that's what airplanes are for!*

ABOUT THE AUTHOR

 Edwin Ritts' museum profession spanned 39 years, during which time he directed art museums in New Brighton, Pennsylvania, Asheville, North Carolina, and Dubuque, Iowa. He also directed the Historic Greenville Foundation in South Carolina, culminating in the construction of the Upcountry History Museum in South Carolina and the Thomasville Cultural Center in Georgia.

Edwin's interest in writing began at Wilmington College in Ohio, where he edited the weekly newspaper and wrote short stories published in the school's annual literary journal.

Edwin and his wife, Susan, have two grown children and four grandchildren. They currently split their time between Dubuque, Iowa and Isle of Palms, South Carolina with their four dogs and three cats.

www.ingramcontent.com/pod-product-compliance
Lightning Source LLC
Chambersburg PA
CBHW072103300726
48975CB00003B/680